THE
SHATTERED
CASTLE

THE ASCENDANCE SERIES
— BOOK FIVE —

THE SHATTERED CASTLE

JENNIFER A. NIELSEN

SCHOLASTIC PRESS · NEW YORK

Copyright © 2021 by Jennifer A. Nielsen
Map by Kayley LeFaiver

Library of Congress Cataloging-in-Publication Data

Names: Nielsen, Jennifer A., author.
Title: The shattered castle / Jennifer A. Nielsen.
Description: First edition. | New York: Scholastic Press, an imprint of Scholastic Inc. 2021. |
Series: The Ascendance series; book 5 | Audience: Ages 8–12. | Audience: Grades 4–6. |
Summary: When King Jaron returned to Carthya, he brought with him a device that
supposedly shows the way to a great treasure, but now everything is going wrong: Castor,
the son of an old enemy, is conspiring against him and wants the throne for himself; his fiancée,
Imogen, seems to have turned against him; and the Prozarian Monarch has invaded his kingdom
and taken Jaron's castle—but Jaron has a lot of experience at hiding and escaping, and
he is not willing to leave Carthya or Imogen in the hands of his enemies.
Identifiers: LCCN 2020056396 | ISBN 9781338275902 (hardcover) | ISBN 9781338275919 (ebook)
Subjects: LCSH: Kings and rulers—Juvenile fiction. | Rescues—Juvenile fiction. |
Betrayal—Juvenile fiction. | Conspiracies—Juvenile fiction. | Adventure stories. |
CYAC: Kings, queens, rulers, etc.—Fiction. | Rescues—Fiction. | Betrayal—Fiction. |
Conspiracies—Fiction. | Adventure and adventurers—Fiction. |
LCGFT: Action and adventure fiction.
Classification: LCC PZ7.N5672 Sj 2021 | DDC 813.6 [Fic]—dc23
LC record available at https://lccn.loc.gov/2020056396

1 2021

Printed in the U.S.A. 23

First edition, October 2021

Book design by Christopher Stengel

To a few superfans:

Abigail and Ava
Anne, Isabella, Samantha, and Ben
Brooklyn
Katie
Nida
Roxy and Rubi
You earned your place here.

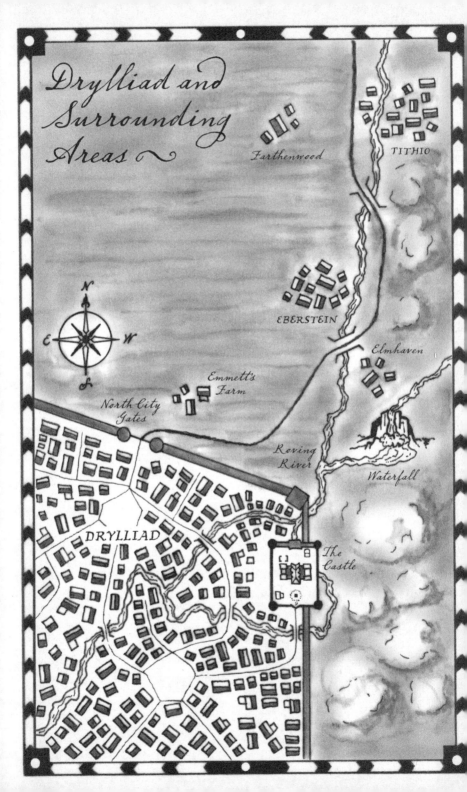

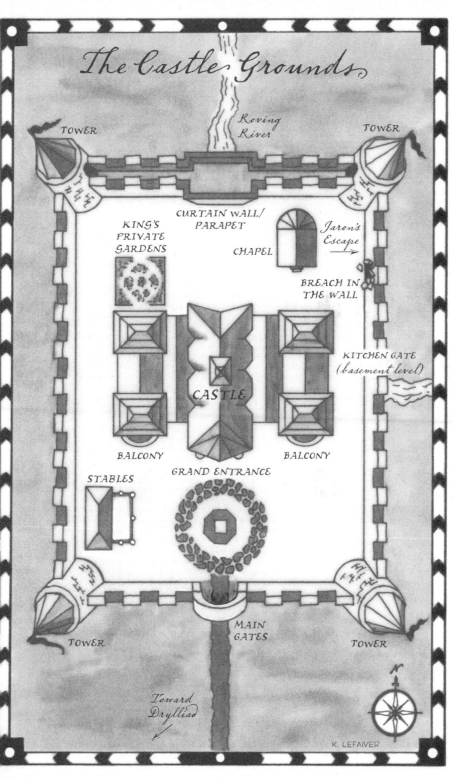

ONE

Throughout the years, I'd faced death more times than I could count, fought a war, endured the loss of my parents, and survived torture, cruelty, and multiple insults in the form of overcooked meat at the supper table. I thought that I had already faced the worst of anything this world might offer.

Then Lady Batilda Lamont came to the castle. Imogen's mother. She looked very much like Imogen — though Lady Batilda's hair was lighter and worn in a tight bun at the nape of her neck. However, Batilda hadn't even fully left the carriage before I ceased to see any true similarity between mother and daughter.

In the same instant she exited the carriage, it began.

"Imogen, your hair . . . surely someone here can work with that."

"Imogen, I'll need a new gown. Several new gowns."

"Imogen —" Finally, Batilda noticed me standing there, waiting to greet her. Her lips puckered in disapproval, or really, her entire face puckered, which I hadn't thought possible until this very moment. "*You* are Jaron?"

I had frozen as something close to panic sparked within me. I had known every kind of villain before, but this was new to me. I had sworn to Imogen that I would be polite and friendly, and I intended to keep my promise. However, no matter how hard I searched my mind, I couldn't come up with a single word that Imogen would approve of.

"*King* Jaron," Imogen corrected. "Mother, he's your king."

Lord Kerwyn, who had been standing at my side, stepped forward. "Madam, it is customary to bow before one's king."

"This boy is our king?" She shook her head, her expression souring with every movement. "And soon he will be my son-in-law. How wonderful."

Her tone implied that she believed having a thorn in one's foot was also wonderful. I was clearly the thorn.

I still hadn't said a word, but my gut had twisted so tight, I didn't know what I should say. Since the moment I'd learned that Imogen's mother would be coming to our wedding, I had expected this to be a difficult greeting. Batilda had sold Imogen to Bevin Conner as a way of paying for her personal debts. She had sold her own daughter.

"Try not to think about that when you meet my mother," Imogen had told me, but now that I was here, I could think of nothing else.

I eyed the balcony overlooking the main entrance, wondering how fast I could scale the castle wall and use it for an escape. That wouldn't be dignified behavior for a king, but I was still considering it.

Kerwyn cleared his throat. "Madam, you will bow to your king."

"Oh, very well." Batilda gave me a bow, but it meant even less to her than it did to me. When she rose up again and looked behind me, her frown only deepened. "I understand that most castles are quite drafty. Will my room have any problems?"

"Definitely." Sensing my opportunity, I eyed Kerwyn. "It was rude for us ever to offer our cold, drafty castle to this gentle-woman. Perhaps you will arrange for a room at the inn —"

"I can manage here, I suppose, if you'll provide me with an extra servant to keep the fireplace stoked. How many servants will attend me?"

I clicked my tongue but didn't sound nearly as disappointed as I'd intended. "What a pity, we ran out of servants this morning. But at the inn —"

"Someone will be assigned to your room." Imogen took my arm, giving me a warning glance that I ignored. "Shall we go inside?"

"I thought you'd never offer. It's blistering hot out here." We came to the grand entry, a large gathering place for guests who wished to move onward into the great hall or the throne room. Those who lived in the castle could go up the master staircase directly in front of us.

Batilda pointed to a woven tapestry hung at the base of the master staircase. "Is that the one you burned? I heard —"

"Mother, stop," Imogen said.

I forced a polite smile, though it caused me physical pain to do so. "No, not *that* tapestry."

"Oh, of course. I would have noticed the burned areas. I also heard — What shall I call you?"

"Mother, you know very well —"

"I've also heard, Your Majesty, that your interests have shifted away from fire and are more in the realm of causing explosions. Is it true that six months ago you blew up four ships in a harbor across the sea?"

"Yes, madam, but I should add, they were not my ships."

They had been the ships of a new enemy I had once thought was extinct: the Prozarians. I had defeated them in battle, and I hoped we had heard the last of them. But during every dark night, I lay awake in my bed, thinking of them, of what was coming. Most nights, I finally drifted off with more new questions than answers. How could I prepare for something I could not anticipate?

Batilda wasn't finished with me. "And is it true that my daughter was on one of those ships that you exploded?"

"Yes, Mother, but it was my plan —" Imogen began.

She got no further before Batilda squared herself to me and looked straight into my eyes. "King Jaron, will my daughter be safe in a marriage with you?"

The question hit harder than Batilda might have known. Truthfully, Imogen would be safer with nearly anyone else in the kingdom, and every one of us in the room knew it. Even Kerwyn, standing behind Batilda, leaned in to hear my assurance that I could protect her.

But there was no truthful way to answer that question. If thoughts of the Prozarians did not keep me awake at night, this question did.

"Jaron has saved my life on more than one occasion," Imogen said.

"Your life would not have needed saving except for Jaron."

Batilda turned back to me. "Is it also true that you were once a thief who went by the name of Sage?"

I hesitated, looking from her to Imogen. This conversation could not possibly be going worse.

"Jaron . . . Oh!" Tobias entered from the great hall and stopped when he saw Imogen's mother. Collecting himself, he said, "Forgive the intrusion, but Harlowe has asked to see you."

Rulon Harlowe was my chief regent, and Roden's father. Harlowe had never aspired to become a chief regent, or really, to be a regent at all, which was the exact reason I wanted him in that position. He and Tobias were also more loyal than nearly all my other regents put together. That wasn't necessarily a reflection of their good characters as much as it was a statement of the spineless, power-hungry nature of most of the other regents.

"Is it urgent?" I asked, nodding slightly as a hint for Tobias to answer.

"The wedding is in three days," Batilda said. "Have either of you given a single thought to which silver pattern you want for the supper?" She turned to stare at Tobias. "What can you possibly want with Jaron that is more important than a silver pattern?"

"I, uh . . ." Tobias looked over at me with the same expression a person might use when the ground beneath them has just collapsed. "No, I suppose it can wait."

"Clearly we have a crisis," I announced, but I didn't get far before a voice behind me stopped me in my tracks.

"King Jaron!" When I turned, the person was already bowing, so at first I wasn't sure who had come to further ruin my afternoon. Tobias gestured at me, signaling that this person, standing with his body bent low in the doorway of the throne room, was the crisis.

To whoever was still bowing, I said, "Can you not rise again, sir? If you need help, Tobias is a physician, sort of."

Then he rose, and I recognized him immediately. This was someone I had not seen in many years, nor did I have the least desire to see him. If he was anything like his father, then I already understood why Tobias looked so concerned.

"Castor Veldergrath."

Son of Santhias Veldergrath, a mold that had infested Carthya for far too long.

His son would be no different.

· TWO ·

I f I'd had any manners, I would have said something more to Castor, such as "Welcome to my castle," or "It's good to see you again."

Only, he wasn't at all welcome here, and none of this was good. It wasn't even tolerable. I knew little of Castor now, though as a boy he had been spoiled and disagreeable. Perhaps the same was true of me, but at least I had charm. Castor was the son of Santhias Veldergrath, a former regent and a man who had planned to kill me, Roden, and Tobias when he heard rumors of Conner seeking a false prince. Turns out he wanted to become king himself, and the three of us were in his way. My first act upon being restored to the throne was to strip Veldergrath of his title and his position as a regent.

If Castor was here now, then more trouble was coming.

So rather than any gesture of politeness, or for that matter, any basic civility, I simply asked Castor, "What do you want?"

He smiled at me, then turned to bow to Imogen. "My lady, it's good to see you again."

"Again?" I asked.

"Most times when I go to market, he's there too," she

said, as if their regular meetings at the market were only a coincidence.

"Since when does a Veldergrath go to the market for himself?" I asked.

"When does a future queen?" he countered, settling his eye on Imogen. "And is this lovely woman your mother?"

Batilda giggled. An actual giggle. I felt nauseous.

He took Batilda's hand and kissed it. "In a different world, you might have been queen."

Kerwyn stayed with them, hopefully to keep control of Castor's flirting, while I crossed the room to speak to Tobias in private. "Why is he here?"

"Harlowe told him to stay in the regents' room."

"No, why is he here in my castle?"

"Let's go to the regents' room, and I can explain on the way."

I turned back to Imogen and caught her eye. She smiled at me, but her brow was pressed low, concerned over what was happening. I gestured with my head that I was leaving with Tobias, and she nodded back at me.

Tobias walked beside me toward the regents' room. "Imogen's mother seems . . . nice."

"I think she breathes fire in her sleep." I ran a hand through my hair. "Tell me about Castor."

"It's not him. There's a bigger problem."

"Oh?" I stopped to stare at him. "So when I asked if it was urgent, and you said no —"

"I got nervous, Jaron. The way Imogen's mother glared at me —"

That made sense. Other than pausing to glare at Tobias,

she'd fixed her eye on me with the same disdain that Mrs. Turbeldy used to have when I'd lived in her Orphanage for Disadvantaged Boys. I knew why Mrs. Turbeldy hated me. I'd offended her nearly every day that I had stayed there. Batilda clearly hated me more.

"So what's the problem?"

Tobias drew in a deep breath. "The regents have resigned."

"Which regents?"

By then, we had arrived at the regents' room. Harlowe was inside and stood to greet me. After a brief bow, he answered my question. "All of them have resigned, other than Tobias and me."

My hands formed into fists. "Why?"

"They've been sending messengers all afternoon, every one with a different excuse. Tobias and I couldn't make sense of it, until —"

"Castor's arrival." Surely there was some connection between him and this new problem.

"Ahem."

I turned and groaned. Castor had arrived again, with yet another low bow that I only saw out of the corner of my eye.

"Forgive me," Castor said. "I was so taken with your future bride and her mother that I didn't realize you had left."

I turned to face him. "If Harlowe tells you to remain here in the regents' room, that is what you do. You will not wander this castle as if it's yours."

His right eye flinched slightly; then he regained his boldness. "Apologies, my king —"

"Am I your king, Castor?"

"Of course. You saw the way I bowed."

"I figured your back had gone out. But if I am your king, then tell me now: Are you the reason why eighteen regents just resigned their offices?"

Castor's smile spread across his face like spilled oil. "With a little more time, it will be all your regents."

"Perhaps we should sit down." Harlowe held out one hand, inviting me farther inside. I kept my eye on Castor as I walked to my chair at the head of the table. Harlowe took his place beside me, with sheets of parchment on the table in front of him — the resignations of the other regents, I assumed. Tobias sat in his usual chair near the end of the table, since he had less seniority than most of the other regents. Castor pulled out a chair to sit down, but I shook my head. "That chair is for a regent. I'll get you another one." The servant attending the door was Errol, who had once worked for Conner in his former estate of Farthenwood. He would know what I wanted. I said to Errol, "The blue chair, please."

Errol barely suppressed a smile as he dipped his head at me, then disappeared, returning a minute later with the chair. Early in our training to impersonate a prince, Conner had put us through lessons in an upper schoolroom. One of the chairs in that room was meant for a five-year-old. I had a fond memory of it.

The chair was placed against the wall for Castor. His lip curled when he stared down at it. "I won't sit there."

"Then you're welcome to stand. I assumed with your back problems —"

"I have no back problems. I was simply offering you a respectful bow, one that I already regret."

"Why did you bother bowing at all? You are clearly behind the resignation of my regents, so what do you want?"

"I want only what is owed to me." Which I figured involved a day or two in my dungeon, but he quickly added, "I am here to restore my father's position as regent."

"Your father has not been a regent for two years. Did he send you here?"

"My father is dead." Castor's words lingered in the air. Again, basic courtesy would require me to express sympathy, but I hadn't been polite yet and I didn't see any reason to start now.

Instead, I said, "Your father was not a regent when he died and cannot have his title back now that he is dead. What a strange request." I turned to Tobias. "Can you imagine that, seating a corpse here as regent? I grant you, I might like him better that way."

"My father's title must be restored so that I can inherit it." Castor arched his head. "My request is within the boundaries of law."

"Which law?"

Harlowe cleared his throat. "It's an archaic law, Your Highness, still in our books, but to my knowledge, has never been used in Carthya in quite this way. In the early days of Carthya, during the time of the three rulers, there was sometimes the problem of one ruler dismissing the regent that another preferred. The law was put in place to allow the eldest child of the regent to reclaim the position so that a family could have the chance to redeem themselves."

"That's a stupid law. Watch carefully." I leaned forward

and snapped my fingers. "There, now it's not a law anymore. I just decreed it."

"I thought you'd say that, so I have another plan." Castor looked at Harlowe. "Tell him."

Harlowe pushed the sheets of parchment toward me, and they were exactly as I had thought, the regents' resignations. "Each one names Castor Veldergrath as his or her successor. Jaron, Castor has the right to be named as a regent."

"And I have the right to review these papers before making any decisions." I stood and pushed back my chair. "As you may have heard, in a few days, I'm getting married, and then Imogen and I will take a little time to ourselves. When that time has passed, I'll begin that review."

"How much time?" Castor asked.

"Eighty years, at least," I said. "But do not worry. This will be my top priority once I'm back to work. Until then, you must leave the regents' room, for you have no place here." Looking at Errol again, I added, "Please see him out of the castle."

Castor stood, his face reddening. "This is a mistake, Jaron. When I return —"

"Be careful that the rest of your sentence does not become treason," Harlowe warned.

Castor closed his eyes and drew in a breath, exhaling with, "When I return for your wedding, my king, I hope you will have changed your mind."

He bowed again and left the room. The instant he did, I turned to Tobias. "Make sure that Castor Veldergrath gets nowhere near my wedding."

· THREE ·

In the rear corner of the castle was the King's Private Study. A grand window facing the rear gardens meant that not much studying ever got done in here, but this was my space, where I was not to be disturbed.

In theory.

I'd only been there for ten minutes before Roden visited, to ask about security for the wedding day.

Amarinda visited within the same hour, to say that Imogen's mother was looking for me.

And Tobias came an hour later. I would have sent him away, but he brought food with him, ensuring I could hide in here for the rest of the evening, so I let him in.

Though of course, Tobias wanted to talk as well.

"I just paid a visit to Master Soring, who is here in Drylliad."

I tended to think of him as Master Snoring, due to the number of times I had fallen asleep during his speeches. It once took him an hour to answer the question of "How are you today?"

Tobias continued, "He was in debt, so Castor Veldergrath bought up his land, then threatened to expel his family if he did not resign as regent. Master Soring told me that Castor also had some information on Mistress Orlaine and threatened to reveal it if she did not resign. Master Termouthe voluntarily resigned. He and Castor's father were old friends. I don't know about the others."

I pinched the bridge of my nose with my fingers. "What do the reasons matter? Castor must not become a regent."

"I agree." Tobias paused. "What will you do?"

"I'm not sure. I have bigger problems on my mind for now."

"The wedding?" My eyes darted, and Tobias asked, "Or something else?" I still didn't answer, and he added, "You've spent a lot of time in here since we returned from Belland. Why?"

Six months ago, a ship I was on had been captured by the Prozarians. The lecherous Captain Jane Strick was their commander, but their monarch was Strick's daughter, Wilta. She was beautiful, brilliant, and deadly to her core. I had destroyed most of their fleet on Belland but had also brought back with me a secret that everyone believed had been destroyed.

Since I had no intention of telling Tobias about that secret, or any other, my only choices were to lie or make him leave.

I was no liar.

"Please leave me alone now," I said to Tobias.

"Amarinda asked me to tell you that Imogen's mother —"

"Do not tell her where I am." This was as serious an order as I had ever given. "Even the devils leave me alone here."

Tobias stood and gathered up my plates. "Imogen's mother was looking for you earlier. But Amarinda asked me to tell you that she has left for the evening. She received a dinner invitation . . . from the Veldergrath family."

I set my jaw forward, closed my eyes, and nodded. "Please go, Tobias."

He did, and when the door was closed, I slumped in my chair and tried to hold my thoughts together. If Batilda was dining with Castor Veldergrath tonight, would she embolden him to come at me harder than before? Or would he make her hate me even more?

The answer was obvious. Batilda couldn't hate me more than she already did. She would only make things worse with Castor.

Needing something to do, I stood and walked to a pillar against one corner of the study. A small metal lever near the floor could be pushed with my foot to unlatch a secret door in the pillar. I opened it and walked down a circular stairway to an entirely separate area that no one knew about except the servants who had constructed it for me. I called this my truly private study.

The small room was bare, other than a table and chair and enough candles for light. In the table, behind a hidden compartment in a drawer, was my great secret.

"Were you a fool to have taken this?" I asked myself, using a Prozarian accent, as I always did down here. Maybe I'd never need to use it, but if I did, I wanted it to be perfect. I answered myself in the same accent, "You have proven yourself a greater fool than usual."

I pulled out the Devil's Scope, still in its satin bag. I had stolen it from the Prozarians along with three separate lenses that had to be inserted into slots on the top of the scope. Viewed together, the lenses were supposed to become an ancient map to what Captain Strick had called the greatest treasure that anyone might imagine.

I didn't know what the treasure was, but some form of wealth was almost certainly part of it, and I couldn't deny how much Carthya needed it. My kingdom would benefit from a fresh supply of gold — the war a year ago had greatly depleted our supplies. Of greater importance was finding the treasure before the Prozarians did. I could well imagine the destruction they would cause if they had funding for it.

I inserted the first lens into the scope, which depicted a cave in a land across the sea known as Belland. My brother Darius ruled there now. When I added the second lens, I saw a moon that showed the viewer when and where to find the third lens. I had found the third lens, though I had let everyone around me, both friend and enemy, believe that I had lost it, never to be found again.

Yet here it was, in my hand.

I slid the third lens into its slot. It should have been the completion of the map, but if it was, I had yet to understand it. Using lines from the two previous lenses and adding new lines, symbols were created in a language I could not read, nor had I ever seen any languages like this before.

Three symbols were engraved into the top of the scope itself. Nearest to the eyepiece was a circular arrow, a symbol of unity, of people coming together as one. In the center was a triangle, a symbol of strength. And third was a circle with three lines running through it, dividing the circle into equal thirds. It was a symbol of the origins of Carthya, of the three rulers who created this land.

I had interpreted the symbols as a message, that one, the circular arrow, was stronger than three, the divided circle.

But even if I was right, it still meant nothing to me. Nor could I interpret any of the other engravings all over the scope. Maybe there was no solution. Maybe the scope lived up to its name, a great joke of ancient devils.

It was too dark down here to study the scope and lenses properly, so I put them back in the satin bag and walked up the stairs. But the instant I opened the door, my heart stopped. Imogen was standing in the center of my study, arms folded, eyes blazing.

"A secret door? Where does it lead?"

"To an underground room."

"Is that where you've been all evening? Hiding down there?"

"I've been here in this study. And I was hardly hiding. Half the castle has come in here tonight."

Her eyes flicked to my right hand, covering my pocket. "But you are hiding something. What is it?"

I huffed, then brought out the satin bag. She knew instantly what it was. With a small gasp, she looked at me, though I couldn't read the emotion. There was too much of it — anger and shock and horror and . . . something else. Betrayal, maybe?

"Jaron, you told me this had been lost back in Belland!"

I had to be careful here. "No, I never told you that. Tobias told you."

"Then you let me believe it. How is that any different from lying?"

"I did not lie to you, Imogen. But I also knew how angry you would be if you knew I still had the scope."

"Because this will draw the Prozarians back to us. They must know you have it."

"They believe it was lost." I stepped toward her. "That's why I didn't tell you, why I didn't tell anyone."

"There's always a reason why you don't tell, always an excuse."

I shifted my weight. "Protecting my kingdom is hardly an excuse."

"You were protecting yourself, thinking only of yourself." She pointed to the scope. "You were thinking of the treasure that promises."

"Yes, I was. And the trouble it promises if the Prozarians get it. You saw how far they were willing to go to find the lenses. Should I have just let them have it?"

"No, Jaron. You should have destroyed the scope, as you let us all believe you did. If you had, the Prozarians would have gone their way and we would have remained at peace. Maybe my mother was right."

I looked up, curious as to what she might mean.

Imogen was shaking her head. "Do you know there was a time when I never had to worry about threats to my life? When Mother sold me to Conner, I thought that was as awful as my life might ever get, and I learned to live with it. Then I met you."

She stopped there, but she wasn't finished. I was still reeling from what she had already said. Did she mean that her life was awful now . . . because of me?

Imogen's eyes darted away, and when she looked at me again, there was something different in her expression than I'd ever seen before, something worse than disappointment or the feeling of having been betrayed.

"Do you have anything else to tell me, Jaron? Any other secrets?"

She waited for my answer, but it didn't come, and not because I had no other secrets but because I couldn't find the words to speak them aloud.

Finally, she shook her head again. "You do place me in danger. You *have* put me, and everyone else, in danger by keeping that scope."

I frowned. "The Prozarians do not know this still exists. As long as it remains that way, they have no reason to come here. And if they do come, it won't be for the scope."

"If they do come, it will be for revenge," she mumbled. "How much longer can your list of enemies get?"

"Hopefully not longer than my list of friends." I stepped closer to Imogen. "We can face anything if we do it together."

"We didn't do *this* together. *You* made this decision; *you* kept this secret." She backed away. "How dare you pull me into this now, as if I had any part in it?"

Before I could say another word, she turned and marched from the room. I sank to the floor, wrung out. In the solitary walls of my private study, I felt exactly how very alone I had suddenly become.

· FOUR ·

I wasn't sure exactly how much time had passed before another knock came to my door. I ignored it, but whoever was on the other side knocked again and then I recognized Kerwyn's voice. "My king, Lady Batilda, mother of Lady Imogen, wishes to have an audience with you."

"Tomorrow, Kerwyn." All but two of my regents had resigned, Castor Veldergrath was clearly planning a takeover of my throne, Imogen was furious with me — possibly for good reason — and I had hurt my foot when I kicked the wall after she left. I'd had enough for one day.

Kerwyn's voice deepened. "You'll want to speak to her, Jaron."

I grunted my permission, then rolled off the hard floor where I'd been sitting so that at least I could be on my feet for Batilda's entrance. As expected, her bow was brief and insincere. Unexpectedly, she was dressed in traveling clothes.

"You're not leaving, I hope?" Four of my five words had been perfectly true. At least my honesty was in the majority.

Batilda glanced around the room a moment before looking directly at me. "What was your mother like, King Jaron?"

That caught me off guard. It was always difficult to speak about my mother, and I rarely did so without finding a catch in my throat. "She was . . . unfailingly loving, even when I failed her. She was kind and rarely too serious about anything. She was an artist." The catch began to choke me, so I simply added, "Why do you ask?"

"I am a mother too, and I love my daughter. I never would have sent her to Farthenwood if I had not been forced into it. That was an incredibly difficult decision, but when our last source of income was lost, I had no other choice."

I looked down, sensing what was coming, but I had no idea what I would say to it.

She paused, as if she was waiting for me to answer the questions she had not asked, but I stayed silent. Finally, Batilda continued. "I know that you love Imogen too, or you believe that you do, and I know that you too must sometimes make difficult decisions."

I thought of the scope again. It was back in its secret place beneath this room. I should have told Imogen about the scope. I should have told Imogen everything before now.

Batilda stood up taller. "However, what I must say now will not be difficult at all, though it will be hard for you to hear. I know all about you, more than you may realize. I've spent much of the day speaking to your servants, your friends . . . and even those who would not consider you a friend, all the while hoping to hear some reason why I should allow my daughter to marry you."

I looked back up at her, feeling my heart begin to race. "That is not your choice —"

"Instead, all I have heard are reasons why she should not, why she must not be connected to you any longer."

"Who said that?" This time she didn't answer, and I added, "This is Imogen's decision."

"As her mother, this decision is my legal right. I have authority over her, and in this case, my king, it even gives me authority over you. You'll find it written in the Book of Faith, page three hundred and five."

My eyes narrowed. "How did you know that?"

"Castor Veldergrath happened to mention it tonight at supper. He's very well educated. He has offered to assist us in working this out."

"Working *what* out?" Shifting my weight, I asked, "Where is Imogen? She should be here and answer this for herself."

"Imogen would prefer not to see you right now, though she refused to tell me why. I hope you will respect her feelings in this matter, and you must honor mine. I will give proper respect to the crown if I must, but I cannot respect the boy who wears it. And I will not allow you to marry my daughter."

Her words left me so stunned, I barely could speak. I'd faced full attacks that had left me reeling, that had wounded me physically and cored through me emotionally. But never had I experienced any blow such as this. I vaguely noticed her bow; then I thought I heard her say that she and Imogen would be staying with Veldergrath that night. By the time she left, I was sitting again on the ground, listening to the clack of her shoes against the stone floor as she walked away, triumphant.

I had never before considered myself defeated, not personally, not in battle. Until now.

· FIVE ·

On the front of the castle, between the second and third floors, was a small ledge that overlooked everything up to the castle gates, and even provided a good view of Drylliad beyond our walls. It was accessible by climbing from a balcony on the second floor. Nobody knew I was out here, except perhaps the passing sentry below, his head cloaked. I'd have to speak to Roden about that. Even on cold nights, sentries were never to be cloaked.

At least he wouldn't notice me out here. I didn't want his attention, or anyone else's. I wasn't sure why I'd climbed to this ledge. Maybe I felt a faint hope that Imogen would realize this was all a mistake and any minute now she'd return.

Except it wasn't a mistake, and both Imogen and I knew it. Regardless of my reasons, I had deliberately kept the truth from her. Even if I could find a way to fix this, there was nothing I could do about her mother. Batilda would never change her mind about me.

I wished Mott were here, and Darius. I could've used Mott's practicality and Darius's faith in love. Truly, I would have liked anyone to talk to right now. Tobias and Amarinda hadn't been married for long; they barely noticed when anyone else was in the room. My adopted younger brother, Fink, wouldn't understand, and Roden would only say I got what I deserved. He'd be equally mad that I hadn't told him about the scope.

I watched the sentry again, noting the gait of his long legs, his posture as he walked. I knew the sentries who patrolled in the daytime but had rarely taken time to observe the night watch.

Something about him seemed familiar. Too familiar. I leaned forward and under my breath mumbled, "Mercy."

I didn't know his real name; I'd never cared to ask. But Mercy was Wilta's top counselor, one of the crueler Prozarians I'd met, and, somehow, still alive. That couldn't be possible. Back in Belland, I'd seen him fall to his death. But this was him.

I crouched low to warn the others, but at nearly the same moment, Mercy threw back his cloak and raised a crossbow that had been hidden. He fired off two shots with perfect accuracy and killed the other sentries within the gates.

There should have been a response from the towers at the curtain wall. Where were my vigils? When I looked to the towers, I saw a glint of metal in the moonlight.

I stood, hoping to get a better view, but that might have been a mistake.

A voice called down from the tower, "He's right there, on the ledge!"

A hiss cut through the air. I jumped off the ledge, barely missing an arrow that hit exactly where I had stood. It bounced off the rock and fell with me to the balcony below.

I landed on my weaker leg and the pain of it echoed through

me, but I barely noticed it. Here, on the second floor of the castle, were the rooms for the royal family and honored residents. One by one, I ran each room through my mind. Most of the rooms were empty, but Tobias and Amarinda and Fink were still here. I had to warn them.

Errol must have heard me land on the balcony because the doors flew open and he asked, "King Jaron, are you all right?" He showed no surprise to see me. It was hardly the first time I'd fallen here.

"We're under attack!" I scrambled to my feet and raced toward him, even as arrows began pelting the balcony. "Get down!"

I dove at Errol as an arrow whizzed beside him, then kicked the doors closed with one leg. I rolled to my feet and yelled at him, "Warn the guard!"

Errol ran, and I turned back to the door at the sound of an enormous boom, followed by the shattering of glass from the nearby windows. I fell backward and rolled, trying to protect my hands and face from the worst of the flying shards.

The castle shook as more boulders slammed into its walls. From above and below, I heard the guard beginning to collect. I wasn't sure where Roden was.

"Jaron!" Fink had left his room and was running toward me. I shouted back, "Get Tobias and Amarinda!" Fink pivoted around, racing toward the far corner of the castle, where their room now was. I followed him but stopped at Kerwyn's room. I pushed open the door and saw a servant already assisting him with his slippers.

"No time for that," I said. "Get to the inner keep."

The inner keep was in the center of the castle, accessible

only through a secret doorway in the cellar that led to stairs even farther underground. The enemy probably wouldn't know it existed, much less how to get inside. There was no safer place for anyone to be.

Tobias, Amarinda, and Fink ran into the corridor. Fink had found a sword by now. Mine was in my room. I started in that direction, but a servant rounded the corner behind them, with my sword in his hands.

"Help everyone upstairs get to safety," I said. The servant nodded and ran one way while I led my friends toward the stairway. We were halfway down when an explosion below us collapsed the castle's main entry.

"Hold your lines!" That was Roden's voice. He was already on the main floor with at least fifty of our men, most of whom had clearly been roused from sleep only minutes ago. "Let no one get past you."

We continued hurrying down the stairs behind them. I paused long enough to look outside at our attackers, who were firing arrows and pushing their way forward. Their numbers were at least four times ours. I had no idea where they had all come from in such a short time, but sooner or later, they would get in.

Roden saw me and called my name. When I locked eyes with him, he gestured with his head to a body on the ground, lying in a pool of blood. Harlowe.

I turned to Amarinda. "Can you and Fink get yourselves to the inner keep?"

"No, I'm staying with you," Fink said.

"Make sure that Amarinda gets safely to the keep."

"Jaron, I can fight!"

"You're not ready for this. Now go!"

He grunted and joined Amarinda to continue running downstairs while Tobias and I ran to Harlowe. Tobias pressed fingers to his neck and nodded to me, though as soon as we rolled Harlowe over, the extent of his injuries became clear. Something must have cut him straight across his middle.

"Can you help him?" I asked.

Tobias only shook his head. "I really don't know. I've never seen anything like this."

"Do everything you can. Please, Tobias." My words weren't necessary. I already knew that he would.

By then, Kerwyn and his manservant were at the bottom of the stairs. They hurried over to us. "Help Tobias bring Harlowe to the inner keep," I said.

Kerwyn began to lift Harlowe's legs. "You're not coming with us?"

"There's something more I need to do."

"Send my servant instead," Kerwyn offered.

I shook my head. "It must be me. Hurry."

The servant picked up Harlowe in his arms while Kerwyn led the way downstairs and Tobias pressed his hand against a wound on the side of Harlowe's head.

"Whatever you've got to do, do it fast!" Roden said. "We don't have much time!"

I was already racing through the great hall, then turned left at the corridor toward the King's Study. The castle shook as the bombardment continued, though finally my army was mobilized and we were beginning to fight back.

I ran into my study; then something broke through the castle walls somewhere above me. I dodged the larger pieces that fell and ran to the stairs inside the pillar. The wall of my study was already crumbling before I was halfway down.

"Advance!"

I knew that voice, better than I wished to. The order came from Captain Jane Strick, mother of the Prozarian Monarch. I had always considered Strick dangerous but never imagined she was capable of something like this.

She led her soldiers through the hole that had once been the wall of my study, and they began spreading throughout the castle.

"Someone find out where those stairs go!"

I tucked myself around a corner at the base of the stairs. The instant the first man came down, I stabbed him, then shoved the next man against the wall and placed my sword at his throat.

"How many of you are here?"

"Five hundred in this wave. Five thousand by morning."

"What is the mission?"

"Revenge, for Belland. And the Monarch says you stole something from her."

The scope.

Imogen had warned me of that.

Imogen. I had to get to Imogen.

I gave the soldier a quick death and grabbed the scope. I started back toward the steps; then yet another explosion came, and rock tumbled onto those same steps. Another second, and I would have been there too.

When I'd had this room built, the workers had called me paranoid for the way I had designed it, with secret entrances and exits. I shoved one of the secret exits open now, taking me out from beneath the castle and into the night. On the hillside above me, Prozarian soldiers continued to stream into the castle. I heard shouted orders from Roden's senior officers to retreat, and only seconds later, cheers came from the Prozarians, claiming victory.

With the scope in one hand and my sword in the other, I began to run, turning back only once to see my castle half in ruins and now occupied by an enemy bent on the destruction of my country.

Determined to have possession of the scope.

And their revenge on me.

If this were only about me, I would have collapsed right there, without strength to go on. But one single thought lit a fire beneath my feet.

I had to get to Imogen.

· SIX ·

By now, the Prozarian army would be spreading out within the castle walls. I tried to piece together what had brought us to this. Mercy must have been on my ship out of Belland, hiding there or disguising himself as one of the pirates, and at some point, he had found a place among the castle vigils. Roden owed me a full explanation for how that could have happened.

Mercy took out the vigils in the towers first, then the sentries, then the way was opened for the attack of the entire Prozarian army. Everything he had planned seemed to have gone perfectly.

I kept to the shadows of my curtain walls, unnoticed, until I found the first gap and slipped through, into the cool Carthyan night.

I'd rarely traveled this way, and certainly never on foot. Once I had some distance from the castle, I noticed an impressive waterfall pouring out from a ledge in the bedrock. Captain Strick's soldiers must have come in the same way I'd just left. There was no other route to the eastern wall.

Roden did have soldiers placed out here as vigils over this

part of the castle. I passed their bodies as I walked, feeling increasingly nauseous as I absorbed how massive the attack was.

Assuming the roads and bridges were being watched, I cut through wooded areas and waded through rivers, pausing occasionally to look back at what had been my castle. The bombardment had ended, so there would be no new damage, but that was a thin dusting of good news in an avalanche of bad. I didn't know whether Roden had gotten his men out, or if they had been forced to surrender, or even if any of my armies had survived the assault. I didn't know if Harlowe was still alive, or if my closest friends had made it to the inner keep.

I stopped only once along the way, to hide the scope high in the hollow of a tree. It would be safer there than with me, especially considering that I hardly expected a warm welcome from Castor Veldergrath.

Dawn was brimming on the horizon when I finally reached Elmhaven, the estate of the Veldergrath family. It was far grander than Farthenwood and twice the size, with its own curtain wall and towers, not too different from what surrounded my castle. Flags bearing the Veldergrath crest flew from every tower, though they did me the courtesy of flying a single Carthyan flag as well.

It was surprising to see how . . . normal the place looked, when not far behind me, everything was in ruins. I climbed to the top of the main gate to enter Castor's property, pausing there to get an understanding of Elmhaven's unique design.

The estate was two stories tall, but divided in half by a wide and active river that flowed through the center. Open arched bridges connected each half of the estate, creating what

I thought was a beautiful property, though one spoiled by the master who kept it.

I climbed down from the gate but landed badly on my weaker leg for the second time that night, which meant I was limping as I walked toward the house.

I was only halfway there when at least a dozen vigils ran from their watchtowers and surrounded me.

"Stop in the Veldergrath name!" one of them shouted.

I turned and widened my arms so that they could better see me. "You will not bow to your king?"

"Of course they will." Castor Veldergrath, wearing night-clothes and a robe, his hair unkempt, pushed through them. He offered me a low bow; then they did the same. "We are only surprised to see you at this hour, King Jaron . . . or at any hour, for that matter. Is there a problem?"

I didn't answer. Instead, I was surveying the windows along the front of the house, wondering where Imogen was staying.

"Perhaps we can discuss this inside." Castor motioned with his arm for me to accompany him, which I did, though I kept one hand on my sword.

The entryway was as wide and grand as I would have expected, with portraits of the Veldergrath family hung at every level. At the base of the staircase was a life-sized painting of Castor's father, Santhias Veldergrath. The expression on his face was not so different as the last time I had seen him, one of anger and disbelief. I wondered if he had ever looked any other way after I took his regency from him.

"This way, my king." Castor led me to a library to my left, but he paused in the doorway. "You must forgive me for receiving you so informally. Please allow me ten minutes, and I'll return dressed more properly."

"I came to see Imogen," I said.

"Ah, yes, of course. I'll have a maid awaken her and help her dress."

"Just tell her —"

"Ten minutes, my king." Castor dipped his head and closed the doors, leaving me alone in his library.

Ten minutes.

If he left me alone in this room, then it wouldn't contain any useful information. I opened a second door leading from the library, but it was only a music room. I doubted anything was here. Continuing on was a game parlor, but a small desk sat in one corner.

I pulled open the drawers and rifled through the papers. Nothing was in the first drawer, but on top of the papers in the second drawer was a letter addressed to Castor Veldergrath, with Imogen's handwriting.

It began, *To Sir Castor Veldergrath, I was startled when I bumped into you in the market earlier today, so I may not have answered your questions as well as I would have liked. My answer is that regardless of the rumors you heard about Darius being alive, Jaron is still king of Carthya. If you wish to discuss this further —*

"My king?"

I shoved the letter back into the drawer and returned to the library, where Castor stood with two well-armed men. They all bowed, but my hand returned to my sword. I didn't like the way they were looking at me.

Castor sat at his desk and invited me to sit as well, but I remained where I was, as did the two men with him. He said, "Is there trouble, Jaron? I observed that you must have walked here . . . or limped here, as it were."

"Where is Imogen?"

"On her way, I assure you. In the meantime, how can I help you?"

I eyed his two men. "Who are they?"

"Two captains of my army, at your disposal if you have need of them."

Now my glare turned to Castor. "Do you have anything to do with what just happened at the castle?"

Castor stood. "What has happened?" When I didn't answer, he added, "I suppose that's information I'm not entitled to have, since I am not a regent." A false smile oozed across his face. "However, if you were to make me a regent, we could discuss this matter more openly. And as a regent, I would be obligated to offer up my armies in defense of Carthya . . . if Carthya is in need of a defense."

Anger burned in my chest. "Answer my question."

He tried to look concerned, or to look anything but thrilled with seeing me in this position, but his eyes were far too bright with anticipation. "So there was an attack. From the Prozarians, I assume. Imogen told me a little of what happened in Belland. Of course they would come here for revenge."

Castor fell to one knee, as did his two captains. "Make me a regent, Jaron, and you shall have my armies."

"What are your numbers?" The question had to be asked, even if it wounded my pride to force out the words.

"I have a thousand soldiers who can be at your service by noon today. By suppertime, I can double that number if I put enough pressure on friends." I only stared at him until he continued, "You don't like me, or trust me. I understand that, and I know it may take some time to prove myself, given who my father was. But I am not him, Jaron. At the end of the day, I am a patriot."

I'd heard similar words before from Conner, who had used patriotism as his justification for the murder of my parents and treason against Carthya. Of course, it was that same patriotism that later led him to sacrifice his life for mine. Despite his own twisted sense of morality, Conner had played a role in saving Carthya. Maybe Castor would do the same.

"I will consider your request after I see Imogen," I said. "But if you are a patriot, give me the command of your armies now."

Castor stood and passed a look to his captains that I did not miss. I saw the subtle change in their postures. I knew what was coming.

I set my jaw forward. "You never told Imogen I was here."

"Imogen would not wish to see you, even if she knew." Castor turned to his men. "Take the king to the dungeons. There are questions that only he can answer."

I withdrew my sword and got in one good stab at the captain nearer to me, but the second man crashed against my side, knocking me to the ground while Castor wrung the sword from my grip. A knife went to my throat, and Castor opened his door for a dozen other soldiers.

"If you wish to live, then make me a regent," he said.

I closed my eyes, fully aware of how devastating this decision would be. "I dislike most of my regents. You'd fit in perfectly with them."

Castor inhaled deeply, smug and self-satisfied, and I vowed in that moment to personally wipe that grin from his face. But for now, I had much bigger problems. Namely, whether he was going to kill me.

"Take him to the dungeons," Castor said. "Prepare him for questioning."

Someone pulled a black hood over my face and a gag was tied around it while others began binding my hands and feet. I believed it was Castor himself who pulled the king's ring off my finger before he whispered, "Thank you, my king. I promise that, in your absence, Carthya will become greater than ever before."

From there I was carried back into the entry, and farther on they pulled me down some stairs. My hands were released long enough to be put in chains, and the same happened to my legs. The hood and gag in my mouth, however, remained in place.

One of the soldiers landed his fist in my gut, hard enough that I reeled backward, slamming against the dungeon's rock wall. I stayed on my feet for the second hit, but by the third, I collapsed, barely able to draw a breath against the pain and through the hood and the gag.

"Enough!" a man with an older-sounding voice said. "He'll be of no use to you if he's injured."

"Let's go," another man said. "The king will be dead soon enough anyway."

Dungeon bars closed behind me, and footsteps pounded up the stairs seconds later.

But I was not in here alone. Somewhere in this darkness, I heard breathing. Someone was watching me.

SEVEN

Only a few minutes of silence passed before the person here in the dungeons said, "Rub your gag against the rock wall. That will loosen the knot."

It was the same voice as the man whose words had stopped them from hitting me a fourth time. I didn't know if he was a friend, but I doubted he was an enemy. I was still struggling to breathe, yet another reason to get this gag out of my mouth.

I sank against the wall and found a place where the rock jutted out farther than elsewhere. Rather than loosening the knot, I used the rock to pry the gag upward, then did the same to pull the entire hood off my head.

I blinked two or three times before my eyes adjusted; then I noticed a man on the opposite side of the room, older than I dared to guess, thin and in rags, but with an intelligence in his eyes that grabbed my attention.

"You are Jaron, the king of Carthya," the man said.

"How do you know me?"

"Only by reputation." He grinned, somewhat crookedly, as if one half of his face didn't cooperate with the other half. "Also, they called you a king after that final hit. That helped."

"And who are you?"

"A captive, same as you. Also a scholar, a scientist, a historian, and an observer of the world. I will give you three questions, no more. But I swear to answer them as completely as I can."

I rolled my eyes. "What is your name?"

He arched a bushy white brow. "Three questions only, and you wish to waste one on something so trivial?"

"No." I leaned forward to study him better. His accent wasn't Carthyan, nor from anywhere that I recognized. Despite the chains on his wrists, he had no sores or markings there, so if he was a captive, he hadn't been held here for long.

I locked eyes with him. "You are Levitimas."

He nodded.

Levitimas was the guardian of the Devil's Scope and the treasure it led to. The Prozarians had taken it decades ago during one of their conquests, though in all that time, they had never succeeded in reading the symbols on it.

Then, only a few years ago, the Prozarians were sick and on the verge of extinction. Levitimas had somehow discovered that they had the scope, and offered to heal them in exchange for it. Their monarch, Wilta Strick, accepted the offer and welcomed him as a friend. But as soon as the Prozarians were healed, she betrayed him, casting him into a prison, never to taste freedom again.

In a search of his possessions, Wilta found the first lens, which led the Prozarians to Belland on the hunt for the other two. I sensed that, somehow, this man knew these items were mine now.

These same Prozarians had just attacked my castle. I didn't know what role Levitimas had played in bringing them here, but I wasn't interested in any conversation with him.

"I have no questions for you," I said. "There is nothing you can do to help me."

That seemed to catch him off guard. He cocked his head. "You are trying to trick me."

"No, you are playing games with me! You are a prisoner of the same people who just attacked my country. I'd think you'd want to help me."

"I am helping you."

To that, I merely snorted and turned away.

This time, Levitimas leaned toward me. "If you had unlimited questions, they would mean nothing to you. With only three questions, you must decide what matters most."

"Very well." If he wanted to make this a game, then I'd play with my own rules. "What is the answer to the question you hope that I will ask?"

Levitimas smiled and pointed a spindly finger toward me. "Clever. The answer is, to live, you must die."

That was hardly encouraging. "And what is the answer to the question you hope I will not ask?"

This time, he sighed and his entire body grew heavy. "I rather think that it is the question you would never ask, because you do not want the answer."

"Tell me, Levitimas."

"She will only turn to you if you first give her what she wants most. There is no other way."

I opened my mouth, with the next question begging to be

spoken, of how he knew about Imogen. He clearly did know, but I couldn't waste my third question on something that likely didn't matter. The answer would be the same no matter how I asked it.

"And your third question?" he asked.

I shook my head. "I'll save that for later."

"As you wish. Now you must allow me the same privilege, of three questions."

"Why? Aren't you the man of great wisdom and knowledge? There cannot be anything I know that you do not."

"On the contrary, there is much I do not understand. Wisdom and knowledge belong to all that is good. Good things are simple to my mind, because I am good. The Prozarians stake their claims on evil, so they are beyond my comprehension."

I understood the Prozarians very well. I wondered what that said about me.

Levitimas added, "I will consider your lack of wisdom when asking my questions."

"How generous of you."

"Do you have the scope and all three lenses, as the Prozarians believe?"

If he answered me in riddles, I intended to do the same. "Your first question is useless. You're the guardian of the scope and lenses, so you must already know where the treasure is buried."

He smiled faintly. "It is useless to know *where* the treasure is buried. I need the lenses to understand *how* to get it."

"I can help you with that. Once you've found the treasure, pick it up. That's how you get it."

Levitimas chuckled. "You were right before. You are no scholar and no scientist."

"But I am a king. So here is the answer to your question. The Prozarians took nearly everything from me tonight. What little I have left will not fall into their hands, nor yours."

He smiled. "I see that you have learned to answer a question without saying anything at all. Very clever. Question two: If you did find the treasure, what would you hope to gain from it?"

This was simple enough. "I want to escape from this dungeon, take revenge on the Prozarians, destroy every single one of Castor Veldergrath's future plans, rebuild my castle, and somehow get the girl that I am supposed to marry to speak to me again. Can your treasure help me with any of that?"

Levitimas stared back at me; then the half of his face that could smile broke into laughter. Nothing about this was funny. I had meant every word of what I'd just said.

"If you believe the treasure can help you with that," he said, still laughing, "then you deserve it more than any of us."

"Agreed."

Again, he flashed me that crooked smile, though this one soon faded. "I've heard them speak of you. I'm beginning to think that everything they said was more truth than exaggeration."

"Then they said I am a fool, or reckless, or that I deserve everything that happened tonight."

"Yes, yes, all of that. But more. They said you were arrogant, incapable of trust, and that one day you would be the reason for the destruction of your kingdom."

I lowered my eyes. The first two were absolutely true, and I seemed to be carrying out the third to perfection.

Levitimas said that to live, I must die. I wondered if that was an answer to the most obvious question ahead of me now: How could I defeat the Prozarians?

Maybe he was telling me that I could not do it. That with my death, someone else would take over and succeed where I would fail. Maybe he was saying that my time on the throne was over. What would that mean for me and Imogen?

Imogen.

The dungeon door was flung open, and footsteps pounded down the stairs. "Jaron?" Imogen called.

Before I could answer, she was there, grabbing the bars of my cell. A round-faced vigil with beady eyes followed behind her. I instantly decided not to like him.

"Castor said there was an attack on the castle," she said. "Is that true?"

I nodded at her; then my eyes flicked to the stairway behind her, where Castor was emerging from the shadows. A second vigil was on his heels, a man I'd seen when I first came to Elmhaven. He was taller, with dark skin like Mott's, though unlike Mott, he had thick hair and an even thicker beard that nearly reached his chest.

Castor said, "You can see that everything is exactly as I told you. The castle has fallen into Prozarian hands. They will come here next, looking for him. Simply by coming here, Jaron has put you in extreme danger."

I said, "Then release me. I'll gladly leave."

Imogen turned to the second vigil. "Open this cell, Captain Reever."

Castor stepped between them. "I explained this to you, my

lady. Jaron cannot be released, for your safety, or his. Indeed, releasing him would threaten all of Carthya."

"Yes, but releasing me might be the only way to save yourself," I said.

Castor went on as if I had not spoken. "There is nowhere in Carthya for him to go. The Prozarians will already be searching everywhere for him. If Jaron leaves, he will be found, and when he is, the Monarch will do whatever it takes to get the information from him that she wants. I understand he stole something from her called a Devil's Scope. Have you heard of it?"

Imogen glanced at me, but I only lowered my eyes. As usual, she had been right all along.

He continued, "Apparently, it leads to a great treasure. If we release Jaron, the Monarch will get the scope and discover the treasure, and the Prozarians will become more powerful than ever. Surely you can see this."

"I do." Imogen stared at me. "Jaron and I have discussed this very thing."

"But as I told you upstairs, I have a plan. It will save Carthya, and save Jaron as well. I want to protect him, even if he doesn't realize it."

I rolled my eyes. There were many things I was beginning to realize about Castor Veldergrath. His compassion and loyalty were not among them.

Castor only briefly glanced at me before turning to Imogen again. He took her hands in his. "My lady, if you wish to save Jaron's life, you know what you must do. And you must act now."

Imogen turned back to me with tears in her eyes. "Jaron, we have to talk."

I only shook my head. "Imogen, please don't."

I had already guessed what Castor wanted her to say, and if I was right, I knew that I could not bear to hear it. What the Prozarians had just done to my castle, Imogen was about to do to my heart.

· EIGHT ·

Imogen opened her mouth to speak but hesitated as thick tears spilled onto her cheeks.

Beside her, Castor's eyes lit with anger, though he tried to control it in his voice. Through gritted teeth, he said to Imogen, "The Monarch could be here at any moment, and then it will be too late. Speak to him now, or you will weep for him later."

I shook my head at Imogen, warning her not to agree to Castor's demands. Whatever he had persuaded her to do was for his own ambitions. It had nothing to do with what was best for Carthya and certainly nothing to do with helping me in any way.

Castor only wanted to achieve what his father never had: to take the throne. He didn't care two coins together about Imogen except for what she could do to help him steal my crown.

Castor pushed further. "Why do you hesitate, my lady? If he cared for you, why would he come here, drawing the Prozarians to you? Maybe you think you still care for him, but think of what the Monarch will do to him when she comes. She wants the Devil's Scope more than she wants to take her next breath.

She will do her worst to Jaron, and we both know he will never tell her where the scope is. How will she get him to talk? Only when the Monarch turns her anger on you. He knows this, and yet he came here. If you refuse to act, my lady, many people will suffer, perhaps you worst of all, and the Prozarians will still get the scope. You can stop this from happening."

I shook my head again as I saw her eyes begin to soften. "Imogen, don't do this."

Castor whispered to Imogen, "Even now, he is thinking only of himself. You must think of all Carthya now."

Imogen nodded and before speaking drew in a slow breath to steady her emotions. "Do you remember, on the night of your parents' funeral, you sent me away from the castle? You didn't want to put me at risk because of the danger you were in."

That got my attention. "This is different."

"If it is, then it's so much worse now. This time, I can save you. Castor's plan is to exile you as soon as possible, far away from Carthya. I know that's not what you want, but it's your only chance to live. I need you to accept that there is nothing more here for you. Or at least . . ." She wiped another tear from one eye. ". . . I will not be here for you."

Pain pierced my heart, the feeling of it splitting apart. "Imogen, this isn't what you want."

"It is. There is nothing more between us, not now and not ever. Accept the exile. Accept that any future for us is over."

I shook my head, feeling hot tears in my eyes. "He's forcing you to say this."

"But it doesn't mean the words aren't true. Goodbye, Jaron."

"Escort Lady Imogen upstairs," Castor said to the

round-faced vigil. "Jaron and I need to work out the details of his . . . exile."

The vigil took Imogen by the arm. My gaze followed her, but she didn't look back once as she climbed the stairs. After the door was closed, Castor turned to me, smiling in victory.

"She is so strong," he said. "So trusting."

"And you are the cancerous boil on the backside of a rat," I muttered. "You lied to her."

"When did I lie? You do have the Devil's Scope, and the Prozarians did attack Carthya to get it, and if I turn you over to the Monarch, she will push you to your last breath to find out where it is."

"You are working with them," I said. "You helped the Prozarians get into Carthya."

He chuckled. "Oh, I absolutely did. In exchange, I will be rewarded with the title of Steward of Carthya. It's not quite the same as being king, but I will get there, soon enough. Perhaps once I find that treasure myself."

I'd been digging one heel into a dirt patch on the floor, and I finally hit stone. Pausing from my work, I said, "Take me to the Monarch. At least she had the courage to attack me openly. You're nothing but a scavenger who slinks in Prozarian shadows, eager to take whatever remains are tossed your way."

"Who are you to insult me?" he said. "You are nothing now, and I am the future Steward of Carthya. You should bow to me and beg for my mercy."

"I am speaking to a traitor and a snake; those are your titles. I wouldn't beg for my last breath of air from you."

"Ah, well, let's find out if that's true."

I turned back to the wall, refusing again to look at Castor. But he crouched to my level and sighed. "If only you could be here to see the great things I will do for Carthya. Until then, I must keep my promise to Imogen."

"You might get away with lying to her, but you will not lie to me."

"Again, I have not lied. You will be exiled, just not to the grassy, faraway shores that Imogen might have thought." He smiled. "You will be exiled from life itself, exiled from your final breath. Imogen and I are expected at the castle this afternoon, but before we go, I will personally handle your *release* from this dungeon. However, first, I wish to know everything about the Devil's Scope. How it works, where it leads to, and where you have hidden it. If I find it first, I will easily destroy the Prozarians and be the sole ruler of Carthya."

"You know that I won't tell you anything."

"You will, or I'll bring in others to loosen your tongue. Are you ready, Captain Reever?"

My eyes flicked to the vigil who remained, and a cold pit settled in my stomach. I knew exactly what was about to happen.

Reever stuck a heavy key into the lock of my cell and opened the door. In one hand was a coiled whip.

He smiled at me when our eyes met. "Welcome to Elmhaven, King Jaron."

NINE

From inside my cell, Reever turned a crank that rolled the chains on my wrists upward, forcing me to my feet, now with my arms held over my head.

Castor walked directly in front of me. "I should be honest with you about one thing. I'd planned to do this anyway, as revenge for the way you humiliated my father. But the fact that I also want the Devil's Scope sweetens my plan."

My voice began trembling, despite my efforts to control it. "The Monarch will find out I was here. She'll know that you tried to get the scope for yourself."

"By the time she hears anything, I'll already have the treasure. And with it, I will take complete control of Carthya."

I smiled with as much cruelty as I could muster. "If that's your plan, then I won't tell you a thing. I'll gladly take a few stripes to see you punished for ignoring her wishes."

He flinched but quickly recovered and stepped even closer. "Then take these stripes, for it will be your final act in a life that will end in a wisp of dust. You are a failed king, a failed groom, a failed person, in every possible way. The best you can do now is to save yourself some misery and tell me about the Devil's Scope. Where is it?"

I stared back at him. "Levitimas and I have just been playing an interesting game where we each get to ask the other three questions. I suggest we do the same. Are you sure you want that to be one of your three questions?"

Reever punched me, hard, and with my arms suspended by the chain, I had to absorb the full force of the blow.

"Where is the scope?" Castor repeated.

I was coughing for lack of air but found it in me to mutter, "It's hidden, you snake!"

Castor shook his head. "Didn't I tell you that he'd be like this, Captain?"

"You did, sir." Reever pulled out a knife and cut away my shirt.

"Answer my questions!" Castor said. "I will not ask again before that whip flies."

"I hope not. I am sick of listening to you speak."

I'd barely spoken the final words before Reever snapped the whip against my back. I had arched it in hopes of shielding myself from the worst of the pain, but that did nothing to help me. It still stung fiercely.

"You have crossed a dangerous line," I spat at Castor through gritted teeth. "And for what? So you could kneel to your country's invaders? At least your father's treason still kept Carthya free."

The whip snapped again, forcing a grunt from me.

"You destroyed my father's reputation, his power!" Castor

yelled. "You ruined my family! Did you think there'd be no consequences for that?"

"I knew there'd be consequences. I just didn't think you'd be this cowardly."

"Reever —"

Castor's order was cut off by the call of a servant upstairs. "Lord Veldergrath, Lady Batilda has asked to see you. She says it's urgent."

"Now?"

"She's waiting in your office, sir."

"Very well." Castor turned to me. "You will stay here with Captain Reever until you reveal the location of the Devil's Scope. After that, in my mercy, I might allow you to die. You'd better wish for that, because I have taken away any future you might have hoped for. Your throne is mine, your castle is mine, and Imogen just severed the last threads that connected you." He began to leave, then turned back to me with a taunting smile. "Perhaps Imogen's mother can suggest ways I might comfort her daughter during these trying times. Lady Batilda is quite fond of me, I think."

When I only looked away, he turned my head back to him with his hand. "You don't know how long I have waited for this day to come. Now I will bring you to your knees as no one else ever could."

"Only to my knees? That's more generosity than I'll offer you before this is over."

Castor grimaced at me, then pointed to Reever. "You make him scream until he gives us the answer."

"Why is this necessary?" Levitimas asked. "The king can

yet be of great help to us. The Monarch would not want you to be hasty."

"We do not take orders from you, old man." With that, Castor spun around and stomped up the stairs.

When Reever turned my way again, I set my jaw forward, determined not to make another sound.

Reever raised the whip. "You heard the master. I've got to hear you scream."

I closed my eyes as the whip snapped again. Only this time, it hit against the stone wall beside me.

Reever looked over at me, clearly irritated that I hadn't caught on. He struck the whip against the wall a second time and said, "If you don't scream, Castor will come back down to find out why."

I tilted my head, still not fully understanding, but on the next snap of the whip against the wall, I did scream. Reever immediately repeated the action, and so did I.

After a minute of this ridiculous game, he finally lowered his whip. He turned the crank to allow me to lower my arms, and my legs crumpled to the ground.

"Did it cut the skin?" Levitimas asked.

Reever looked at my back. "Yes. Forgive me, my king."

I was in no mood for forgiveness. "Don't you dare ask that right now. Not when my back is on fire." After a minute, the sting had eased enough that I could think. I mumbled, "Tell me what is happening."

"Those of us in Castor Veldergrath's service are called Stewardmen. Some of us serve only because we were forced into it. Jaron, you are our king."

I rolled my head enough to glare at him. "If you were truly on my side, why didn't you release me and put Castor in these chains instead?"

"Then the Prozarians would only install another steward to the throne, or take over the rule of Carthya themselves. If we act fast, Castor Veldergrath can be defeated."

That didn't make sense to me, but it was possible that I was too tired, and too much in pain, to gather any details.

"I must go now and report to Lord Veldergrath." Before he left, Reever added, "He wanted me to stay until you told me where the scope is. What should I tell him?"

"Tell him that immediately after I defeat the Prozarians, I will come for him. He should get as far from Carthya as he can."

Reever sighed. "I can't say that. What should I really tell them?"

I glared at him until he understood that was my message. He shook his head and left the dungeon.

Levitimas said, "Are you determined to make this bad situation worse?"

"Is that your third question, Levitimas?"

"No. It was only a warning."

I tried to lean against the rock wall of the dungeon, but the rock was rough and it hurt my back, so I leaned forward, head down. Levitimas said nothing, which I appreciated. I needed the time to think; I had everything to think about.

I wondered how many of the Stewardmen were on my side. Captain Reever had only said "some." I'd rather he had said "most" or "all but two or three." Until I had proof otherwise, I couldn't trust any of them.

I also had to consider that Castor's ambitions didn't stop at becoming the Steward of Carthya. He wanted to be king, and he somehow believed that Imogen could help him achieve that.

But she couldn't. Imogen was not a royal, nor even of noble birth. Yet he clearly wanted something from her.

And I wasn't at all sure what she wanted. I remembered every single word she had spoken to me down here, but had she meant those words, or was she saying what was necessary to get me to accept exile?

For that matter, why had she accepted exile for me? She knew I'd never agree to leave Carthya.

There was so much I could not understand.

Nor could I hold my thoughts together when the injuries to my back demanded my attention. I tried to find a way to sleep that didn't leave my back stinging with pain, but every movement hurt, every angle hurt. All of me hurt.

Levitimas had said that Imogen would only turn to me again if I first gave her what she wanted most.

What did she want? Trust?

I did trust her, completely and absolutely; that was never a problem. No, the problem was that she no longer trusted me. I had failed her one time too many.

Which meant she had no reason to continue loving me.

I glanced up and saw Levitimas staring at me. I couldn't read his expression, though I was sure he could guess at exactly what was on my mind. I hated the unfairness in that.

So I turned away from him, closed my eyes, and did my best to sleep.

· TEN ·

I couldn't have been asleep for long before I heard a familiar clacking of heels on the stone stairs. I blinked, hearing the sound of my name, and then Batilda was there, staring at me through the bars of the cell with the same beady-eyed vigil who had come down with Imogen earlier.

Reluctantly, I sat up, but only stared at the stone wall in front of me, humiliated to be in this situation. I felt like an exhibit on display, to be laughed at and mocked.

And it seemed that was the way Batilda intended to treat me. She didn't laugh, but she spoke to the vigil as if I were not directly in front of her. "So it's true," she mumbled. "The castle has fallen."

"Jaron has fallen, but the castle remains," the vigil said. "Any damage to the castle will be repaired as soon as possible, under the direction of Master Veldergrath."

"Imogen told me she had arranged for Jaron's exile." Batilda continued staring at me. "Why is he still here, and left in this state of injury?"

"The exile will happen soon, as promised," the vigil said. "You told Master Veldergrath you would not discuss Imogen with him before knowing whether Jaron was alive. Here is your proof."

For the first time, I looked over at them, specifically at Batilda. I shook my head and said, "Do not discuss Imogen with Castor Veldergrath. He is using her."

Batilda stared back at me, though there was little mercy in her eyes. She said to the vigil, "Imogen can speak her own mind. Whatever she chooses to do, I will not stand in her way."

The vigil smiled. "That is good enough. Thank you, Lady Batilda. I will see you upstairs to pack for your return to the castle."

"Yes, but . . ." Batilda glanced my way again. ". . . Jaron is still a king. He cannot be left this way."

"The time of kings in Carthya has ended. *Jaron's* time has ended."

"Allow me to wrap his wounds."

"You are the mother of a queen. We have servants who will do that."

"Then give him your coat. At least do that much for him."

"My lady, this is a Stewardman coat! It's made of the finest wool."

"I don't care if it's been spun from gold!" Batilda said. "Am I the mother of a queen or not? Give him your coat!"

The vigil grunted, then removed his coat and gave it to Batilda.

"What will happen to Jaron now?" Batilda asked.

"His exile will be arranged, but the master will personally take care of that detail. Until then, I'm sure you have much to do to prepare to return to the castle."

The beady-eyed servant held out an arm to escort Batilda upstairs, but she said, "He cannot wear such a fine coat with these wounds. Open the cell for me, then go upstairs and fetch me some bandages. That is the least we can do before his exile."

The vigil mumbled something under his breath, but he did as she instructed, opening the barred door between us; then he stomped up the stairs, muttering even louder.

Instantly, Batilda knelt beside me and whispered, "Imogen wants to know if the others are safe."

My brow furrowed as I tried to grasp the sudden change in her behavior. "What?"

"The others. Her friends?"

"Oh." I closed my eyes and saw their faces pass through my mind. "I don't know."

"Imogen has a plan, and she asks you to trust her."

"What plan?"

Batilda shrugged. "She said you would know."

I rolled my head enough to look at her. "I should know her plan? How could I possibly know that?"

"She said that you would know what she is thinking."

My sigh came as heavy as my chains. "I never know what she is thinking, Lady Batilda. I only know that, on my best day, I'm usually five steps behind her."

"And this is not your best day." Batilda heard a sound behind her, then stood and gave me the coat. "A sword is at the top of the stairs. It would be better to go left. I must leave before any vigils return."

Before leaving, she closed the cell door but stopped it from swinging entirely shut. At the base of the steps, she paused to look back at me, saying, "You're too young for all this."

Her shoes clacked up the stone steps again, but my focus was on the cell door. It was unlocked, but it wouldn't be long before that beady-eyed vigil returned with the bandages.

After the dungeon door above us closed, Levitimas let out a low whistle, then said, "I think that could have gone better."

"You said I would have to die in order to live," I replied. "But I've got a better plan."

He frowned. "Are you sure? I thought mine out quite well."

"And I've barely thought mine through at all, but I will not stay in here a minute longer." Angling myself to reach the pin hidden in my belt was no simple matter, but I retrieved it and picked at the locks on my wrists. Once I was free of them, I looked up at Levitimas. "I will bring you with me."

"Whatever you have in mind after you leave this dungeon, I doubt you will survive," he said. "I am certain that I would not."

"But you've got to try. You've got to do something!"

"I am. I'm waiting to find the treasure."

I groaned. "I will help you find it. Please, Levitimas, you must come with me."

"That treasure will offer what you think you want most," he replied. "But if you are not careful, it will take what you value most."

I put a hand on the bars of the dungeon. "I have to find it, before the Monarch does. Then I will reclaim my kingdom and rid the world of the Prozarians forever."

"It will not be as simple as you suggest," he said.

"Nothing with me is ever simple."

"No, I would never think that. Until we meet again, be at peace."

I slid on the Stewardman coat Batilda had left here for me. It was dark blue with two wide leather stripes that crossed in the back and went straight over the shoulders. A handsome-enough coat, except the wool was like a stiff brush against the wounds on my back.

I closed the dungeon door and hurried up the stairs, pausing in front of the door at the top before pushing it open. Peace was the last thing I had in mind.

· ELEVEN ·

Because I'd been hooded when they carried me to the dungeon, I wasn't sure exactly what to expect when I opened the door. Fortunately, I entered a small room without windows or decoration. A cot was set up in one corner, perhaps for a vigil, when necessary. In the opposite corner, a rack was mounted to the wall for the storage of weapons. My sword wasn't there, but I did see a sword, more or less. It was simple and rusty, the balance on it was terrible, and I doubted it was sharp enough to cut through cream, but it was the only weapon here. This must have been the one Batilda had mentioned.

I hoped no one would challenge me before I escaped. This sword wouldn't defend me against a single toothpick.

I opened the next door and heard a commotion in the corridor to my right. Batilda seemed upset as she explained to whoever was with her that "Jaron didn't look well. Master Veldergrath must promise that he will be cared for before he is exiled."

"He will be treated better than he deserves," a male voice replied. "That is Master Veldergrath's promise."

Their voices were coming my way, so I darted toward the

left and quickly rounded a corner. At best, I had ten seconds before they discovered my absence.

This route led me into a turret with stairs leading upward. I had no idea where they went, certainly not to an easy exit, but I had no other choice. I ran up the stairs and opened a door to find a working area for servants. Three maids were in there now, but I saw a couple of objects on a nearby table that I wanted, so I put my head down, greeted the women, and then reached across the table to grab a knife and a thin wooden carving board.

"What are you —" a maid started to ask.

"I'm borrowing these . . . permanently." I smiled and ducked out of the room as quickly as I had entered. Back on the stairway, I paused long enough to slide the knife into my boot and then to place the carving board against my chest, belting it in place beneath the Stewardman coat. If any trouble was at the top of these stairs, I needed some form of armor.

I entered the next level to find myself in a long hallway with doors on one side, probably rooms for the servants, based on the plain walls and simple furnishings. On the other side of the hall was a single door, leading to the upper arched bridge that I had seen when I first came to Elmhaven. If I could get across the bridge, Imogen's room was likely somewhere on that other side.

I opened the door and stepped onto the bridge. A branch of the Roving River flowed directly beneath me, its mighty current louder than I would have expected from up here. I started across but was only halfway to the door when it opened and Castor stepped onto the bridge ahead of me. My sword was at his side, which infuriated me.

He smiled and chuckled when he saw the sword in my hand. "You'd defend yourself better with a soup spoon."

I squared my footing to him. "I agree. Do you have one I can use?"

He laughed. "Sorry, no."

I glanced behind me to see three Stewardmen cross onto the bridge. The man in front held a bow with the arrow already notched into place.

My options were narrowing. I climbed onto the ledge of the bridge, hoping to find a possibility for escape, but all I saw was the river below. Farther below than I wished it was.

I looked over at Castor again. "Your father was a smart man. He was wrong, and he was evil, but at least he was smart. What a pity you are only two-thirds the man that he once was."

"I am twice what he was. Within a single day, I have dissolved your kingdom, lured you to my dungeons, and now, on the eve of my becoming the Steward of Carthya, I am about to send you to a permanent exile."

"Your stupidity shines with every word," I said. "Nothing that you are planning will actually work."

"I will be king, Jaron. Once you are no longer in my way, of course."

I turned around again and saw the archer raise his bow. From this height, the fall into the river would likely kill me.

You must die if you want to live.

Levitimas's words rang in my ears. I didn't know whether he had anticipated this moment or not, but one thing was certain: The archer's arrow was meant for me.

He fired, striking me square in the chest. The thrust

knocked me off balance, and I fell backward until I hit water and sank to the river bottom. I tried to get to air but had no idea which way was up or down. The current carried me over a sharp rock that reopened the wounds on my back. Blood rose up to the surface while I struggled not to inhale water.

I was some distance downriver before I finally floated to the surface, but I could scarcely move. All I could do was stay on my back and let the water carry me away.

A single sound penetrated from somewhere in Castor's estate down to me. A scream of my name. It was too late by then to do anything, for I was already too far away.

But I wished I could, even if it would make things worse for me.

That scream had come from Imogen.

· TWELVE ·

I let the river carry me beneath Castor's gates, and onward still until I was far from Elmhaven, and far from anywhere. I hadn't slept at all the night before and hadn't eaten since the few bites I had taken last evening. My strength was sapped, every muscle in my body ached, my back stung fiercely, and Imogen's final words to me, pushing me as far from her as possible, echoed in my ears. I felt beaten down in a way I never had before.

Finally, I rolled from the water, realizing only then that an arrow was sticking out of my chest. I plucked it out, then unbuttoned the Stewardman coat. There, still against my chest, was the wood carving board. The arrow had pierced it deeper than I had expected.

I sent the carving board and arrow downriver. I'd lost the sword when I fell, but at least the knife was still in my boot.

After several minutes, I tried to stand, but my legs immediately crumpled beneath me. I couldn't lie down either, not with the wounds on my back. So I sat, hunched over and shivering inside the coat of my enemy, with no idea of what to do next.

There was almost nothing I could do physically. It had

been extraordinary luck that I'd survived that fall into the river. I never should have come out of that water.

After a very long time of staring at nothing, I pushed to my feet and remained there, balanced only by holding on to a nearby tree, while trying to decide where to go from here. I took one step toward Elmhaven, but in my condition, I had no chance of helping Imogen, nor was I sure that she wanted my help, or even my presence. I turned to walk toward the scope instead, but it was safer in the hollow of the tree than in my hands. Finally, I began walking toward my castle, or what was left of it.

I didn't make it far. I was bruised and exhausted, and my spirit was crushed. After realizing I'd only wandered in a wide and miserable circle, I gave up and leaned against a nearby hill where I could close my eyes and think.

I must have slept at some point, and for quite some time, because when I awoke, a morning glow warmed the horizon and my clothes had dried. Somewhere nearby, I heard the sounds of marching, though at first I couldn't tell if they were coming closer or moving farther away. I crouched low, then crept forward until I saw soldiers passing beside me on the road, all of them in the green-and-white colors of the Prozarians and moving toward Drylliad.

Their uniforms looked clean, and the men looked cleaner. I didn't think any of these soldiers had been part of the initial assault on my castle, which was a concern. The Prozarian I had questioned in the King's Study told me there'd be a force of at least five thousand coming to join the first five hundred already at the castle. This must be them.

"You're under Veldergrath's command?"

I froze, hearing a voice behind me, then turned to see a Prozarian officer with both hands on his hips, staring at me. I looked down at myself and remembered the Stewardman coat.

"You're a deserter, I assume?"

I stood and finished buttoning up my coat. "Not at all. I'm on my way to Drylliad with a message for your monarch. I stopped to rest last night and must have fallen asleep."

"What is the message?"

My next words would be risky, but I hadn't seen this man before and I hoped he had never seen me. "Jaron attempted an escape from Elmhaven last night but was shot in the chest with an arrow and fell into a river far below. Master Veldergrath believes he is dead."

"Has anyone located the body?"

I looked directly at him. "Yes, he was recently found by a Prozarian soldier who happened to be in the area."

The man brushed a hand over his jaw. "The Monarch will not be happy about this news. You should tell her yourself."

I shook my head. "She will never believe the news if I tell her. She ought to hear this from one of her own men."

"Perhaps you're right, but I'm not telling her. It'd be best coming from Commander Coyle. You're welcome to march along with us to Drylliad."

That was the last thing I wanted, but I did want to return to Drylliad, and this might be the least suspicious way of getting in. I just had to hope that Commander Coyle was nobody I would know or recognize.

I nodded and followed the man back to the road in time to join up with the last rows of marching soldiers, who only gave me disinterested glances before facing forward again. That was fine by me. Surely there had to be soldiers here who had also been at Belland. At the very least, I needed a hat.

The boy marching beside me looked to be near my own age, but the worry on his face could not be missed.

"What's your name?" I asked him.

"Haddin."

"Are you all right?"

"You live here in Carthya," Haddin responded. "Is it true, what they say about their king?"

"Only the worst parts. What have you heard?"

"That he will show you his right hand and steal from you with his left. That his mind never stops creating mazes of plots and plans."

So far, I rather liked Haddin. "Is that so?"

"There's more. I've heard that the king cheats death with nearly every step he takes."

"Ah, well, if that's true, then you have no need to worry. I have just come from Lord Veldergrath's estate with a message, that the king is dead."

Although I had spoken the words with confidence, Haddin didn't seem convinced. "But what if that is only one of the king's many lies or tricks?"

I took offense at that. "A trick, maybe. He avoids lies."

"What's the difference?"

"There happens to be a great difference —"

Haddin shrugged. "Doesn't matter. Our monarch said we were not to believe anything that she does not tell us herself."

Which complicated my task greatly. It was not enough to spread rumors about myself. I needed to persuade Wilta to believe me. I had no idea how that would be done.

It would certainly require some creative tricks, and a great act of deceit.

· THIRTEEN ·

When the castle towers came distantly into view that afternoon, orders were issued down our lines that we were to rest, as we would likely need our strength once we entered Drylliad. A few scattered homes were here on the outskirts, but the farmers working their fields merely dropped their tools and hurried their families inside. Nobody seemed interested in challenging this large group of soldiers, and I hardly blamed them for that. They had no chance of winning.

I'd have no chance either if anyone around me decided to look at the newcomer who had joined their ranks. It was one thing when we were all facing forward to march, with me at the end of the lines. It was quite another the way they were now talking with one another, relaxing. One soldier began watching me, far more closely than I wanted.

I immediately left the road, headed toward a few of the homes, but Haddin followed me. "The Prozarians are never to break their lines without orders."

"So get back to your line."

"The commander will ride along the lines soon for an inspection."

"He's not my commander, Haddin."

"No, but he won't like to hear that anyone has wandered off."

"Then don't tell him."

Haddin sighed and began hurrying back to the road. From where I stood, I watched as a large man in a Prozarian uniform rode down the lines. The soldiers saluted him, and he returned the gesture, occasionally stopping to ask questions. Haddin returned to his place in line and motioned for me to join him, but I did not move.

I could not move, because I knew this commander.

The soldier who had found me asleep earlier had called him Commander Coyle, a name I had not heard before. Back in Belland, I had called him something else: Lump, a substitute he had tolerated only because he clearly hated his first name, Rosewater.

Lump's real name was Commander Rosewater Coyle. He would know me at a glance.

Lump was speaking to Haddin now. I turned and immediately walked toward the nearest home. It was little more than logs bound together by river grasses with bundles of dried hay for a roof, and a door that only leaned against the entrance.

I entered the home without knocking and found myself facing the farmer's sword, such as it was. The craftsmanship was crude and the blade looked dull, but all I had was a stolen knife, so I was in no position to compare weapons.

This man must have been in his late thirties, though the

lines on his face made him look older. His clothes were as ragged as mine ever were in my years as Sage, but his eyes were sharp and focused.

His family huddled behind him, a wife and five children, and he was clearly determined to protect them. He raised his sword at me, then blinked and immediately fell to his knees. "King Jaron? Forgive me, we did not expect you."

His family followed his gesture, but I immediately asked them to rise. "I didn't expect to be here either. What is your name, sir?"

"Emmett. Only Emmett."

If he had no family name, then he had been born in poverty and likely had little expectation of rising from it. But he seemed to be a good man.

I began unbuttoning my coat. "I need a favor. It shouldn't be dangerous if you do exactly as I say."

Emmett stepped forward, or rather, he limped forward, quite noticeably. My shoulders fell, along with my plans when I had entered this home. Emmett had no chance to pass for me.

"Never mind," I said. "Stay here. Do you at least have a hat?"

"I'll go out there as you." A boy who looked to be about Fink's age emerged from behind his father. "That's what you need, isn't it? Someone to go out there and claim to be you?"

I shook my head at his offer. I wouldn't risk anyone so young.

"My son can do this," the farmer said. "We know what you've done for Carthya. Let us help you."

I had little choice but to agree. Reluctantly, I removed my

coat and handed it to the boy. While he buttoned it, I opened the door a crack, and sure enough, Lump was riding up the hill.

"Listen carefully," I said. "Tell the truth as much as you can, that this is your family's home and you're only here to say goodbye. Ask him to allow you that and then swear that you will catch up to his men before they enter Drylliad."

Emmett's wife came out from behind her husband. "You're sending my boy into battle?"

"Not if he does this right." I straightened the collar of the Stewardman coat and looked directly at him. "Make that soldier believe you."

The boy nodded and walked outside just in time for Lump to arrive. His voice wavered at first, but he quickly recovered. "Commander, I am the one you are looking for."

"You were just marching with my men?" Lump asked. "How old are you?"

"Fourteen, sir."

"I did not think Lord Veldergrath had boys so young among his armies."

"Lord Veldergrath? Oh, well, he has never asked my age. I only stopped here to say goodbye to my family. If you'll allow that, I'll return to your ranks before you enter Drylliad."

Silence followed his request, and I began to worry that Lump might try forcing him to leave now, which would be a disaster. But finally, he said, "Very well. Tell your family that there is good news. Carthya is on the verge of surrendering. With some luck, no fighting will be necessary."

I felt the eyes of Emmett and his family fall heavily on me, but I was focused on what was happening outside. Nor did I want to explain anything that Lump was saying.

"Thank you, Commander," the boy said. "I'll join you soon."

Lump rode away, and after a minute, the boy walked back inside. He watched me carefully as he began unbuttoning the Stewardman coat. "Carthya is surrendering?"

"Not if I can help it. I need one more favor: that you all will keep me a secret." I took the coat from the boy and began dressing in it again, wincing once more as the rough fabric brushed against my back.

"Of course we'll keep your secret," Emmett said. "And my wife can wrap the wounds on your back."

I shook my head. "I can't fight in bandages."

"Get him one of your father's shirts," Emmett's wife said to her son. "That will be better than the coat alone."

I was slow to put the shirt on but fully grateful. When I finished with the coat as well, I thanked them and said, "I need to go now."

"How will you fight without a sword?" Emmett stepped forward. "Take mine."

I waved my hand against his offer. "You may need that."

"Not as much as you will need it, I'm sure."

I nodded in thanks and slid the sword through the buckle of the coat. In exchange, I gave him the knife from my boot. That, at least, would give him something for defense, if necessary.

"You're still easy to recognize." His wife reached for a sewing box and pulled out a bit of fur, which she gave me. "Put this under your hat when you need to change your look." She gave me some other rags as well. "Stuff those inside your coat to widen your shoulders. They'll have to look twice at you to recognize you with those."

"Take my hat too." The boy pulled a hat off a hook beside the door. I put everything but the hat in my pocket for now. I could hardly return to Haddin looking like . . . whatever I would look like with these items.

"Thank you, all." I turned to leave, then stopped. The poverty of this family was apparent, but I felt close to collapsing with hunger. I had spotted half a loaf of bread on their table, and I wanted to ask for it, but I didn't dare. Not after taking a valuable sword, and a shirt and hat, and after putting their son at risk to save myself.

I gave them a polite nod and said, "You have done more than enough for me."

I walked out the door but heard the boy running behind me. He tapped my arm and held out the bread. "Mother said that, in our hands, this bread might save us for a day but, in your hands, it might save all of Carthya. Please take it, King Jaron."

I nodded gratefully, then accepted the bread. I finished the last bite upon rejoining Haddin in the lines.

He shook his head at me. "The commander said he only allowed you to leave because you were so young. I thought that was strange, considering you're my age."

"Strange indeed," I said. "But I've got to be old enough to take on whatever we find in Drylliad."

"The commander says the worst is over," Haddin said. "We control the castle; we control the city. There's really only one problem that remains."

"What is that?"

"The girl that Jaron was going to marry. What was her name again?"

Something began to twist in my chest, a feeling I recognized from many times before when something awful was about to become far worse. "Her name is Imogen."

"Yes. Now that Jaron is gone, I've heard rumors that Imogen is the only remaining threat to us. At least, that's what the Monarch believes. I'll bet a month's wages that will be our assignment when we get to Drylliad."

"What assignment is that?"

Haddin shrugged. "Imogen will have to join us, or she'll follow Jaron's fate."

My fists curled. If they intended to go after Imogen, then I would not waste time with diplomacy or compromise. If the Prozarians had any intentions of harming her, then there would be no option now other than for me to destroy them.

· FOURTEEN ·

Shortly before crossing through the gates into Drylliad, our lines were brought to a halt because of what sounded like a disturbance ahead. It was loud enough that Lump's shouted orders to "get him under control" could be heard even from the back of the line, where I was.

Haddin furrowed his brow and leaned in to me. "What do you think the problem is?"

I couldn't think of a single person who could have caused so much commotion, with one exception: Mott. He must have returned to Carthya.

Without answering Haddin, I pushed my way forward, ignoring the reminders from other soldiers that we were to remain in our lines. When I was near the front, I saw him; I saw Mott's bald head and large frame. He was fighting three to four soldiers at any given time, and a half-dozen bodies were sprawled out on the ground in various stages of consciousness, but Mott was also losing strength as new men continued to attack him.

Finally, Mott was brought to his knees and placed in chains. Lump, one of the few people I'd ever seen who could match Mott's size, stepped forward, his hands clasped behind his back.

"We meet again," he said.

Mott didn't answer. Instead, his head was lowered as he sought to regain his breath.

Lump continued, "I thought you stayed in Belland. What brought you here?"

"To attend the king's wedding, as a surprise." Mott looked over the group. "Though this was not the surprise I had expected."

"I'll give you a bigger surprise, though you may not welcome it," Lump said. "There are whispers among my men that Jaron is dead."

Mott swung his head sharply toward Lump, his eyes widened with alarm. "That is impossible!"

"I have not verified the claim myself, but we both know how reckless Jaron is. He was never meant for a long life."

"Yes, he was." Mott blinked once, then bowed his head and his shoulders slumped. I felt awful watching this, but Lump had been correct. My life had always been one of balancing on a narrow beam just above the grave. It shouldn't be hard for Mott to believe that I had finally fallen in.

Lump wasn't finished. "Did you come alone, sir? Or did Darius come with you?"

"I came alone," Mott mumbled.

"Really? You took the trouble to come all this way for Jaron's wedding and his own brother would not come too?"

"Darius had business in Belland that required his attention. I came alone."

Mott spoke convincingly, but I knew him well enough to know when he was lying. Darius was here in Carthya too, though I had no idea where, if he was free, or if he had also been captured.

"Take him with us," Lump ordered his men. "We'll see what the Monarch wants to do with him."

The soldiers marched on, and I waited where I was until Haddin brought up the end of the line. I took my place and ignored his many questions. A thousand other concerns required my attention instead.

Those thoughts came into sharper focus when we crossed through the gates into Drylliad. At the top of the hill in the distance, I saw the upper turrets of my castle. The curtain walls prevented me from seeing most of the structure, but I saw enough to have hope that maybe the damage wasn't as bad as I had thought.

Other than Prozarian soldiers on patrol at nearly every road we crossed, Drylliad itself was uncommonly quiet. There were no markets, no wagons, no people moving about for their daily business. I hoped this only meant that families had safely isolated themselves in their homes, and nothing worse.

"I heard someone say that all citizens have been ordered to go directly to the castle," Haddin said. "That's where they'll announce our victory to the people."

"Has Carthya surrendered?" I asked.

Haddin shrugged. "It must have."

"Under whose authority?"

"I don't know."

As Haddin had suggested, within only a few steps, soldiers

on horseback began riding through the streets, announcing orders for all men, women, and children to come to the gates of the castle at once.

I lowered my head as people began cautiously leaving their homes, clutching their children tightly in their arms. Until now, I had thought there was no more room in my heart for so much to hurt, but I was wrong. The ache overfilled and began spreading through my chest with each new family that stepped out of their home. They looked personally defeated, as if life had gone out of them, as if all they could do was to put another foot forward and hope for a chance to survive. Maybe that was how I looked too.

Since I was at the end of the line, many of the families simply followed us, their conversations becoming louder and bolder the longer we walked.

"I expected more of Jaron," one man said.

"I heard he ran from the castle during the attack," a woman replied. "My sister's a maid there and saw him. He abandoned the castle and everyone inside to the Prozarians."

"Now he's abandoned all of us," a second woman said. "If only his brother had taken the throne, as he was meant to do."

"If only," I mumbled.

Haddin must have been listening to their gossip too. He elbowed me. "Did you ever hear the story about Jaron as a child?"

"Which one?"

"Apparently, he set fire to a tapestry —"

"I've got to go." I ignored his protests and didn't look back as I cut away from the line of soldiers and the families following us. The closer I got to the castle, the more certain it was that someone would recognize me.

So instead, I retraced steps I had not followed in two years, since the time I had used this route to bring Conner, Roden, Tobias, and Mott into the castle.

The Roving River ran beneath the lowest part of the castle, a deliberate design to allow the current to carry away our waste-water and food scraps. A metal gate prevented unwanted guests from traveling upstream to enter the castle on their own. Likely as not, I was one of those unwanted guests now, but I also knew where the gate key was hidden, so I would easily get in.

However, once I passed through the gate, I realized my job would be far more complicated than I had expected. Rubble from the attack had fallen into the river, blocking the flow, which now had spilled over its banks, creating a sort of muddy lake where dry land had once been.

As much as possible, I tried to stay on dry ground, though that required me to scramble over large fallen stones and other debris that scraped at my arms and legs. From there, I followed the river upstream, passing the very place where Roden and I had once fought shortly before I was made king. For some rea-son, the memory made me smile now.

Otherwise, with nothing else down here, I dunked myself in the cleaner part of the river, then climbed up the narrow lad-der and pushed through a door in the floor to enter the kitchen.

Because of whatever mandatory announcement that was to be made, the kitchen was empty. I started toward the hidden entrance to the innermost keep, but from the doorway, someone called to me, "What are you doing here, boy? Everyone is to be present for the announcement."

"What announcement?" I asked.

"Everything that Lord Veldergrath promised us if we followed him," the soldier said. "Come on, we don't want to be late."

No, indeed, I did not.

FIFTEEN

The man who had found me in the kitchen was a Stewardman, and he waited for me to squeeze off the extra water from my coat before I joined him. I was glad to have a hat to hide my face, but I worried that wouldn't be enough. The first chance I got to slip away from him, I made my way up to the second floor, to the place I had retreated to once the castle attack began.

Most of this floor seemed intact, other than a gaping hole in one corner of the castle wall, and the glass on the balcony doors and nearby windows was gone. Log beams had been inserted to hold the upper floors in place. Rocks and other debris from the damaged wall were everywhere on the ground, though several servants were working in the area to clean and begin making repairs.

Voices were headed toward me, so I ducked into the nearest room in the corner of the castle, a smaller room reserved for the queen's personal maid.

I shut the door nearly all the way, leaving it open a crack so that I could peer out. While I did, I tried to change my appearance using the items the farmer's wife had given me earlier. I felt ridiculous placing a piece of fur over my hair and stuffing my coat to broaden my shoulders, but if it kept me from being recognized, it would be worth it.

Outside the room, I heard footsteps and angled myself to see who was there.

"How do I look?" That was Wilta's voice. I couldn't see her face, but I saw a curl of her red hair against a green dress trimmed with white ribbons — Prozarian colors.

"Monarch, there is no one more beautiful than you." I recognized Mercy's voice, slathering praise on her like over-buttered toast. I truly hated Mercy. Even more now that I knew he was the one who had made the attack on my castle possible.

"The princess of Bultain is also quite beautiful, I've noticed." Captain Strick had a far more military look than her daughter and would be a challenging opponent in any duel. "We have searched the entire castle but have not found her, nor the regent she recently married, nor a few others."

"Find them," Wilta snapped. "Didn't I say that every person who matters to Jaron must be accounted for? What about Roden?"

"No sign of him either," Captain Strick said. "But he has an entire army with him, so it's only a matter of time —"

"It is your fault they got away. You have been so intent on celebrating that you fail to realize we do not yet have a victory."

"We nearly do," Mercy said. "Castor Veldergrath himself confirmed the news about Jaron."

Wilta turned on him, and from where I stood, I saw Mercy backing up. "You are useless, Lord Trench! We came here for the scope, and Castor Veldergrath's archer just ruined my last hope of finding it. Tell me why I should celebrate Jaron's death?"

Mercy bowed his head. "No, Monarch, you are correct."

"Jaron humiliated us back in Belland," Strick said. "We came here for revenge, and now we have succeeded."

"I want the treasure!" Wilta nearly screamed the words. "That is all that matters!"

"We can still find the treasure," Mercy said. "If Imogen will confirm that he had the Devil's Scope, then we only need to know where he hid it."

"Where is Castor?" Wilta's footsteps could be heard, as if pacing. "He should be out there with me when I am announced to the people."

Strick said, "He is still speaking with Imogen in the king and queen's private sitting room. Apparently, she is not cooperating with his plans."

I glanced to my right. Was Imogen really so close? The next three rooms beside me were reserved for the king and queen. The center room was a private sitting area. Was Imogen truly in there, and with Castor?

"Perhaps it is better if you first greet the people alone," Mercy said. "I'll go out now and get their attention."

In the same moment, Imogen must have walked into the queen's apartment, the room directly beside me. Even from where I stood, it was easy to hear her conversation with Castor.

"It's too soon," Imogen was saying. "It will be hard enough on the people just to hear of Carthya's defeat."

"It will be worse if that's all they hear. We owe them the comfort of knowing life in Carthya will go on as usual for them."

"I will feel as false as I will look," Imogen protested. "One month is all I ask."

The maid's room, where I was, had a second door that connected with the room where Imogen stood. I had been slowly opening that door but stopped when I had enough of a view to see Castor and Imogen facing each other. I couldn't see Imogen well, but Castor's face was flushed with anger.

"One month is not acceptable," he said.

"But it's all I can give you. We should go; the Monarch is waiting."

"Wilta is intolerable," Castor said. "The sooner I can get her out of Carthya, the better. For now, let's put on a smile and pretend we care anything for her."

Imogen accepted his arm, and they left the room, while I returned to watching everything I could from the first door I had already cracked open. Castor bowed to Wilta, though from Wilta's tight expression, I was certain she had just heard what Castor had said about her.

Out on the balcony, Mercy must have said something that caused the people below to applaud, though it wasn't nearly loud enough for how crowded I knew that courtyard must be. Not everyone greeted his news happily.

He finished even louder than before with "It is time to welcome your monarch!"

Wilta frowned back at Castor and Imogen. "The people will learn to love me, but I will always hate them."

In an instant, her scowl turned to a smile. She walked out, waving her arms to muted cheers from below. Castor and Imogen waited inside the castle.

Wilta called down from the balcony. "To my Prozarians, this is the day you have long awaited. Carthya is ours. No one is left to challenge us. To all Carthyans, it is my sad duty to inform you of the death of King Jaron. With his loss, you are invited to join in our cause. I am your monarch now, and I command you all to kneel before me."

Cries of alarm and murmurs rose up even to where I still was, hidden inside this room. Then I also heard shouted orders, certainly from Prozarian soldiers on the ground, commanding the people to kneel.

Gradually the noise quieted, and a minute later, Wilta nodded and held out her arms. "Very good."

"Hail to the Monarch!" someone cried from below.

"Hail to the Monarch!" the people repeated.

I had to force myself to remain on my feet, so harsh was the blow of realization that hit me. All of them must have knelt. All of them had just acknowledged her as their ruler.

Carthya was no longer mine.

· SIXTEEN ·

Wilta had made it official, claiming her title as the Monarch of Carthya, now a conquered country. *My* country, conquered. I truly could not understand how this had happened, and so quickly.

My mind raced through every possibility of what I should do, though everything ended with a single question: Should I reveal that I was still alive?

If I did reveal myself — race onto the balcony and show myself to the people — I could ask them to fight with me, and they would.

But I knew how that would end, and how fast it would be over.

For now, I had to let my people believe that I was gone. It was a cruel decision, particularly to those I most cared about, but it had to be done.

Out on the balcony, Wilta continued her speech. "We shall go on to other conquests, bringing the countries that surround us to their knees, and move onward again, until I am the only Monarch in all the lands. Carthya, you will be part of that victory. Fight for me, and be part of our growing empire. You are all Prozarians now, and I am your monarch!"

A cheer rose from that, as unenthusiastic as the others. When the noise dimmed, Wilta said, "I cannot always be here in Carthya, of course, so in my absence, you will have a steward. He will be the caretaker of this land, to collect your taxes and tributes, to settle your quarrels, and to carry out our new laws. I give you Steward Veldergrath!"

My heart sank. I'd known this was coming, but to hear it still infuriated me. If the Prozarians had wounded Carthya, then Castor Veldergrath was the infection that prevented its healing. I would not rest until he was personally defeated.

"Let us greet the people." Castor took Imogen's hand and led her out to the balcony with him. Shouts immediately began to rise from the crowd below, that of "traitor" and "betrayal." Obviously not what he had expected.

"My people!" Castor tried to yell above them. "Listen to me!"

But the anger was such that he could not make himself heard. Finally, Wilta hissed at him, "Go back inside!"

Castor went first, this time abandoning Imogen to leave the balcony on her own, and Wilta followed. She put herself directly in front of Castor, waving a finger in his face. "That could not have gone worse! You promised me that the people would welcome your reign!"

"They will," he said. "I assure you that they will. They're just upset right now, from the news about Jaron."

Now Wilta turned to Imogen. "And you are still not cooperating. Tonight will be your last chance. When the nobles come for our official welcome, you will do whatever it takes to get them to accept Castor as their steward, or by tomorrow, you will be replaced."

Imogen merely dipped her head at Wilta but said nothing.

Wilta stormed down the stairs, screaming at everyone she passed along the way. Castor immediately turned to Imogen. "Is that what it will take, Imogen, to help me succeed? The threat of execution?"

"Allow me to speak to my mother again," Imogen said. "She will advise me."

"What good will that do? Jaron is gone! I am your only hope of gaining the throne."

"The throne? Is that what you think I care about?"

Castor grabbed her arm. "I think you care about your mother. Refuse to cooperate, and I will make sure she scrapes by in poverty for the rest of her days. I think you care about Amarinda, who will become a widow, if you make that necessary. When I find Jaron's supposed brother, Fink, he will live out the remainder of his days in the dungeon. Do you care about any of them?"

Imogen pulled her arm away and looked Castor in the eye. "You will not threaten me, and you will not threaten those I care about! What I do tonight I will do for the good of my country, not because you are small enough to issue threats against the innocent."

Castor's spine stiffened, and he turned to one of his vigils. "Lady Imogen wishes to spend time in her room. For her own safety, remain at her door. She is not to leave until the gathering tonight."

I stood back while Imogen was returned to her room, the vigil closing the door sharply behind her, then standing at watch in front of it. I wanted to sneak inside, but for now, I had to get into the dungeon.

I started down the servants' staircase, but a Prozarian passing by pointed at me. "You, get to work. There is much to be done before tonight."

When our eyes met, he looked directly at me without a flicker of recognition. In a lower voice than I'd normally use, I said, "I was separated from the other Stewardmen. Do you know their assignment?"

"We all work together now. Join the workers carrying debris from the main floor."

"I will watch for them, sir."

Once at the bottom of the stairs, I spotted a soldier escorting a man in chains toward the dungeons. Levitimas. They must have been transferring everything here to the castle.

"I know the dungeons," I said to the soldier. "I could take that prisoner in."

"Then do it."

Soon I had one hand on Levitimas's chained arm and began leading him downstairs toward the dungeon.

Levitimas glanced over at me and smiled. "So it's you."

"Don't smile," I muttered. "Don't say anything here."

"Someday you'll have to tell me how you survived. I'll write that into the book of knowledge."

"You must speak more quietly."

"I see you did as I suggested. You died. Now you can begin to live. That is good."

I stopped walking and turned to face him. "No, none of this is good; none of this is right. I have no idea what I'm doing."

"None of us do; that is the secret to life," he responded. "No one begins to obtain wisdom until they admit they lack knowledge."

"All I know is this problem is bigger than me," I said. "I need help."

"You certainly do. Have you done as I suggested? Have you given her what she wants most?"

"Levitimas, I can't —"

"Then she will never turn to you again." He straightened. "Take me to the dungeons. I've lived so long in them, I'm quite uncomfortable up here."

As we walked, I said, "What is this book of knowledge that you mentioned?"

"Is that your third question to me?"

I groaned. "No. I have bigger problems right now than a book."

"You act like someone who is defeated. Jaron —"

"Don't say my name."

"The Prozarians can be stopped as they are now. But if they find the treasure, they will become unstoppable."

"And that's my fault? Why didn't you stop them when you had the chance? You found them with the plague. You offered to heal them if they returned the scope to you. They tricked you and imprisoned you, and yet you still healed them!"

"It wasn't the plague. A terrible disease, yes, but with a few of the right herbs, they were healed." He paused, then added, "And not everyone has been healed."

Again, I stopped. "Are they still sick?"

"Is that your third question?"

I let out a string of curses, grabbed his arm again, and together we continued toward the dungeon. However, once we turned the corner to enter, I stopped, struck by the damage farther ahead. Half a wall must have collapsed directly over the royal crypt, nearly blocking the corridor and entirely blocking the entrance. I froze as I stared at it.

"You will see your parents' tombs again," Levitimas whispered. "They're behind all that damage, I assume."

"I must be a great disappointment to them now." For all my father's weaknesses, the castle had never suffered a loose brick, much less destruction of this magnitude.

But the entrance to the dungeon was intact. I had to knock and announce my business before the door was unlocked from the inside and opened. Here was a landing large enough for three or four men, though usually only one person remained as vigil at the door. It was that vigil's job to escort us down a narrow flight of stone stairs and unlock one of four cells.

Other than a few torches that cast heavy shadows on the walls, it was also quite dark down here, which might keep any vigils from recognizing me. Even so, I moved farther into the shadows and did my best imitation of the Prozarian accent to say, "This is a special prisoner. He must be kept in one of the nicer cells."

"The entire dungeon is overfull already," the vigil who had opened the door replied, but he reached for a set of keys hanging from the wall. "Follow me."

We descended a rounded staircase until we reached the

cells below. The castle had a second dungeon in an upstairs turret, reserved for a special prisoner. That's where I had held Conner for a time, but I'd rarely been down here. I hated these dungeons.

Each cell was separated by rock walls and had thick bars on the front. The vigil unlocked the first cell he came to, one full of Carthyan soldiers, each with a chain on his leg. *Where was Roden?* I wondered for the hundredth time.

Or Mott. He should have been here. "There are no other prisoners?" I asked.

"Should there be?"

"I was told a man would be down here, the companion-at-arms to the king."

One vigil whispered to the other, who nodded. "We know of that man, but he broke free before we could get him down here."

"He is here, in the castle?"

"If he is, we'll find him soon enough."

I doubted that. Mott was too clever. Besides, I had fully expected them to see through what little disguise I had. If they didn't recognize me, they wouldn't find Mott.

Remembering Levitimas was still beside me, I pointed to the nearest cell. "That one will do."

"I'd prefer that one." Levitimas pointed to the cell on the opposite side of the small path where we stood. "If it's all the same to you."

The vigil sighed and walked down to open the door. I walked Levitimas in, still keeping my head down.

"I have orders to question this man," I said to the vigil. "You are welcome to wait here with me until I finish."

"How many questions?"

"Several. It could take hours."

The vigil cursed — a creative new word I decided to adopt for my own vocabulary — and gave me the keys. "Make sure every door is locked before you leave or it'll be my head."

"Of course."

After he'd left, Levitimas said, "You seem disappointed that your friend is not here."

Disappointed didn't even begin to describe how I felt. I had no access to Imogen, nor did I have any idea where Roden was, but I had been certain Mott would be here. I was glad he had escaped, but I desperately wanted to talk to him. It didn't matter whether he advised me, scolded me, or simply assured me that all would be well. I just needed someone near me on my side. With every passing minute, I felt the walls closing in on me.

I was running out of time before Carthya would forever be beyond my reach.

· SEVENTEEN ·

In the darkness of the dungeons, I immediately began removing the chains of the prisoners in the cells. As I did, one of my soldiers whispered, "Why are you doing this?"

I wanted to tell them who I was, I really did. But a few of the prisoners were in Stewardman uniforms, same as me. I couldn't take any chance of them betraying me yet again.

"I am a friend to the king," I said, attempting to disguise my voice.

"Then you must have heard the rumors, that the king has fallen."

"It is no rumor," a Stewardman said. "My eldest brother is a friend to the archer who shot him at Castor Veldergrath's estate. Veldergrath rules us now. He will be a better king than Jaron ever was."

I closed my eyes and tried to steady my temper. After a slow breath, I whispered to the soldier in front of me, "Does anyone know what happened to the Captain of the Guard?"

He leaned forward to whisper in my ear, "Captain Roden called a retreat of any men who could get away. Not all of us could. We believe they've got more of us locked up elsewhere in

Drylliad, but we don't know how many. We do think the captain escaped though, because we've overheard the order given to search for him."

I thought he was finished, but in the same whisper, he added, "You should know, my king, that I do not believe the rumors."

I smiled at that a little, then in an equally low voice replied, "Leave this dungeon in five minutes, all of you who are free. All those loyal to the king are to gather at Farthenwood in two days. Make weapons there; prepare yourself in any way you can."

I stood to leave, but one of the Stewardmen said, "You will not help us too?"

I turned to them. "Why would I help traitors to the throne?"

"Because we serve Lady Imogen."

I cocked my head, grateful for the darkness. "What do you mean?"

"She sent her mother here, not one hour ago, trying to get us freed. Her request was refused, but her mother promised us that Imogen would find a way to free us. I thought that's why you had come."

"Why are you in this dungeon?"

He shrugged. "Castor Veldergrath suspects us of disloyalty to him."

"Where are your loyalties, then?"

"With Carthya, as before."

That was enough for me. I gave the keys to the soldier I had spoken to earlier. "Set these Stewardmen free and bring them with you. You have five minutes." I clapped him on the shoulder, then ran toward the stairs.

I hadn't even started up the first one before I encountered the vigil who had given me the keys. "They told me to stay with you . . ." he began.

I withdrew the sword given to me by the farmer. "And now I'm telling you to move into the first cell."

"It's filthy!"

"I agree. Get in there." I ordered the soldier who had recognized me to put him in chains, adding, "You should gag him too, if anyone is willing to sacrifice a dirty sock for the job."

I ran up the stairs a second time. Two vigils were stationed on the landing at the top. One started to reach for his weapon, but I used the flat end of the sword to strike him hard against the head and he collapsed to the floor. I turned my sword on the other vigil but found him on his knees.

"Leave me alive, and I swear, I'll do anything you ask."

"Then forget you've seen me here. You will even deny it to your friend when he wakes up. "

"If he wakes up."

"*When* he wakes up. Now hush. Where are your loyalties?"

"Some of us serve only because Master Veldergrath forced us to do it. Many of us hold loyalties to Lady Imogen."

"So do I." I replaced my sword. "If I were you, I'd spend the next five minutes pretending to be unconscious. It might save your life."

From there, I lowered my hat farther and left the dungeon. The kitchen wasn't far away, but because of the destruction around the crypt, I had to take a longer route to reach it. I was surprised to find it a bustle of activity, with the cooks and serving staff all preparing food that looked and smelled better than anything I'd eaten in some time. In fairness, I'd barely eaten anything in over a day.

An unattended tray was near the kitchen entrance, waiting for a maid to deliver it somewhere. On it was a variety of meats and cheese, with a bowl of sliced peaches in the center. If anyone saw me swipe the tray, they said nothing. I carried it two flights up a back stairway, which emptied out very near my room.

I stopped in my doorway, noticing something different and horrifying. In the corner of my room, Batilda's trunks were stacked, some of them opened. I rolled my eyes, silently listening for the devils' laughter over this new joke. Imogen's mother had taken over my room.

This was unacceptable.

I kicked the door closed behind me, then sat at my desk, thoroughly irritated. If the manners I used to clean the food off the tray would make Batilda's toes curl, then so be it. As I ate, I noticed a paper sticking out of one drawer. I pulled it out and saw a note Errol had once written as instructions to other servants on how to manage me. I'd enjoyed it so much, I had kept it.

I smiled and read down the list. At the very bottom, underlined, were the words *Even if he ignores everyone else, he will always listen to Imogen.*

I ran my finger over her name, as if that would somehow bring me comfort. "What is your plan, Imogen?" I whispered to myself. "Tell me, and I will listen."

Something inside me whispered back, in an answer I did not want to hear, "It's her secret."

· EIGHTEEN ·

After eating so much, I began to feel my exhaustion, but I couldn't sleep yet, and certainly couldn't sleep here. The last thing I needed was to be interrupted by Batilda screaming to the entire castle that not only was I alive, I was also tucked into my bed, ready for capture.

What I did need was a way to move about the castle without being recognized. A Stewardman coat and hat lined with fur might be passable in the darkness, but I couldn't limit myself by only being out at night.

I had to find a better disguise. My eyes wandered to Batilda's trunks.

I opened the first one, and my mind immediately began turning with possibilities. Wearing a Prozarian uniform, or even dressing like one of the Stewardmen, would always draw too much attention to me. I needed to become someone who was rarely noticed, someone who melted into the background like a faded curtain.

It was an offense I was guilty of far too often. I was so used to having servants pass by on their duties, there were occasions when I forgot they were in the room. Based on the busy activity in the kitchen, it appeared that the Prozarians had merely shifted the servants' duties to working for them, so I hoped my servants had become equally invisible to their eyes.

I pulled an old blue tunic from my wardrobe and stripped it of any decoration. I belted it, then did the same for a dark overcoat I used to wear. It would be warm for this season, but it would keep the sword covered.

Digging through Batilda's trunk, I found a hat that could be altered for a simple cap. I pulled off all its decorations, but I still needed a way to cover my hair. Then I grinned.

Beneath the hat was a wig, something Batilda had probably brought for the wedding. It was pale blond, a little lighter than her hair, and very different from my own.

I tried on the wig and, looking at myself in the mirror, began pulling out all the pins keeping the hair in place. Then I pulled the strands together and tied them at the nape of my neck. I used the sword I'd borrowed from Emmett to cut the hair shorter, and when I replaced the wig and used the hat, I grinned, perfectly satisfied. I almost didn't recognize myself.

From there, I cleaned up the best I could, cramming the Stewardman coat under the bed. I also needed to get rid of the ribbons and patches from my clothing, and the remains of Batilda's wig, or these items would easily lead back to me. I stuffed everything into my pockets and started toward the door, then froze when I saw the handle turn.

If this was Batilda, I felt certain that she would reveal me. Anything to please Castor. Anything to add misery to my life.

I grabbed the wig and hat and darted beneath my desk, in the far corner of the room. I put a hand on my sword, ready for when I was discovered.

The door opened, and someone entered. They were making an attempt to be quiet but also began what sounded like a thorough search of the room, looking through the wardrobe, beneath my bed, behind the curtains. A search under the desk was inevitable.

The person laid something heavy on the desktop. From the way it clunked down, I was sure it was a large knife, or more likely a small sword. I tightened my grip on the sword at my side, hoping I wouldn't have to use it. I wasn't entirely sure I *could* use it, not with such a dull blade.

Whoever was here began eating what little food I had left on the tray still on my desk, and at some point kicked the side of the desk, hard enough that it might've cracked the wood. It reminded me of the way I had kicked at the wall of the castle after Imogen had left, hurting my foot in the process. Whoever was here must have done the same. I heard a whispered string of curses, and then the person tossed themselves on my bed.

I immediately grinned. This was Fink!

Then I felt bad for grinning because he sniffed a few times and I realized he was crying. Maybe because he had just kicked a heavy wooden desk, but I hoped at least a couple of those tears were for me, if he had heard the awful news about my death.

He must have, for this time he let out another chain of curses, attaching my name to the end. I thought about what Imogen had been telling me for a while, that Fink cursed too much. Maybe she was right about that too.

My bed creaked as if he had sat up. He sniffed again, then muttered, "At least you won't be around to stop me this time."

Muffling my voice with one hand, I said, "I'm always around to stop you."

Fink yelped and must have leapt off the bed. His footsteps pounded all over the room until he finally peeked under the desk.

"You? . . . How did you . . . ?" Fink finally gave up on his questions and dove toward me, wrapping his arms around my neck.

One hand pressed too hard against the wounds on my back, and I pushed him away, drawing deep breaths to control the sting.

Fink's brows furrowed. "Are you all right?"

"I'm still aboveground, so I could be worse."

Fink crawled out, and I followed him. "Is it only your back that's injured?" he asked.

"Yes."

"Good!" He kicked my leg, possibly as hard as he'd kicked the desk. "You want to have secrets and plans and keep me out of your business, and that is fine. I can always figure them out another way. But this went too far. I thought you were dead! I thought I would have to fix this by myself."

I smiled. "How were you going to fix this?"

"It's not a great plan, but it's all I had." Fink shrugged. "I know what's happening here. Castor is going to try to claim the throne. I figured I'd challenge him for it."

"You'd walk downstairs, demand to see the Steward of Carthya, tell him you have a greater claim to the throne than he does, which you don't, by the way, and he'd apologize for the inconvenience and step down. That's your plan?"

"I already said that it wasn't a great plan. Besides, do you have anything better?"

"Not by much." I pushed my hair back from my face. "You're supposed to be in the inner keep."

"Mott came in and helped us all get out."

"Mott did? Where is he now?"

"I don't know. He was helping Harlowe get into a wagon in the courtyard, but Harlowe is hurt really bad. Tobias still doesn't know if he'll live. Nobody saw me leave."

"What about Kerwyn, and his servant?"

Fink lowered his eyes. "They left that first night, hoping to help more people get to the keep, but nobody came back. Tobias went out later to look for them. He found Kerwyn and his servant, but . . . the Prozarians must have found them first. Kerwyn is dead, Jaron."

I closed my eyes and tried to take in that awful news. Kerwyn had been a good man. No, he was better than even that. He loved Carthya and our people. He had also been one of the few at the castle to always accept me as I was. He had crowned me king and had been an invaluable counselor and friend ever since. Even if one day I rebuilt this castle to twice its former glory, it would never again be what it was. This place would never be the same without Kerwyn.

"Are you all right?" Fink asked.

I should have nodded and reassured him that everything was fine, but it really wasn't, and I certainly wasn't all right. I shook my head but could not speak.

Fink shoved his hands into his pockets and scuffed his boot on the floor. "What are we going to do now?"

Forcing down my emotions, I turned to Fink. "Last I checked, I had an army. Have you heard where they are?"

"No, but I can find them."

"Absolutely not. You are going back to the keep."

"Do you remember making me a knight?"

"It wasn't a real oath. I just wanted to make you feel better."

He huffed. "What about everything I did in Belland? You trusted me with items the Prozarians would have killed to find. I protected them, and I did it on unfamiliar land. But I know Carthya. I know Drylliad and the land around it. I can find Roden."

"This is different. The area is crawling with Prozarians, and Castor has his own armies that will be watching for you."

Fink folded his arms. "Give me a chance to do this. Maybe I'll find them, maybe not, but I am not hiding in that keep for another day."

"These people are not playing games. They learned from Belland. They know how I think and how I plan."

"That's why they're winning! This entire attack was designed for exactly the way you think. But nobody understands how *I* think, not even me. Maybe my plans are terrible, but believe it or not, yours are worse; they are *always* worse."

I thought about Imogen once again. For the first time, I began to understand that maybe I was in *her* way, that my strategies were endangering Carthya. Hers could save us.

Fink continued, "I learned from Belland too, in a good way. You think I'm not ready to fight or to help, but how will you ever change your mind unless you let me prove myself? Let me do this, Jaron."

Reluctantly, I nodded. "Find Roden, and tell him to meet me at Farthenwood in two days. You will stay there with him until I come. Be safe. Promise me that."

Fink began backing out the door. "I promise." He stopped, then added, "I do have one suggestion. Put one of the ribbons from Imogen's mother in your hair. Jaron would've hated it, so that will make you less obvious."

I grinned and headed toward Batilda's trunk again. "One more thing," I added as he began to leave. "Don't curse so much. You're better than that."

"I learned it all from you," he replied with a wink; then he was gone.

· NINETEEN ·

I used a privy to dispose of all the unwanted items I'd pulled off my disguise, and then emerged as any castle servant would. I had the tray in my hand that I'd taken from the kitchen, and quickly realized my theory was true. Nobody gave me a second look.

I moved through the corridors, amazed at how open others were about discussing private issues as if they were alone. This was exactly what I had hoped for.

I was so invisible, in fact, that I was able to pass directly by Captain Strick and Mercy and receive no attention other than a quick scolding for not having moved out of their way. He went on to tell her that there had been a prisoner breakout from the dungeons, except for one single prisoner. I could guess who that was: Levitimas, who, for reasons I could not fathom, would still be down there.

The main floor was the busiest, with soldiers working as builders and repairmen on the castle entrance, trying to clean up the damage and, where necessary, even bringing in new rock for repairs. Their efforts would take months to complete, and though I appreciated the free labor, I wasn't about to wait months before making my move. I didn't even want to wait days for it. The longer I waited, the deeper the Prozarians' claws would sink into my country.

Lump entered the corridor, and I immediately turned to the wall, pretending to examine it for damage. "Enough!" he said to all the workers. "Guests are already arriving. Gather your things and go clean up."

The workers did as he said while I quickly ducked into the throne room. I'd only come in here to avoid Lump, but what I saw made my gut churn with anger. There on the dais, Wilta was seated on what had once been my father's throne and was now my throne. She was wearing a particularly grand dress, green again, and her hair was piled high on her head, topped by a crown. No guests had yet arrived, so she was at her finest, shouting orders at the servants in the room.

Mercy entered from a rear door, one reserved for royals and the high chamberlain. He bowed to Wilta, then stood at her left, in Kerwyn's place. That infuriated me as well. Kerwyn had been killed only a day ago. It was an insult to his memory for Mercy to stand there. Seated at Wilta's right, in what had once been my mother's throne, was Castor. The king's ring was on his finger, and my sword was sheathed at his waist.

I had to look anywhere else, or I knew the heat of my glare would catch his attention. I'd only been watching him for a few seconds, and I'd already compiled a list of at least twenty ways I would one day ruin his life.

I didn't see Imogen, which bothered me, though I supposed it would be worse if I had to see her at Castor's side again. It took everything in me not to march onto the dais and confront him immediately.

By now, the room had begun filling with people, mostly former regents and nobles who had been here many times before. It was customary for the royals to stand at the door and greet each person upon entering. I hated the task, so I'd solved it by avoiding having any parties here, though when we did, I performed my duty.

Neither Wilta nor Castor could be bothered to leave their thrones. Maybe Wilta worried that if she left her throne, Castor would take it. Maybe Castor worried if he ventured out into the crowd, they might try to hurt him. I certainly would have tried.

"You there!" a soldier called to me. "There's a draft. Close the doors onto the garden."

I nodded and headed that way. I did close the doors but went outside. I simply could not look at the stolen thrones a minute longer. Once I was alone, I cut over to the King's Gardens. My private place.

Here, I could take a few minutes to mourn for Kerwyn and his servant, and for what must have been a terrible number of my soldiers who fell during the Prozarian attack. Here, I could remind myself that this wasn't over yet. I simply had to figure out how to finish this with so little help on my side.

Debris from the attack still littered the gardens, and a rock had fallen on a privacy wall, taking a huge chunk out of it. I was halfway through that gap when I stopped, almost unable to move. I'd found Imogen.

She was seated some distance away from me, speaking in a

low voice to someone I could not see. A minute later, that figure left, but she did not. Instead, she lowered her head and became silent, completely unaware of my presence.

It wasn't far from here that I'd once ordered Imogen to leave the castle, in hopes of protecting her. She had turned the situation around and ended up protecting me. She always did that, I realized. Without Imogen, I wouldn't be alive today.

I removed my hat and wig, and walked toward her. I knew the risks if I were seen. For now, it was vital that Wilta and Castor both believe I was dead. But Imogen needed to know the truth.

So I crept closer, hiding behind the shrubs and trees until I was almost near enough to whisper her name and be heard. If only we could talk, just long enough to understand each other. There was nothing I wanted more.

She sniffed, and then a small gasp escaped from her. I peered around a tree and realized she was crying, or rather, trying not to cry and failing at it.

The sight of it pierced my heart. If those tears were for me, then even if this fraud of my death was necessary, I was still the cause of her pain.

Which led me to wonder about other tears I had caused her. How she must have felt to discover I'd been holding on to the scope for the past six months, studying it, poring over its markings, and I had never once breathed a word of it to her.

I wanted to promise myself never to keep a secret from her again. I would have promised that, but I still had other secrets, including one that would be awful for her if it was revealed, or awful for us. There would be no us if I told her everything.

Maybe there was no *us* now.

I had to speak to her, to hear her voice. I needed to know about her plans and tell her about mine. If she and I worked together, we could fix this.

So I waited until she had turned in my direction, then stepped out from behind the tree.

She was still some distance from me, but she definitely saw me because she froze and then new tears fell to her cheeks.

Every part of me ached to go to her, to beg her forgiveness, or even to hear her voice. But I couldn't. Because nothing in her expression invited me closer. Instead, she only stared, and I did too, and there we stood for so long that I began to wonder if this was all we had left, just to look at each other. I had expected that this moment would have lifted my heart. I was wrong.

"Imogen?"

She turned at the sound of her mother's voice behind her, and I ducked back into the shadows.

"Yes, Mother?"

"Castor asks that you come to the throne room. He is concerned for you."

"Castor is only ever concerned about himself."

"Everyone is waiting. Imagine how it looks for him to be claiming the throne while you are out here in the gardens crying for Jaron."

"Imagine how it looks to other Carthyans to see my mother's friendship with the Prozarian captain!"

"You know very well why I am doing that. Now you must make things right again between you and Castor. It's the only way. Without Jaron, everything must rest on your shoulders now."

"My last words to Jaron . . ." Imogen shook her head. "I was cruel to him."

"You did what had to be done, and you must stay strong for the more difficult choices still ahead."

Imogen sighed. "Yes, you're right."

She started to follow her mother into what remained of the castle. I tossed a pebble ahead of Imogen's path, and at the sound, Imogen turned back to look at me. Her face lit with a smile, then her lips parted, as if she wanted to say something. And the smile that had so briefly warmed her face faded.

Silently, I held out my hand to her. I needed her help if we were going to fix Carthya, if we were going to fix *us*. She took a single step toward me, then glanced again at her mother. When she turned to me once more, her eyes were sad again, almost more so than before.

Maybe because now she had a choice. She didn't have to go into that throne room; she didn't have to stand at Castor's side. She didn't have to walk away from me.

But that's what she was about to do.

I lowered my hand and nodded at her, though it crushed my heart to do it.

I didn't know whether Imogen walked away because she wanted to, or because she felt she had to, but I was beginning to understand that tonight was part of a larger plan.

A plan that didn't seem to include any future with me.

· TWENTY ·

By the time I made it back into the throne room, Imogen was already on the dais with Castor. He was standing and holding her hand midway between them, which looked awkward and forced, but Imogen's smile was more convincing than I would have liked.

Wilta stood beside Castor, eyes forward, but this time her mother repeated the announcement that had been given earlier from the castle balcony. ". . . Castor Veldergrath shall be the Steward of Carthya, subject to our monarch, and yours. Hail Wilta Strick, your Monarch!"

"Hail to the Monarch!" the people cried out.

"Hail to your Steward, Castor Veldergrath!"

"Hail to the Steward!" the people echoed, several of them my former regents.

Castor stepped forward with Imogen, and my gut twisted. "As is the Carthyan tradition, the betrothal is to the throne. With the unfortunate loss of King Jaron, it is appropriate that I offer marriage to his betrothed."

A cheer arose around me, but I nearly collapsed in place. This was what they had been discussing all this time, never quite saying the words but speaking so plainly I should have known.

Castor had promised the ultimate revenge on me. He wouldn't get that through taking my throne or my title. His revenge would be to take Imogen.

And his revenge was working. I already felt myself splitting in half.

Castor continued, "You have loved her, and I will love her as she loves me. With our marriage, we will forever unite Carthya to Prozaria. To Imogen, and to our marriage!"

My head was spinning. This could not be possible; it could not be part of Imogen's plans, not now that she knew I was alive.

But she did know it, and there she was, beside him.

He looked to Imogen, who merely stared forward and said, "Thank you, Steward Veldergrath. I will consider your offer."

The people cheered her words, but my eyes were on Castor, who looked furious. Obviously, Imogen was supposed to accept his proposal just now, and that did worry me. She would not be allowed to defy him, not if she was supposed to get the people on his side.

From where she stood on the dais, Imogen found me. Our eyes locked, and though there wasn't the slightest betrayal of recognition in her expression, I felt some hope that she had looked for me at all. Then, in an almost imperceptible move, she shook her head at me.

What did that mean?

What did that mean . . . for us?

The announcements were followed by a celebration in which Carthyan nobles, several of my former regents, and other notable men and women of the country greeted Castor as their steward, though most turned away with grimaces and sighs. I felt some comfort in that. The nobles didn't like me any more than I liked them, but that was only because I was arrogant, rude, and impossible to work with. Castor was worse.

"Pardon me!"

Imogen's mother had inadvertently backed into me. I put my head down and realized she was in a conversation with Captain Strick.

Batilda returned to her conversation. "You must forgive my informal appearance tonight. I had the most lovely wig intended for this evening. I must have left it at Elmhaven."

"Prozarians do not wear wigs," Strick said. "It is a wasteful luxury."

"I agree, of course. I only hoped there might be an exception, in celebration of tonight's announcement." Batilda thought a moment longer. "It didn't go the way I had expected."

"The announcement was supposed to be for a marriage. Your daughter humiliated Lord Veldergrath up there. You had better speak to her, before Wilta does it."

"I will, Captain Strick. I don't know why she changed her mind like that."

"Obviously, Jaron is too fresh in her mind. We will never have control over this country until Jaron is forgotten. That will be the next phase in our plan."

I wanted to hear more, but looking beyond them into the corridor, I saw a sudden rush of eight or nine Prozarian soldiers racing down the stairs. Their swords were raised. Something big was happening.

I left the throne room and hurried to catch up to the others, asking the nearest soldier about the disturbance.

"We found one of the escapees," he said as he brushed past me.

It probably wasn't Levitimas. But the soldier might not be talking about the dungeon escapees. There was also the escape from the innermost keep.

At the bottom of the steps, someone shouted, "There he is!" The group gave chase, and I followed, all of us racing to the northwest corner of the castle, where my private study had been before the Prozarians turned it to pebbles and dust. That's when I caught my first glance of Tobias. He was a fast runner but not fast enough, and the Prozarians had him trapped in a corner.

He turned, raising a longsword that took both hands for him to manage, and yelled, "Take one step closer and I will strike you down!"

I admired his boldness and courage, and for a few seconds, his threat seemed to work, but then whoever was commanding the soldiers ordered, "Get him on his knees."

Five soldiers rushed forward. To his credit, Tobias got in at least one good swipe, though with a longsword, it would have been impossible for him not to hit someone. The remaining four soldiers disarmed him and quickly forced him to his knees.

Tobias looked up at them. "When I kneel, it is only to Jaron, the true king of Carthya."

"Then you kneel to a grave." The man who had spoken kicked Tobias in the side, and he fell to the ground.

"Where are the others who were with you?" the commander shouted.

"I saw them," I said. "Follow me."

The commander left orders for three of his men to bind Tobias's hands and to care for the soldier he had injured. As I led the others away, I heard Tobias say, "I'll see to his wounds, if you don't tie me up."

Five soldiers were with me, including the commander. I led them into the kitchen, which was bustling with activity for the celebration upstairs. I looked around, hoping to see a woman I'd always called Cook. She was sending a tray of food out the door, so I waited until she was looking directly at me before I said, "Did I just see three Carthyans run through here?"

"When?" She began to shake her head.

This time, with more meaning, I added, "Did you see them, *Cook*?" A smile spread across her face. She recognized me.

"Oh yes," she said, perhaps with too much theater in her tone, but it would have to do. "Oh yes, I did see them. Big and mangy and—"

Before she enjoyed this too much, I interrupted. "I think they jumped into the river below."

She suppressed a smile, for she knew very well that as a boy I had escaped the castle on several occasions by opening a latch in the kitchen floor and jumping through it into the river. My tutors never followed me, because they knew how disgusting the water was once the kitchen staff dumped all their food scraps into it.

But Cook clearly understood the game I wanted to play. She opened the latch and said, "Why, yes, they did jump."

The soldiers looked down into the river, more clogged than usual because of the preparations for the guests upstairs. The commander frowned up at me. "You expect us to jump into that river?"

"No, you'd be a fool to jump in there," I said. "We have one of the escapees. The Monarch would never expect you to pursue the other three."

"I will jump," one of the soldiers said. "I want the gratitude of the Monarch when I capture those prisoners."

With a nod from his commander, he held his nose and jumped, immediately followed by a second soldier.

"The rest of you should get in there too," the commander said. The other two soldiers took their turns, and I realized the commander had begun staring at me. His eyes narrowed. "Aren't you —"

"In you go." I yanked on his coat to pull him forward. He lost his balance and fell into the river.

Behind me, Cook began laughing. "It reminds me of old times, my king." She dipped her head at me, then returned to her duties.

I peeked down the hole again, watching the commander float downriver with the others. They'd be caught by the rubbish gate before long. I'd have to try not to cross paths with them, at least until I was better armed.

I closed the latch to prevent them from climbing back into the kitchen, then turned, immediately crashing into the last person I ever wanted to see here: Mercy.

He reached for a sleeve of my coat, but I wheeled around and picked up a tray full of dishes, throwing them at him. They crashed to the floor, leaving him with several cuts on his face.

A soldier appeared behind him and picked up a frying pan,

a big one intended for me. I ran instead to the hearth where a kettle was boiling. I picked it up and threw the liquid toward the soldier. He ducked, so most of it landed on Mercy, who screeched with pain.

The soldier leapt forward and tackled me to the ground, then called for the cooks to bring him a knife. No one responded. When he called again, it became obvious they had fled the kitchen entirely.

The soldier pressed his knee into my gut and looked over at Mercy, whose skin was already showing the marks of burns.

"What do you want me to do with him?" he asked.

"Insolent servant boy! Throw him in the dungeons," Mercy said, with his hands pressed over his eyes. "I've got to do something about this burn."

He turned and immediately bumped into a brick pillar. If he could see, it wasn't much.

By then, at least ten other Prozarians had gathered around the kitchen. The soldier got off me, and I checked my stomach, certain that he had left a permanent indentation there.

Tobias was already chained in one cell when I was brought into the dungeon. The Prozarians shoved me into a second cell. I raised my trouser leg for them to put the chain on it, but a soldier kicked me off my feet and added a few more kicks to my gut and ribs until he was satisfied. Someone chained my leg; then they closed the bars.

"You must be named Weakling," I said to the soldier who had kicked me, though I was sure the very opposite must be true.

He said, "If you think that was bad, wait until the Monarch

hears what you did to her counselor. You will wish you were already dead."

"Some would say I already am," I replied.

"I will stay as vigil," Weakling said to the other soldiers. "Go and inform the Monarch what has happened to Lord Trench's eyes."

I tried to get back to a sitting position, but I'd barely slept since yesterday's attack and felt the weight of exhaustion now. Tobias was speaking to me, I knew that, but I only mumbled, "Let me close my eyes for a minute, Tobias."

"I thought you were dead," he whispered.

"Let me sleep, or there's a chance I soon will be," I replied.

I quickly drifted off, expecting pleasant dreams. After all, I was living in the nightmare.

· TWENTY-ONE ·

I wasn't sure of the time when I awoke. I felt as though I had slept for hours, so perhaps it was morning, but there was no way to be sure. The dungeons were colder than I'd realized, and I was shivering. This was something else I'd have to look at changing after I got my castle back.

I was still in my servant's clothes, but my sword was gone. I sat up and leaned against the dungeon wall, still aware of the cuts on my back and now fully aware of what Weakling's boot had done to my gut. Truthfully, I had always expected to be locked in these dungeons one day, though I had thought it would come when I was young and my father was trying to teach me some sort of lesson.

Unexpectedly, our vigil this morning was Haddin. He was staring directly at me.

"You marched into Drylliad with me yesterday," he said. "So are you a servant who disguised himself as a Stewardman, or are you a Stewardman in disguise?"

I frowned. "That's not your business. Leave us alone now."

"No, I'm the vigil here."

I pointed at Tobias. "Do you see that regent in the cell

across from me? When he wakes up, he'll need my help to escape. Think of how difficult that will be if you're still here."

Haddin leaned toward the bars. "The regent is planning to escape?"

"I expect both of us will, and when we do, you'll be blamed for it, if you're still here. Go upstairs."

"I'll stop the escape," he replied. "What finer way to prove myself to my superiors?"

"You have no superiors among the Prozarians," I said. "You're a decent person, Haddin. Don't compromise that by serving those people."

He straightened. "I serve willingly."

"What a pity." I forgot him and turned instead to Tobias, calling his name. He seemed determined to remain asleep, so I grabbed a small rock from my cell and tossed it across the path between our cells. It hit him on the shoulder, but he merely rolled over on the hard stone floor.

"We need to talk," I said.

"Now?"

"I'm awake now."

"I was awake last night."

"Yes, but I'm awake *now*. Sit up. Let's talk."

While Tobias groaned and pushed himself to a sitting position, I turned to Haddin. "You're still here?"

"This is where I've been assigned."

"This is also where we're going to say things that you will not want to have heard." He remained where he was and I added, "That sword at your side."

He put his hand on the pommel. "What of it?"

"I'm going to use it against you in about two minutes unless you leave this area."

He frowned at me, then turned and walked upstairs.

Tobias leaned toward me. "I can't believe that worked!"

"It didn't work. He'll be back, and he won't be alone. So in what little time we have, I know about Kerwyn, but tell me about Harlowe."

"His injuries are serious, but if Mott gets them safely away, Amarinda knows what to do. Where will they go?"

I wouldn't take any risks by telling him about Farthenwood, so I simply replied, "Hopefully far enough to stay out of Castor's reach."

Tobias arched a brow. "Why is that?"

"Harlowe is next in line for the throne, and you after that. Both of you stand in Castor's way to holding the crown. Levitimas, are you still here?"

His voice called from the cell farther down from me. "Where else would I be?"

"Enjoying freedom, if you had escaped with the others last night."

"How would that have benefited me?" he replied. "I am here to find the treasure."

"But you know where it is. You have known all along. You could have escaped and sought it yourself."

Even from here, I heard Levitimas sigh. "Would you consider yourself a patient person, Jaron?"

"Only if nothing else works." My leg had been bouncing for the last ten minutes, eager to move. Tobias snorted, which I supposed was his opinion on that question.

Levitimas spoke again, "I have never been their prisoner. I have merely waited for events to unfold that will allow me to get what I want."

"I hope whatever you've waited for all these years is worth it."

"This is my life's work. I have collected a thousand years of history to be added to the life's work of scholars from a thousand years before that. All that I must do is find their book. It is hidden with the rest of the treasure. Nothing in this world matters more to me than that book."

Much as I tried, I could not understand patience like that. "So why didn't you find the treasure and get the book? What were you waiting for all this time?"

His laugh was soft, as if I'd made a joke. "I suppose I was waiting for you. I will help you find the treasure, but only on one condition. You must promise to give me the book."

"I already told you, I don't care about the treasure anymore. I've got bigger problems." Such as the sound of the dungeon door upstairs, opening again. We were out of time.

Levitimas continued, "Jaron, you are the Monarch's captive now, and whether you care about it or not, she will force you to find the treasure for her."

"Then tell me where it is, and you and I will get it right now."

"How can you not already know?" Levitimas asked. "Do you understand so little of your own history?"

If I did, this wasn't the time for a history lesson. Boots were pounding down the circular staircase toward us. "Right now, I am far more concerned with Carthya's future. Can anything in the treasure help me with that?"

"The book can. But you must promise that to me."

"You can have the book, Levitimas, but I hope there's more to the treasure than that."

"The treasure is at once everything and nothing. Except for the book."

"How can Jaron find the treasure?" Tobias asked Levitimas. "The scope and lenses were lost in Belland." Neither of us answered him, and after a very long pause, Tobias said, "Oh, Jaron, you didn't."

I set my jaw forward. "They were always going to come. We knew that from the moment we left Belland."

Seconds later, three vigils arrived. Haddin had returned with Weakling and a third soldier who I didn't bother naming because I doubted he'd be around much longer. He looked cruel enough that I'd have to go after him first.

"Levitimas, I have one other question for you." I leaned forward and glared at each of the three soldiers who had come. "You've been a captive of the Prozarians for a long time. I can't tell which of these three vigils is the stupidest. Maybe you can advise me?"

The vigils looked at one another; then Weakling rattled the bars of my cell with his sword. "Be quiet."

As they wished. In a whisper, I said, "I only ask because the stupidest one will think he's going to survive the next few minutes. The other two will have the good sense to leave while they can."

Weakling laughed. "You're hardly in a position to make threats."

"Yes, obviously I am *now*. But my threat remains the same."

Haddin started to reach for the set of keys hanging from the wall, and while I would have welcomed a personal visit,

Levitimas spoke instead. "Tobias, tell me something about Carthya."

I leaned my head against the wall, then sat forward again when the rock scratched my back. So there would be a history lesson after all. I groaned. "Must we do this now?"

"It might save our lives."

"I highly doubt that."

But Levitimas's distraction did seem to work. Haddin replaced the keys, and the postures of all three Prozarians relaxed.

"Carthya is more than a thousand years old," Tobias said. "Founded by three siblings: Ingor, Faylinn, and Linus, all who left their homeland to establish a kingdom of their own. At first, they ruled as equals. While the three rulers worked together, Carthya was the strongest country in the land. As the story goes, Faylinn had a book that taught them to build powerful weapons and how to trade with foreign kingdoms to build wealth, which they did, with great success. But over time, disagreements arose among them. Each became so focused on what they wanted most, they began to see the others as threats. You see, Ingor wanted Carthya to become a trading empire — the wealthiest country in all the lands. Faylinn wanted an educated country — the wisest of all lands. Linus wanted to fight, to be a nation of conquerors." Tobias paused and glanced over at me. "We should talk more about this."

"This one lesson is plenty." I should have saved my sleep for now.

I'd closed my eyes to rest again, but I was fairly sure that Tobias made a face at me before continuing. "Faylinn tried to persuade her brothers that Carthya was strongest when their three goals were all united as one. But the two kings saw the wishes of the others as threats to their own desires. In the end, Ingor killed Faylinn. Then Linus killed Ingor and all those who supported him, and became the sole survivor of the rulers."

"Jaron Artolius Eckbert the Third," I said. "Proud descendant of someone who'd kill his own brother and sister to get his way." I pushed my hair out of my eyes. "What more do we need to talk about, Tobias?"

He hesitated. "Not here."

"I disagree. Your story almost bored these vigils to death. Keep talking, and I won't have to do anything to them." I looked over at the vigils. "Have you forgotten I'm going to hurt you all? You're almost out of time, and I promise to leave scars. Get out of this dungeon, now!"

"We're waiting for further orders from the Monarch," Haddin said.

"You won't be conscious when those orders come." I pointed to Weakling. "You ought to switch your sword to the opposite side. Where you have it now, I'll have no trouble grabbing it from you."

He frowned but stepped back, placing his hand on his sword. When he thought I wasn't looking, he quietly rotated the belt to his other hip.

Levitimas sighed. "You kick against the bricks of walls you have built yourself."

"He always has," Tobias added.

"Maybe so." I kept my eye on Weakling, and my smile widened. "Far better than to remain locked within them. Let's get out of here, Tobias."

· TWENTY-TWO ·

I had already slid the pin out of my belt, but there was no way to hide what I was doing from the vigils, so I simply exchanged glares with them as I worked.

"Stop that!" Weakling said.

I only grinned back at him. "If I stop now, how will I get free of these chains?"

The mean-looking one reached for the keys. "We told you to stop!"

"Yes, I know. I heard you before."

He shoved the key into the lock, withdrew his sword, and swung open the cell door. In another two steps, he was close enough to reach me, but when he did, I yanked the chain off my leg and swung it at his face, hard. Something cracked, a cheekbone, I thought. He swung around in a dizzy half circle before falling to the ground.

Weakling rushed in at me but, from habit, reached for his sword where it no longer was. I grabbed it and left him with a deep cut on one side. He fell to his knees, then collapsed beside the other vigil.

From outside the cell, Haddin immediately raised his arms high. "I won't fight you."

I smiled. "As I suspected, you are not the stupidest of the vigils. Take the keys and unlock the regent's door." I nodded toward Tobias's cell. There was no point in making the same request for Levitimas. I knew he wouldn't leave.

Haddin began unlocking the door but said, "I think I know who you are."

I advanced on him, looking him square in the eye. "Do not say my name, do not think it, understand? We could be friends, Haddin, which is far better than having me as a foe."

"There's nowhere for you to go after you leave this dungeon," Haddin said. "The castle is filled with your enemies."

"Then I need you as a friend as well." After Tobias's chain was released, I told him, "The keys to get us out of this dungeon are at the top of the stairs. Go find them and wait for me."

Tobias nodded and hurried upstairs while I turned to Haddin. "I can save your life, but it may require you to lie to the Monarch. Can you do that?"

"I'm loyal to the Monarch."

I rolled my eyes. "That wasn't my question."

Haddin glanced at the two men locked in their cell. Both of them needed medical attention. "They can be saved, if you hurry," I said, raising the sword I had taken from Weakling. "What do you choose?"

Haddin lowered his voice. "I can lie."

"If anyone hears that you and I marched into Drylliad together, you will be sent to this dungeon until you are forgotten.

Neither of us wants that, so for your sake and mine, deny any knowledge of me. Now take those keys and go help your friends."

Haddin nodded and began unlocking the cells for his companions. I turned to run up the stairs only to see Tobias walking down again, his eyes fixed on me.

"What's wrong?" I asked.

Emerging from the shadows behind him was Lump, with a knife at Tobias's back.

I thought about cursing, but I was trying to cut back, for Fink's sake. So instead, I simply expressed my sympathies for every mirror Lump had ever passed by in his life.

"Give me that sword," Lump demanded.

I frowned at him, then reared up and threw the sword behind me, into Levitimas's cell. He stepped away from it. "I don't use weapons."

"Nor does Tobias, and look where that got him," I replied.

Lump clearly didn't appreciate the way I had rid myself of the sword, but he said, "So you're alive."

"Disappointed?"

"Relieved. The Monarch was furious with Castor." He glanced behind him. "Were you going somewhere?"

"I can't defeat the Prozarians from here." Then I gestured to the two Prozarians I had injured. "Well, not all of them."

Lump's face tightened. "If it were up to me, I'd beat you senseless right now."

"But it isn't up to you. Take me to the Monarch. Tobias is coming with me."

"You can't order me to do anything."

"No? Then why are you here?"

"The Monarch heard a prisoner down here was making threats and causing trouble. She suspected it might be you. I have orders to bring you to see her."

I rolled my eyes. "That's the same order I just gave you. Why did we have to argue?"

"Because Tobias wasn't included."

"Let's not hurt his feelings. Tobias is coming."

Lump blinked hard, then gestured at me to walk up the stairs ahead of him with Tobias directly behind me. We continued up another flight of stairs and around a corner until we came to the door to the library.

I stopped there. "Who is inside?"

"Captain Strick and Lord Trench."

"Who is Lord Trench?"

Lump rolled his eyes. "I believe you call him Mercy."

"Trench." I chuckled. "Let's call him Lord Stench. It will be our joke."

"The last person to call him that was sent to our dungeons for life."

"It's still worth it." I scrunched up my face. "All right, go in and make any excuse necessary to get Strick and Stench out of that room. And do not tell them about me."

"Why not?"

"What if the Monarch doesn't want them to know? What will she do if you ruin this secret?"

He considered that but added, "I can't leave you alone out here."

I rolled my eyes. "We'll wait around the corner until they're gone, I swear it on the tombs of my ancestors. Now go."

Reluctantly, Lump went into the library while I began looking around, wishing for something to eat. I already regretted promising to be here when Lump returned, because otherwise, we could have gone down to the kitchen.

"I guess we're stuck here," I said to Tobias. "You had a reason for telling Levitimas the history of the three rulers. What was it?"

His eyes widened. "I thought you didn't know the story."

"I've heard it my whole life. Tell me why it matters now."

"Did you wonder why Castor invited Batilda to supper after she came to the castle?"

"Obviously to get back at me."

"Yes, but not in the way that you think. Do you remember when Castor first greeted Batilda in the great hall? He told her that in a different world, she might have been queen."

I closed my eyes and let that sink in. "Batilda comes from one of the three rulers?"

"Go back a thousand years, and she is a direct granddaughter of Faylinn. The records were in the inner keep; I saw them for myself, but I've never seen these records anywhere else. Somehow, Castor must have this same information. In a different world, Batilda would be queen, and Batilda's daughter —"

"Imogen has royal blood," I whispered. "Does she know?"

"I'm not sure, but I'm certain that Castor does know and that's why he invited them to his estate the evening of the attack. He wants a friendship with them."

"He wants far more than a friendship," I said. "He plans to marry Imogen."

Tobias nodded, as if he had already expected that. "She is

a queen, by birth. If Castor marries her, he will become a king. He will have almost as much claim to the throne as you do." He hesitated, then added, "I hate to say the rest, because I know how selfish it will sound, but it's something I have to think about. You said it yourself. If Imogen refuses to marry Castor, then there is only one other way for him to become king."

"He'll have to kill you and Harlowe." I pressed a hand to my temple. He wouldn't ask for their resignations anymore. Not after they'd already refused him so forcefully.

The library door opened, and we backed away from the corner even farther. We heard Captain Strick leave first, her boots stomping away from us as she mumbled to herself something about Wilta and "spoiled child." That was followed by a tapping noise on the stone floor. Curious about the sound, I peeked out enough to see Mercy pass directly by us, holding a cane that I recognized as belonging to Lord Kerwyn. Kerwyn used to take it with him on long walks.

Mercy's eyes were entirely wrapped, obviously because I had burned them, and he was using the cane to feel his way forward. I considered tripping him so that I could take back Kerwyn's cane, but a castle servant ran up behind him. "The Monarch suggested that I guide you to your room," he said.

I immediately lowered my head and turned away from the servant, though Mercy still managed to bump into the wall, rather hard.

"Walk slower!" Mercy snapped. I wondered if the servant had meant to do that to him. I hoped so.

Lump came around the corner next. He said, "The Monarch will see you now."

We walked in. Wilta was seated at a desk, her long red hair curling over her shoulders. She was clad in a royal-blue dress. That was Carthya's color, which could not be an accident. She looked up as we entered, her face showing only the barest hint of surprise.

She stood and walked a circle around me, removing my hat and wig. "Alive! Well, this changes things."

"It will change too many things if anyone else knows. Let this be our secret, Wilta."

She smiled and stepped back. "I'll consider that." Her eyes shifted. "Hello, Tobias."

He nodded briefly, and I said to Wilta, "Tell Lump to wait outside. We have a lot to talk about."

"Very well." She waved Lump away, and when he was gone, she said, "I always believed you were still alive. Castor was a fool to have fallen for your trick."

"He wasn't the first fool I've tricked."

Wilta flinched when she recognized my insult. "Has it only been six months since Belland?"

"Hard to say. You've aged quite a bit since I last saw you."

Her mouth pinched shut. "I understand that Roden fled with your armies during our attack. You are alone, Jaron."

"I'm here," Tobias said.

She glanced over at him with a wry smile. "Yes, I'm sure he takes great comfort in that."

"I do," I said. "I fully expect that Tobias will be the key to our victory."

Her smile widened. Hardly a sign that she agreed with me. "Is this the time when you threaten me?"

"That's not necessary. My previous threats still stand. Remain here and the Prozarians will be destroyed."

"We will stay until we find that treasure. Where are the scope and lenses?"

"Hidden."

"You know that I will do whatever it takes to get them."

"It is for your own sake that I am keeping them hidden," I said. "I'm doing you a favor."

"How?"

"Not everyone around you is as loyal as they pretend to be."

"Oh? Who are you talking about?"

"You must know. Who would have the most to gain if you were no longer the Monarch?"

Wilta shrugged that off. "They would only lose. Do you know what I do to people suspected of disloyalty?"

"Frown at them?"

"Yes. Right before I order their deaths."

"Ah."

"Everyone in my service fears me, and they should."

"Fear of a leader may be the most powerful reason to betray a leader."

"If you know of anyone who plans to betray me, tell me their names."

"I'm still figuring that out. If something happened to you, who would rule?"

"My mother. Normally, she never could become the Monarch. In the Prozarian tradition, when a Monarch dies, their eldest child takes the throne, not the husband or wife. But since I have no child, power would go to her until she had another child."

"And if something happened to your mother?"

"Lord Trench would rule." Wilta shook her head. "They are both loyal to me. All who serve me are loyal!"

"If that's true, it will change when the treasure is found." Wilta stared back at me, hesitating long enough that I was able to add, "Whether you want to believe it or not, and whether I want it to be true or not, I am your best chance to survive."

· TWENTY-THREE ·

Something about what I had said must have struck Wilta as funny, because she began laughing. "*You* are my best chance to survive? Didn't you just threaten to destroy me and my people?"

"I said that you would be destroyed, not that I'd be the one to do it. Someone else will."

Wilta's mouth slowly widened into a smile. "Lies," she whispered.

"That cannot be," Tobias said. "Jaron does not lie."

Wilta flinched slightly, though she quickly recovered. "I have no reason to believe you."

"You have one very good reason. If I am correct, and there is a plot to kill you, then you owe it to yourself to find out who that person is."

Wilta's eyes flared with a sudden anger. She raised her arm and pointed toward the door. "My people love me! They serve me willingly!"

I caught her arm with my hand and raised the sleeve, revealing the same scars I had seen when we had first met on the pirate ship. She had claimed they were wounds given to her by Captain Strick, as a way of convincing me that she was a captive.

Her arm was worse now. There were more scars, and bandages to cover what I suspected would soon become scars.

"What are you doing?" She tried to pull her arm away, and when I didn't release it, she opened her mouth to call Lump back in.

"Do they know you are still sick?" I asked. I pulled her in closer. "No, you haven't told anyone, and why? You think if the people know, they will remove you from the throne."

Wilta's eyes shifted, and she said, "They have no power to remove me."

"Then who does?"

"I can only be removed by the votes of the commander of my armies and my highest counselor."

"Captain Strick and Lord Stench."

"Trench," Tobias corrected me. Then he stepped forward. "Mind if I look at your arm?"

She hesitated only a moment before lifting her sleeve again and holding out her arm. Tobias took it, leaning in close and running a finger up one of the scars.

"This isn't plague." He looked over at me. "I don't know what this is, but it isn't plague."

Wilta pulled her arm away again and lowered her sleeve. "A ruler must surround themselves with people they trust, and I keep my circle very small. My mother prepares my food each day, and Lord Trench delivers it. If either of them wanted to get rid of me, they could have done it long ago."

A knock came to the door. Through it, Lump said, "Monarch, the Steward of Carthya has come to see you. He insists that it is urgent."

Wilta eyed me. "Shall I let Castor enter? What a fun reunion that would be, all of us together with the king he tried to kill and a regent he wants to kill."

I pointed to the curtains. "Tobias, go hide there."

"You think that will save him?" Wilta walked back to the desk and pulled out a quill and paper. "Tell me how to find the Devil's Scope. Do it, or I'll give Tobias to Castor right now."

"Tobias is the one person in this castle who can help figure out your sickness."

"He's a boy who has read a few books. He's of no use to me." She shoved the quill into my hand. "Give me the Devil's Scope and I'll hide you too."

"No, I must speak to Castor." Or hit him a little.

"Didn't you ask me to keep you a secret? What will he do if he knows you're alive?"

"Monarch?" Lump knocked again. "My lady, he says this is urgent."

"I need one more minute," she called, and pushed the paper in front of me.

I huffed, and then I began writing, angling my body to steal the knife from the desk while I wrote down the location of the scope. It was followed by one of my better insult poems, though with more time I might have composed a masterpiece.

I handed the paper to Wilta, who read it over, and even managed a smile over my poem, although she clearly failed to appreciate the talent in rhyming "warthog scat" with "Prozarian rat." Then she folded the paper and said, "You'd better get behind a curtain too."

"Absolutely not. Curtains are a terrible place to hide."

"What?" Tobias asked.

"Stay still or you'll make it worse," I hissed.

In the corner of the library was a small alcove, meant to be a quiet reading nook. From there, I could easily listen in on Castor and Wilta's conversation. I stood out of sight and kept the knife I'd just stolen ready in my fist. Wilta hadn't noticed that I'd taken it.

The door opened. From my angle, I watched her put the note I'd written into Lump's hand. "This paper contains an errand that must be fulfilled at once. Send my mother."

"Yes, Monarch."

Castor entered next but remained in the doorway. "Forgive my intrusion." He bowed to her, every bit as low as he had once bowed to me, which I saw as further proof that he was planning to betray her too. Castor cleared his throat, then closed the library door. "Monarch, am I the steward of this castle or not?"

"What do you want now, Castor?"

"I want Tobias. I understand from my men that he was captured last night and taken to the dungeons. However, I just went down there but was informed that he was gone. I wanted to inspect the dungeon for myself, but your vigils denied me entrance."

Wilta's tone already showed her irritation. "If they said Tobias wasn't there, then he wasn't there."

"This is my castle now. My men and my money are repairing it, and yet I am unable to enter my own dungeons."

I actually agreed that Castor should enter my dungeons — as a prisoner. I'd mention that to Wilta as an option.

Her voice sharpened. "This is your castle subject to my authority and my will. You have no power except what I grant to you, which includes where you may and may not go."

"How will the people bow to me if I must always stand in your shadow?"

"They only bow to you *because* you are in my shadow! There are others with stronger claims to the throne."

Castor cleared his throat. "Then allow me to find them! Rulon Harlowe is injured and probably near death, but I cannot find him anywhere. Now Tobias is missing too. I must be allowed to deal with them myself."

"Neither of their deaths will matter if Jaron is alive. Is there any possibility of that?"

I tightened my grip on the handle of the knife I had stolen, then leaned forward, curious as to his response.

He laughed. "I saw the arrow hit him, and saw him fall. I saw the blood that washed down the river with his body."

"And have you recovered the body?"

"Monarch, the Roving River runs nearly the entire length of Carthya. It could have carried him all the way into Mendenwal. But I assure you, he is dead."

"Very well." She was silent for only a moment before adding, "Forget about Tobias and Harlowe. If you wish to keep the throne, you know what must be done."

Again, Castor's reply came quickly. "Imogen still refuses to accept my offer."

"That is unacceptable. Since you are unable to persuade her, I will speak to her myself and inform her that the marriage will happen, with or without her cooperation."

"Thank you, Monarch. She has proved herself uncommonly stubborn."

"But she is not more stubborn than me. Goodbye, Castor."

A few seconds passed in which I was certain he must be bowing to her; then the door opened and he left.

My temper was nearly at a full boil when I burst out of the cove. "Why did you do that?"

"Do what?"

"I just told you how to find the scope, and in return, you encouraged the marriage to Imogen!"

She faced me. "Of course I did. Because now you will make my job easier."

"You want me to get rid of Castor for you." I rolled my eyes. "No, he's your problem now."

"He's *our* problem. He's also vain and short-tempered, and irritates me to my core. Find a way to stop him, or watch the girl you love become his wife."

"*That* is no game."

"It is a game where you and I are on the same side. We share a common enemy. As long as you are fighting Castor, I will help you hide, and help your friends. Cooperate with me, and I will be a friend to you."

"We are not friends, Wilta," I said. "I don't think you

even understand friendship. People stay close to you for power, or out of fear, or because they want a piece of your beloved treasure."

She narrowed her eyes. "And why do they serve you? How long can a person tolerate someone as arrogant, as cruel-natured, and as reckless as you? Even your parents pushed you away, did they not?" Her smile was ice cold. "You really are alone now."

By then, Tobias had left the curtains. "He's not alone, Wilta. Jaron is my king and my friend."

"Jaron is no one's king, not anymore. Let's see how long you remain friends with him now." She stepped toward me. "You question the loyalty of those close to me, but if you had any understanding of loyalty, how did Castor escape your attention? How did Imogen?"

"She has never betrayed me."

"She will, the moment she agrees to marry Castor."

"That marriage will not happen," I said. "Castor and his Stewardmen will be defeated first. You will be defeated first."

"You speak as if you have any control over what is happening." Wilta pointed to the door. "All I have to do is give Commander Coyle a single order, and your life is over."

"I have to do even less than that." I pulled out the knife and threw it toward Wilta, where it grazed her shoulder before embedding itself in the wood shelf behind her.

Her mouth fell open in shock or maybe in outrage, but she quickly recovered. "If that was intended as a warning, it did not frighten me." But her hand was shaking as she flung open the door and shouted to whoever was now on the other side, "Kill anyone who attempts to leave this room and let no one enter." She glanced back at me. "For your sake, that scope had better be in my hands within the hour."

"And for your sake, have someone bring me and Tobias some food. We're hungry."

· TWENTY-FOUR ·

I wasn't at all happy about being trapped in here, and neither was Tobias, but at least it gave us a chance to talk in private.

Tobias slumped against the wall. "Wilta was wrong about you not having any true friends."

"That's hardly the worst thing someone has said to me."

"No, but I saw you flinch when she said it." Tobias waited a bit, then added, "The knife throwing was a surprise. Did you intend to —"

"I meant to miss. I just needed her to take my warnings seriously."

"But why should she?" Tobias asked. I turned to him, and he spread out his hands. "I've heard you make threats before, dozens of times, but that's when you have an army at your back, or at least, you know where your army is. I'm all you've got now, and that won't be enough."

I frowned at him. "In the first place, I made the threat knowing it was only you and me. Besides, we also have Mott —"

"Who is somewhere protecting Amarinda and Harlowe.

I think he'll take them to Farthenwood." Tobias eyed me. "But he's not here."

"We have Roden —"

"Who's missing."

"And Darius. I told that soldier to send them to Farthenwood."

Tobias frowned. "Darius . . . will be in hiding with Amarinda?"

"You've married her already. Will you think about my problems now? Imogen will be forced into marriage, probably very soon. She's got some plan, apparently, and she seems to think I know what it is."

"Isn't it obvious?" Tobias countered.

I tilted my head. "Don't insult me. What is her plan?"

"Didn't Captain Reever say that she was trying to get the Stewardmen on her side?"

This much was obvious. "Because whatever she has in mind, she'll need their loyalty." My eyes widened. "You think Imogen is planning a counterattack of her own?"

"Everything points to that. If she is, then she has to find Carthya's armies. Until she does, she needs to keep Castor and Wilta distracted."

"Which she can do if she keeps them fighting with each other." But that distraction could not last forever. I mumbled, "Do you think she will marry him?"

A very long pause followed before Tobias let out a heavy sigh. "Yes, Jaron. I think eventually she will have to. Imogen could claim the throne for herself right now. Why hasn't she? Because at some point she will need something from Castor, and agreeing to the wedding is the only way she will get it. He'll have a priest in front of them that same hour, before she can change her mind." Tobias hesitated, then added, "Besides, marrying Castor is the only way she'll get control of the Stewardmen."

I shook my head. "We can't let her go through with it, not if those are her reasons."

Tobias waited even longer to answer this time. "She needs the Stewardmen, but that's not her real reason. The final part of her plan is the most obvious."

"Not to me."

"How can you not see it? Imogen is doing what she always does; she is protecting you!"

"No, it's different this time." My shoulders slumped. "She might protect the king, as a duty to her country. But she is finished with me. Imogen made that clear."

"You should have told her about the scope," he said. "You should have told all of us." He glanced over at me. "And for as hard as you worked to keep that a secret from us, you certainly didn't waste time in telling Wilta where it was."

"I didn't waste time in saving your life. You remember that part too, I hope?"

"You could have written down instructions to anywhere in Carthya. You could have tricked them."

Now I closed my eyes and leaned my head against the wall. "They know my tricks, Tobias, and they have plenty of their own."

"Then get new tricks."

"If you play games with a cheater, you won't win by cheating. You only win by creating new rules. That's what I've got to do."

"Maybe." Tobias was quiet for a moment. "But I felt more confident of winning when I knew you were the cheater."

"Me too."

I was nearly asleep when the door was opened by two Prozarian vigils, both of them well armed. Mercy followed them in, with his eyes still wrapped and using Kerwyn's cane to keep from tripping as he walked.

Also, I noted, none of them had brought us any food. Now I was irritated.

"Is Tobias in this room?" Mercy asked.

Tobias eyed me, clearly alarmed. I opened my mouth to speak, but he shook his head at me and said, "I am Tobias."

"Take him with us," Mercy said.

"I can help with your eyes," Tobias said. "In exchange, perhaps you will release my servant, locked in here with me. He has duties to attend to."

"A castle servant from the kitchen threw boiling water on me," Mercy said. "Did your servant do that?"

I had been looking at what I could see of Mercy's bandaged face. His nose and cheeks were dotted with small welts. Those burns were caused by something worse than boiling water. That cauldron must have had oil in it.

"Did you see the servant?" Tobias asked.

"It happened too fast, but all the servants are being questioned, and when I do find him, I will have him killed."

"It could not have been my servant," Tobias said. "He is not allowed in the kitchen."

"Very well. Regent, you will come with me."

Tobias looked over at me, his eyes wild with fear.

I stepped forward. "Take me instead —"

"I'll go with you." Tobias quietly shook his head, warning me again. "I am the regent, and he is only a castle servant. I'll go."

The two vigils grabbed each of Tobias's arms, but I lowered my voice and used an Avenian accent to say, "Regent, I must remind you of your promise to the Monarch."

Even with his bandages on, Mercy wheeled around toward me. "What promise was that?"

I looked at Tobias, whose eyes had suddenly widened to the size of dinner plates. "He is the regent, sir. It is not my place to speak. It's only that the Monarch specifically mentioned some concerns about her top counselor. What was his name again?"

"Lord Trench."

"Oh, that's right. The way she spoke about him was . . . curious."

"I am Lord Trench, her top counselor."

"Really?"

"Who did you think I am?"

"A lowly servant, like me. If you are Lord Trench, then I suggest we all forget this conversation ever happened. It wasn't so important. Isn't that correct, Regent?"

Tobias's eyes continued to widen, more than I thought possible. He arched his brows, clearly asking what he was supposed to say. I only shrugged back at him.

Mercy looked in the direction where he thought Tobias was. "What did she say, Regent?"

I stepped forward. "Sir, he may have promised secrecy to the Monarch. You would not wish him to risk facing her anger."

"No, but I can risk you." Mercy gestured with his cane, and the vigils released Tobias and grabbed my arms instead, shoving me against a wall. My back stung when they did, but it was vital that I not show any sign of pain there. That would identify me in an instant.

"Tell Lord Trench what you know," one of them said.

I whispered, "Could we speak in private? What she said is *about* Lord Trench."

Mercy passed his cane to that vigil. "Beat the servant with this until he speaks."

I turned my head away. "No, I'll talk. I was in this room earlier with the Monarch. Someone suggested that you and Captain Strick intend to take the treasure from her and betray her. If she does suspect you, then you'll be dismissed from her service long before the treasure is found."

"Did she say that was her plan?"

"No," Tobias said, finally catching on. "But with your damaged eyes, you won't be able to help decipher the scope once it is found. She may decide that she has no further use for you."

Mercy pressed his thin lips together. "I see. Fortunately, I am already two steps ahead of her. Release the servant. Regent, you will come with me."

I didn't like that. "Wait — I have more information for you."

"You are only trying to protect the regent, but you cannot help him any longer."

"As his servant, I am obligated to go with him."

Mercy laughed. "You will wait here until the Monarch

sends orders to have you killed. Until then, don't try anything foolish. The vigil outside your door will be well armed."

They left, and the door closed in front of me. After a few minutes, I crept to the door to listen. Of course I was going to try something foolish.

TWENTY-FIVE

There was no noise out in the corridors, no footsteps of anyone passing by. I knocked on the door. "Hello?"

I used the same servant's voice as before. Other than the Avenian accent, I realized that with this slightly lower tone, I sounded a lot like my father.

There was no answer, but I knew someone was out there. I'd heard the shuffle of their feet.

"Were you ordered to ignore basic manners?" I asked. "Hello?"

"Whoever is in there, keep quiet!"

"I'm trying to help you."

Another pause. Then, "How?"

"I wanted to warn you that you'll be in serious trouble with the Monarch in ten or fifteen minutes." I calculated that in my mind. "Possibly twenty minutes. Either way, she'll probably kill you, and that will be partially my fault, so I'm giving you a chance now to run and hide."

Silence. Then, "Why will I be in trouble?"

"Because I'm going to escape."

I turned and looked around the room for anything that

might make noise. I pulled heavy books from the shelves and dropped them on the floor. I tipped over a reading chair, then tiptoed to the door and waited.

It took longer than it should have, and frankly, I had long since lost patience with this new vigil before the door finally unlocked and opened, barely. I grabbed the edge of it with both hands and yanked it toward me, then slammed it forward again, knocking the vigil to the ground. He fell backward and might've fallen unconscious for a moment. Certainly it was long enough for me to take his sword — the fourth sword I had borrowed over the last three days. He sat up until his chest reached the sword's point.

"Give me the keys to this room."

He scowled, but he did hand over the keys. I used the sword to direct him back into the library and shut the door. "If your monarch asks me how I escaped, shall I tell her the truth, that you were stupid enough to fall for a simple trick? Or shall I tell her that you fought heroically and that my escape was through no fault of your own?"

He blinked a few times. "Why would you help me —"

"Answer my next question and I can save your life."

He shook his head. "I am loyal to the Monarch."

"More than she will be to you, I'm sure."

I started to leave, but he called, "Wait! What is your question?"

"Tell me which direction the regent went just now."

"Lord Trench said they were going to the regents' room."

"Did he say why?"

The vigil nodded, then added, "The regent was told that someone there wanted to see him."

I cursed under my breath. Castor was obviously behind this, but why was Mercy carrying out his orders?

"I'll tell the Monarch you fought heroically. And if I were you, I'd lie on the floor and moan and pretend that I hit you hard." He was already on his way down when I ducked out the door.

I rounded the corner, passing a thick group of Stewardmen who were at work repairing the northwest corner of the castle. I ducked past them, all the while thinking of how I might get inside the regents' room. I'd have no success listening through the walls. They were made thick to prevent servants from eavesdropping. I never fully understood why that was important. The regents rarely said anything worth gossiping about. Nor could I simply enter as a servant. I had no reason to interrupt their meeting, and any excuse I gave would draw too much attention to me.

Down the corridor from me, I caught sight of Errol, carrying a tray with a teapot and cups on it. I hurried over to him and reached for the tray. "The king is thirsty."

"Castor is not a —" Errol turned, and I arched my brows at him. "Jaron?"

"Hush. I am a servant of Carthya, the same as you," I said. "But I need this tray, and your coat. Now."

Errol removed his blue servant's coat and gave it to me. It was fine on length but tight in the arms, so I hoped I wouldn't have to do any fighting. I belted my most recent stolen sword beneath the coat and buttoned up to hide most of it. I hoped that wasn't a mistake either. The sword would be difficult to reach in a hurry.

"Where were you going just now?" I asked Errol as I took the tray from him. If this tea was for any of the Prozarians, I'd add some laxative herbs to it. A lot of laxative herbs.

"I was told to bring it to Lady Imogen."

"Where is she?"

"In the queen's apartments. Castor has locked her in there."

I closed my eyes and took a breath. "Get her another tray. I need this one."

Errol handed it to me again, and I carried it back to the regents' room. Without knocking, I opened the door, careful to hold the tray high on my shoulder, blocking any view of my face.

"What is this? We're in a meeting." Castor was in my chair, the one reserved for the king. I had a hot pot of tea on the tray. I wondered about throwing this at him and scalding his eyes, the same as I had done to Mercy.

I glanced over at Tobias, who was sitting in the same small blue chair I had once brought out for Castor. I gestured at him to say something. I couldn't risk Mercy recognizing my voice, nor Castor for that matter.

"Uh . . ." Tobias sat forward. "It is customary for tea to be brought to the regents' room at this time every day."

"Very well." Castor turned back to Mercy, who was still bandaged and staring straight ahead, in a chair beside Castor. "You were saying, Lord Trench?"

"I understand that Carthya's high chamberlain was killed during our initial assault."

"Lord Kerwyn was unfailingly loyal to Jaron," Castor said. "He would have had to die anyway."

"Yet the fact remains that you are in need of a new high chamberlain."

"Who do you propose for the task?" Castor asked.

The tray had only three teacups on it. I'd have to make do with them. As slowly as possible, I began setting them down, at all times keeping the tray between me and Castor.

Mercy cleared his throat. "Do you wish to remain a steward? Or does the title of King Castor ring in your ears?"

Castor laughed. "Are you putting yourself forward as my high chamberlain? You cannot possibly believe that I would choose my enemy's counselor!"

Mercy caught the error before Castor had any chance to correct it. "You consider the Monarch your enemy, sir? Perhaps I do as well. It has recently come to my attention that she has become suspicious of me. So I believe we are on the same side now more than ever."

Castor frowned. "I already have enough trouble with the Monarch. If I agree to make you my high chamberlain, that will only make things worse."

Mercy pointed to Tobias, or about where he thought Tobias was. "I brought this regent here because I know you want him dead. Promise me the title of high chamberlain, and I will give Tobias to you right now. Do whatever you want with him."

For a moment, Castor smiled; then he brushed his hand toward me, so focused now on Tobias that he didn't even once look my way. "You, servant boy, get out!"

If I could have thought of any reason to stay, or any way that I could have helped Tobias, I would have done it. But for now, I kept the tray high on my shoulder, closed the door behind me, then stepped across the corridor into the gallery to try once again to collect my thoughts.

My eyes drifted to the walls around me, and immediately my blood burned with anger. One of the gallery walls was empty. Someone had come through here and removed every painting of my family from back to my grandfather's childhood.

Wilta had said it herself, that this was the next phase in her plan to control Carthya, to make sure I was forgotten.

Not only me, but my family too. I stared at the empty wall, my eyes tracing the darker shades where the frames had once hung, feeling fury rising in me. I was ready to march back into the regents' room now, sword in my hand, but then I heard Errol's voice once again as he followed a far-more-familiar voice coming closer through the corridor.

"My lady," Errol was saying, "if he knows I let you out —"

"I let myself out," Imogen said. "Don't come with me, Errol, or you'll be in trouble too."

"Thank you, my lady."

I remained hidden in the gallery while Imogen marched into the regents' room, leaving the door open. I could easily hear now.

"Castor, how dare you do this? Tobias is my friend!"

"My dear Imogen, I asked you to remain in your room, for your own safety."

She ignored that. "Tobias, leave this room, now."

Castor raised his voice. "Imogen, we've discussed this —"

"My lady," Tobias said, using a more formal address for Imogen than he usually would, "I can be of use to Lord Trench. If he is willing, I can help him with his eyes."

"Tobias is not going anywhere!" Castor's tone sharpened further. "You brought him to me, Lord Trench. He is my prisoner now."

"Lord Trench." Tobias spoke more forcefully. "I am the closest thing to a physician inside these castle walls. Nobody else here will know what to do for your eyes."

A chair was pushed back, and Mercy said, "Until you accept my offer, Steward Veldergrath, you have no authority over my decisions. The regent will come with me. Now, if you wish to change your mind about my offer, perhaps we can discuss the regent's fate again. Tobias, guide me out of the room."

I ducked deeper into the gallery again and desperately wanted to follow, but I couldn't. Imogen was still in the regents' room with Castor, and no doubt he would be furious with her.

I unbuttoned the coat that I had borrowed from Errol and reached for my sword. If necessary, I would use it.

· TWENTY-SIX ·

I mogen was the first to speak. "Castor, we already discussed Tobias. You swore to me that you would not harm him."

"I swore that I would not harm him if you married me. But you keep finding reasons to delay answering."

"You know very well why I can't accept your offer today. I need more time."

"No!" he shouted. "You have had all the time you need! The Monarch has ordered us to marry. How does it look to her if you still refuse me?"

"How will it look to the people if I agree to marry you on the same day that I should have been marrying Jaron?"

Blood rushed to my ears. With all that had happened, I had completely forgotten that our wedding was supposed to be today, almost at this exact hour. So much had been lost over the past few days, but the realization of what today should have been put a knot in my throat.

Castor only snorted. "Jaron never cared about you. Your mother told me all about the wrongs you have suffered because of him." He stepped closer to her, and now his voice softened. "I will be kinder to you, Imogen. I will be everything he was not. Agree to the marriage, I beg of you."

"Castor, I need time."

His voice filled with fury once again. "Close the door, Imogen."

She started to close it, but I immediately darted into the room and raised the tray again, saying in my lower voice, "Is everyone finished with the tea?"

"Just hurry," Castor snapped.

I closed the door and did anything but hurry in my collection of the teacups, not one of them touched. That gave me an excuse to go slower.

"I will try to give you an answer tomorrow," Imogen said.

Castor pulled Imogen to him by her hands. "Tomorrow for your answer, and the day after that for our wedding. I am sorry to be so demanding. It is only the strain of trying to rule beneath the Monarch's boot. She has not been fair to me. She will not honor our original terms."

"In what way?"

"She says that I have disappointed her and I fear she already wants to replace me, but I will not be removed from the throne, Imogen, not after all I've done to come this far. She is forcing me to make plans of my own."

"What plans?"

"A simple way of assuring the defeat of the Prozarians and Jaron's armies, all while leaving the Stewardmen untouched."

Imogen's tone sharpened. "What is the plan, Castor?"

"At some point, Roden will return with what is left of his armies. When they come, I have ordered the Stewardmen not to fight. We will stand back and watch as the two sides destroy each other. We will be the last surviving army."

"It won't be that simple, Castor."

"No, I will win. *We* will win, together." He kissed her hand. "You don't know what I have suffered since I arrived at this castle. No one bows to me; no one calls me by my title. I am treated here as the enemy. The last meal I ate was coated in salt. Did they do any of that to Jaron?"

Imogen smiled. "He used to complain of overcooked meat."

"But they did bow to him, and they still bow to him, even in death! That's my problem. The servants, all the people, are still loyal to Jaron." He stepped back, clearly angry. "How is that possible? While he ruled, I heard nothing but how reckless he was, how little he cared about his nobles. He skipped meetings, including three that I tried to arrange before he forced me to finally act on my own!"

I knew exactly which meetings he meant. Kerwyn had presented Castor's requests to me, and each time I was quick to say no. More specifically, I told Kerwyn I'd rather eat off the stable floor than endure any meeting with Castor.

But Castor wasn't finished. "Jaron created enemies wherever he went, and invited danger into Carthya the way others might invite guests" — Castor gestured to me, somehow still not seeing me — "as if to a tea party. Now that he is gone, all I've heard is the people saying they never had a better king."

"As if they believe he is somehow still here with them."

I hesitated in my work. Imogen must have recognized me.

Castor continued, "I must warn you of something. During

our meeting just now, Lord Trench mentioned that the Monarch wishes to dine with you tonight, in the King's Gardens."

"Wilta wants a supper with me?" Imogen sounded concerned, and for good reason. Wilta and Imogen were not friends.

"She has a special request, one you will not be allowed to refuse."

"Oh?"

"Jaron's memory must be destroyed, to break the people's loyalty to him. The Monarch will ask you to speak publicly about the wrongs he has done to you."

"Jaron has done nothing!"

"Your mother says differently."

"Castor, I will not tell lies about Jaron!"

"She will only ask that you tell the truth, and there is much of it to be told. Why else did you come to Elmhaven that night if not to escape from Jaron's tyranny?"

Castor moved toward her again, but this time, she turned, both to keep him from looking at me and to keep herself away from him, or at least, that's how it appeared to me.

He took her hand anyway and said, "Are you with me, Imogen?"

"I am always on the side of Carthya," she said.

He pulled her closer. "But are you with *me*? Because if you are not, if all this is only a game to you, then I can still take the throne as king. All I must do is rid Carthya of its last two regents, and I will start with Tobias. Are you with me or not?"

Silence fell between them, enough that I took the chance of peeking out from behind the tray, and when I did, I nearly became ill. Imogen was kissing Castor. Not a simple, meaningless kiss, but truly kissing him.

She knew I was here; she had to have known it was me, the third person in what had suddenly become a very crowded room. I felt nauseous.

They were interrupted by a knock at the door. Someone called from the other side, "Steward Veldergrath, we have a problem."

Castor sighed, then snapped his fingers, presumably for me. "You there, escort Lady Imogen up to her room. Be sure a vigil is left at her door when you leave."

I nodded and started to move toward the door, but Imogen wasn't coming with me. She said, "Do not keep me in that room any longer, Castor. I must —"

"As I said before, it is for your own safety. The Monarch only keeps you alive because of me. It is better if you remain there until the supper tonight."

"But I —"

"I have arranged everything," he said. "Do not question your king."

He kissed her once more; then I picked up the last teacup and followed Imogen out. I stopped the first passing Prozarian soldier, thrust the tray into his hands, and said, "The Monarch wants these delivered to the kitchen."

Imogen didn't say anything at first and didn't even acknowledge that I was directly behind her. I followed her toward the stairs without a single idea of what I should say if we did get the chance to speak. Castor's last words to her echoed in my ears: "Do not question your king."

Couldn't those same words have come from me, only days ago?

Imogen had asked me to be fully honest with her. My response had been that I would not trouble her with the details, and not to question my decisions.

I should have told her that I had the Devil's Scope.

That's why she was so angry with me.

I thought about everything she had said to me in Castor's dungeon. I deserved every single word.

But our conversation wasn't nearly over yet.

· TWENTY-SEVEN ·

Once we reached the main staircase, there were few enough others around us that Imogen turned her head slightly to whisper, "You're angry."

"Why do you say that?" I asked.

"I heard you seething behind that tray."

"Maybe because I had to listen to you and Castor. You certainly answered his question of whether you want to marry him."

Her eyes darted. Hardly the answer I wanted. "Did you hear his threat, that if I don't, he will kill Tobias and Harlowe?"

"Yes, Imogen, I heard all of it. Is this what you want, or do you think that this is what you have to do?"

This time, her expression changed to one of deep sadness. "How often have you sacrificed yourself for Carthya, suffered so that this kingdom might stand? Would you expect less of me?"

I searched Imogen's face for any sign of affection while emotions ran through me in waves, flooding my senses and overwhelming my thoughts. I was deeply ashamed of my actions that had brought us to this, but confused as to how I could ever make things right. It meant everything to be near her again, but the happiness I might have felt was replaced with the devastation of watching her look back at me as if I were a stranger.

Why wasn't she saying anything? Why wasn't I?

Words slowly formed in my mind. I hardly dared to say them, but I couldn't walk away from her without knowing. "Precious little of my life is real, but you always were. I need to know if you still love me, Imogen. Tell me whatever you must, but let it be the truth."

I stared at her, with no idea how she would answer, and that terrified me.

After a moment, in a gentler voice than I deserved, she asked, "What does truth mean to you? Is it putty to be shaped and molded to get whatever results you want? Is it a mirror you distort, while telling a person to trust what they see in it? If I do not speak an outright lie, have I then told the truth? How can I answer your question so that you will know it is real?"

Her words hit me hard enough that I had to step backward to absorb them. The worst part was that I had no idea of what to say next.

Before I could answer this time, Captain Reever spotted Imogen below him on the stairs. "My lady, may I speak with you?"

Reever was the man who had whipped me inside Castor's dungeons. Was he taking orders from Imogen now?

As a servant would, I lowered my eyes when he climbed the stairs. She said to him, "Will you wait for me in the sitting room?"

"Yes, of course." He retreated from sight, and Imogen turned back to me. We were alone again.

"I have a plan. I need to know if you trust me."

I locked eyes with her. "Yes, absolutely, but . . ."

"But what?"

I shifted my weight while warnings flashed in my head to stop speaking, or I'd make things worse. But I was having a hard time thinking of any way they could get worse. When I didn't answer, she walked up the rest of the staircase without me.

I followed. "Why did you agree to Castor's suggestion to have me exiled? You must have known I'd never leave Carthya."

"I never assume that I know anything with you. What if that's just another secret?" She waited for me to answer, and when I didn't, she said, "I must go. Captain Reever is waiting."

"Imogen . . ." She turned, and I added, "There are reasons for the secrets I keep."

"What reasons?" When I didn't answer, her eyes fluttered as if she was holding back tears. "If you can't tell me the reasons, why should I ever expect to hear the secrets?"

What was I supposed to say to that? She knew my history better than anyone, which should have been enough for her to know my reasons, and they were simpler than she might have realized: I had never learned any other way.

Imogen finished walking to her room alone while I trailed behind. She stopped in the doorway, then turned back to me. "The sitting room needs to be cleaned. A good servant would see to it at once."

With a slight smile, I dipped my head at her and entered, closing the door behind me.

Captain Reever was standing near a window, but when he looked back, his eyes narrowed.

Imogen said to Reever, "Pardon the delay. I —"

When I looked to see why Imogen had stopped speaking, I saw Captain Reever down on one knee, staring at me. "I can see that it's you," he said. "My king."

I pulled off my hat and the wig. "How did you know?"

"Your eyes. I saw that same expression after the whipping."

"After the *what*?" Imogen turned from me to Reever. "You whipped him?"

"Yes, my lady. On Castor's orders."

"When did that happen?"

"Right after you agreed to the exile, my lady."

Imogen looked to me for an explanation, but I only lowered my eyes. I hadn't wanted her to know.

Reever soon filled the silence, saying, "There is no good news. We have been searching for the captain of the guard, as you asked, my lady, and those who escaped with him."

"Did you find Roden, then?"

"I'm afraid not. In fact, one of Castor's loyal officers is downstairs right now asking for permission to widen the search. Not only to include Captain Roden, but also for other armies collecting against him."

"What other armies?" I asked.

Reever looked around before lowering his voice. "Castor heard a rumor that your elder brother, Darius, is still alive. He believes that Darius has returned to Carthya. Could that be possible?"

I froze long enough to hear Imogen answer, "Yes, that is possible." She quickly added, "If you find him, or Roden, or anyone on our side, you cannot allow them to be harmed."

"I won't have any control over that. I am not in command of this group, and Castor's orders are to leave none alive."

"This mission must fail," Imogen said. "Captain Reever, we need every person in Carthya who is willing to fight with us. If you can avoid finding Roden or Darius, then avoid them. But if not, you must protect them. Can you do this?"

"I will do what I can, my queen. But that is not the worst news."

"What else?"

"We captured a boy in the royal stables who was planning to leave Drylliad. He fought us like no one could, but finally we got him in our control. We brought him back here to the castle for questioning, thinking he was only a thief. Castor knew him though. Said his name is Fink." Reever turned to me. "Your brother?"

I nodded, barely able to speak. Finally, I managed to ask, "What are Castor's plans for him?"

Reever frowned. "He's in the dungeons now. So is Tobias. Lord Trench said he was useless in healing his eyes."

Imogen drew in a sharp breath. "If Castor finds out Tobias is there —"

"I believe that Castor already knows where he is. Just before I came up to see you, I heard him order a double watch of Stewardmen in front of the dungeon. But the Monarch asked him to inspect the castle repairs, so I think Tobias has a little time."

Imogen nodded. "Thank you, Captain."

He offered her a deep bow and then glanced at me. "Any orders, sire?"

"Imogen's orders are enough. Thank you, Reever."

Once he left, Imogen immediately faced me. "We have to get inside those dungeons before Castor does."

"I'll take care of it." I dipped my head at her and began to leave but heard her say my name.

I turned again and saw her expression had softened. She looked so afraid now, so vulnerable, but I stayed where I was. In a softer voice than before, she said, "I agreed to the exile because I thought it would give you a chance to escape, nothing more." I nodded, but she quickly followed that by asking, "Why didn't you tell me that you'd been whipped?"

"Would it have mattered?"

"Of course it matters! If I hadn't agreed to your exile . . ."

"What happened was not your fault." This was why I hadn't told her, though I suppose not telling her was yet another secret. In a softer voice, I added, "Castor's plans for me were always the same."

She drew in a slow breath and murmured, mostly to herself, "I've got to stop him."

My heart began to pound. "Imogen, I need to explain something —"

A knock came to the door, and I quickly donned the wig and hat again, just in time for Batilda to enter. Her eye briefly fell on me, though I quickly turned away. "Imogen, you should not have male servants alone with you. People will talk."

I returned to straightening up the room, which needed no straightening up at all. I could not leave Imogen now, not with so much unfinished between us.

Imogen, however, was still focused on our last conversation.

Rather than address her mother's concern, she asked, "Did you know that Jaron was injured in Castor's dungeons?"

"I visited him soon after it happened." Batilda sat in a chair and began straightening her dress. "I did everything I could to help him and even gave him the chance to escape with the sword, as you asked. But after the arrow struck him during that escape, I didn't see any point in telling you, especially not with everything else you were suddenly facing."

I didn't know what Imogen thought about that explanation, but I could accept it. Even now, Batilda believed I never made it out of that river. Besides, there were far bigger issues on my mind.

Batilda continued, "I am trying to help you, Imogen. I know how difficult this must be."

"I don't know what to do." Imogen closed her eyes, and I wondered if what she was about to say was only for her mother, or if it was for me as well. "The Monarch wants to have supper with me tonight. She's going to demand that I marry Castor."

"How will you answer her?"

"There is no good answer. If I refuse marriage, he will go after Tobias and Harlowe, and anyone else who stands between him and the crown. But how can I accept him?"

Batilda sighed. "You must accept him, Imogen. The Monarch will not allow you to refuse." She found another wrinkle on her dress and straightened it too. "And you need to accept him; it's the only way your plan can work."

"But something has changed, something I didn't know before." She glanced at me and shook her head. Was that a message to me, a warning?

"What hasn't changed is your responsibility to Carthya. Without you, the people would have no hope. Be the queen that you are, and think of them."

"Yes," Imogen mused. "I am a queen. That is my choice." When she spoke again, I had no doubt that her words were for me. She knew I was still listening. "We are running out of time to save Carthya, and to save that which we love most."

I understood perfectly.

And I loved Imogen the most.

· TWENTY-EIGHT ·

After that, a maid entered to begin preparing Imogen for her supper that night with Wilta, leaving me no reason to remain in the room, nor could I stand it in here any longer. Desperate to be alone, I crossed through the maid's room, opened the window, and ducked out to the ledge.

Finally, I found an area wide enough to sit and did so, pushing my fingers through my hair and covering my mouth with one hand.

My thoughts were splitting apart. Both Fink and Tobias were in the dungeons now, and I had no way of getting to them. Nor could I save them from Castor, not even if Imogen agreed to marry him. Castor would not take any chances on someone coming forward to claim the throne.

Imogen had a plan to stop him, but that still did nothing to defeat the Prozarians, and Wilta would fight to her last breath to remain in Carthya until the treasure was found — if it was even here at all.

I couldn't allow her to get the treasure, but I'd have little help in stopping her. Roden and my entire army seemed to have vanished. I'd already lost Kerwyn.

Amarinda. Mott. Darius.

I couldn't save everyone, but over the last several days, it had become clear that I couldn't save anyone.

The faces of all those I cared about flashed through my mind, their images turning to smoke with the next face to appear.

That is, until I saw Imogen's face. She had stared back at me with doubt, with anger, and even with pity, but I had hoped to see some evidence of her love. Instead, she had accused me of having multiple truths, none of them entirely real, and how right she was. Maybe she looked at me and saw only disappearing smoke as well, someone she never could quite hold on to.

And never would. Imogen was going to marry Castor.

I needed Mott here, to advise me and tell me what a fool I was. Or Kerwyn, to remind me of who I was, and where my priorities should be. Or Amarinda, who knew Imogen better than nearly anyone.

Tears filled my eyes. No, what I really needed were my parents. For so long, I had done this on my own. I needed them now.

Threats had come to Carthya before, but I had always known the route ahead of me. As king, I was obligated to fight for Carthya, and I wanted to do it. Every other consideration fell in line behind that.

But not this time. I didn't know how to fight this one. I didn't know if I could, and if I could do it alone.

Only one option stood out to me: If I had to do this alone, then I needed to be closer to the Prozarians, not farther away. I had to see Wilta again. She would be furious that I had ignored her last orders to me, but I could work past that. I had to.

My greatest enemy might be my only solution.

I stood again, skirting along the castle ledge, passing the king and queen's shared sitting room first, and then the king's bedroom next. I peered in and saw evidence of someone having used this room. Was this Castor's room now?

I cursed and would have kicked the wall except that it would have cost me my balance. This had been my father's room. I had no objection to Imogen staying in the queen's room. My mother would have loved her and been overjoyed for her to have the room, but in all my time as king, I had never once crossed the threshold into my father's room. I simply couldn't. To think of Castor spoiling that place was intolerable.

To make things worse, my sword was laid out on a table near his bed. The room was empty, so I pried his window open and slid inside. This was not how I wanted things to be the first time I entered the place that had belonged solely to my father.

I paused as my feet touched the floor, *his* floor, with the same rugs still here as when I was young. I was now in the very place I had stood when my father announced he was sending me to Bymar, to learn to become a proper prince. He had been so frustrated with me then, and my final words to him in this room were anything but kind.

With some effort, I crossed the room to pick up my sword. It felt comfortable in my grip once again, but when I stared down at my hand and saw it bare of the king's ring, now on Castor's traitorous finger, I was doubly furious.

I drew in a deep breath, fighting my instinct to go out in search of Castor right now. My bare hand was a reminder of my situation, of the greater problems that Carthya faced. To solve them, I still had to pass as a servant. If I took back my sword, Castor would know I was alive, for no one else would have dared to remove it from this room.

So with great reluctance, I replaced the sword, but something else caught my eye on the mantelpiece of the fireplace.

A fresh string of curses erupted from me in a continuous flow with every step I took toward it. There, in the center of the mantelpiece, was the ring I had intended to give Imogen when we were married. This was no ordinary ring. This had been my mother's.

And now Castor intended to use it for *his* marriage to Imogen?

I picked it up and dropped it into my boot. This time, I didn't care about the consequences — he would never use *this* ring!

But to protect the servant of this room, I found a piece of parchment and wrote on it, "She is only keeping you alive until she finds the treasure."

This way, at least, Castor would know that someone other than Errol had been in his room. It would also likely create some well-deserved paranoia. I tucked the note under his pillow, then climbed outside again. The rocks that made up the castle wall from here to the ground were so uneven that it was a simple thing to scale down them, as I'd done countless times. Castor had said that Imogen and Wilta would be eating in the King's Gardens. That's where Wilta would be.

I had hoped to have the advantage of surprise, but the instant I crossed through the hole in the garden wall, Lump was waiting for me.

"We knew you'd show up here." He pinched my arms behind my back, then dragged me into the center of the gardens, where Wilta was seated at a table that had been placed there specifically for her supper.

Lump brought me directly in front of her. "Just as you expected, Monarch."

Wilta remained in her seat but leaned back and folded her arms. Her mouth was a thin, tight line. "You disobeyed my order to remain in the library! Did you think I'd overlook that?"

"No, but I hoped you would," I replied. For that, Lump twisted my arm farther.

Wilta said, "It doesn't matter, because now I have figured out how to control you. I simply arranged one supper with Imogen, and you have followed. Unless . . . you really came to see me."

"All I want to see of you is your defeat. Nothing more."

Lump pulled on my arm again. "Stop that!" I said, kicking backward at him.

"Release him," Wilta said. "He thrives on defying pain."

"No, I thrive on defying you." I smirked at her. "Though I suppose it's the same thing."

Wilta took a sip of tea and calmly said, "We found the Devil's Scope, exactly where you said it would be. If you had cooperated with me sooner, I wouldn't have had to threaten Tobias." Now she leaned forward. "Why are you here?"

"Castor is threatening Tobias. I want you to order him to stop."

"Tobias is a threat to Castor's authority. Our agreement does not allow me to interfere with this problem."

"Then change the agreement."

Wilta tilted her head. "Lord Trench was looking for him earlier. I suggested that Tobias might be able to help with his burned eyes. Were you the one who threw that boiling water at his face?"

"I threw something at him that was boiling." Which was all I intended to say on the matter, and I had far more pressing concerns than Mercy's scalded eyes. "There is something else I must ask."

"Oh?" This seemed to entertain her. "You dare to ask for anything, after causing me every sort of trouble, and confessing to a horrid attack on my chief counselor?"

"I did you a favor by attacking him. Now, as a favor to me, will you release my brother Fink from the dungeons?"

"Why would I do that?"

"Because somewhere beneath your crust of greed and evil, I think there's a decent person who doesn't want innocent lives lost."

She tossed her hair behind one shoulder. "You are wrong. I have no concern for anyone's life, innocent or not. And Fink is not innocent. He helped to blow up my ships in Belland."

"That wasn't personal. He just likes to see explosions." I tightened my focus on her. "Release him, Wilta, and I'll tell you what I know about Mercy."

She took another sip of tea, then said to Lump, "Fink is too young to be any threat to us. Release him."

Lump nodded and dismissed himself, leaving Wilta and me alone. She stood and walked closer to me. "Tell me about Lord Trench."

"I was in the room when he came to Castor, asking to be made the high chamberlain. He offered to betray you."

Wilta only shrugged. "Clever as you think you are, you were tricked. I sent Lord Trench there, to test Castor's loyalty. A test he failed, by the way." She took my hand. "I prefer this, you know. You and me working together rather than against each other. I know we've been enemies in the past, but it doesn't have to be that way. We could be friends."

I slid my hand free. "I have enough friends."

"And more than enough enemies. You and I together could easily defeat Castor."

"My grandmother could defeat Castor. My focus is on how to defeat you." My eyes met hers. "That is still my plan, Wilta. It must be."

Her expression hardened as she backed away from me. "How dare you come here, asking for my help? You want me to release Tobias? Well, I won't! Instead, I will have him delivered to Castor tonight."

"Then you would destroy the one person in this castle who can help you with your sickness."

"Tobias is no older than either of us. I doubt he knows enough to be of much use."

"Give him a chance. If he can't help you, then you've lost nothing."

"Why should I believe you? You asked me to keep you a secret, and I have. You asked me to release Fink, and I have. How many times have I proven myself a friend to you, and you return that by ignoring my orders, insulting me and my servants, and announcing your intention to defeat me. No one has betrayed me more than you."

"I cannot betray you because I have never pretended to be on your side. Everything I am doing is for only one of two reasons: your defeat, or stopping the wedding."

"Ah." Wilta stopped mid-tantrum and raised a finger in the air. "So we are back to the reason you came here tonight."

"I came to ask you to release Tobias."

"You came because you knew Imogen would be here." Wilta took my hand again, this time interlocking our fingers. "You think you want a future with Imogen, but I have heard that Imogen ended that possibility in Castor's dungeon. Look at all that I can offer you instead. If we worked together, I would be Monarch and you could be Emperor. Think of the empire we could build together. But I need your help."

"You want me to find the treasure for you."

"Do you know where it is?"

I hesitated before answering. "Almost."

"Let's work together, as friends. Give me what I want, Jaron, and then I will help you."

I thought of Levitimas, and his advice to me about Imogen. But was it really for Imogen? Or had Levitimas been telling me that *Wilta* would only turn to me after I gave her what she wanted?

She continued, "Can you deny that you want to find the treasure too? It is wealth and knowledge and power — truly it is everything!"

"None of that matters to me right now."

Now she stepped back, a wicked smile on her face. "Wasn't today supposed to be your wedding day?"

"Yes, but —"

"But Imogen broke the betrothal, and broke your heart too, I imagine. There is nothing so special about her. Why do you still care for that girl when she clearly no longer cares about you?" I must have flinched, because Wilta smiled, knowing she had hit her target. "I insist that we go forward with the wedding."

My eyes narrowed. "What are you —"

"Oh, not your wedding. Imogen's. When she comes for the supper, I will order her to marry Castor tonight. By sundown, she will be his. Castor will declare himself king, and you will feel a kind of pain I never could inflict on you any other way."

I set my jaw forward. "You will not punish Imogen because of your anger with me."

"Not everything is about you, Jaron. Ordering the marriage is the very reason why I invited her here tonight." She chuckled. "But, for a price, I will let her choose what she wants."

I didn't like the way she had laughed, nor the sudden gleam in her eye. "What is the price?"

"You must agree to my rules, and they are quite simple. During supper, I will give Imogen the choice between Castor and you. If she chooses him, then they will marry tonight, and you lose the game and lose the girl. Your penalty will be that you agree to find the treasure for me."

"The penalty will be that she marries Castor. That has nothing to do with any treasure."

"But she might also choose you, and if she does, you two can be married tonight, as planned. I will restore you to the throne after you and I negotiate a peace between our two countries."

I shook my head. "We are not playing this game!"

She shrugged. "Refuse my terms, and I'll order the marriage as soon as she arrives. So, will you agree or not?"

There was no other choice, and it might be the only chance I had left to stop that wedding. So I nodded and silently prayed I had made the right decision.

· TWENTY-NINE ·

Shortly before Imogen was due to arrive, I nestled into a gap between two thick bushes. From here, I could easily see where Imogen and Wilta would sit to eat their supper, and where I could hear their conversation. I felt the guilt of listening in on them, but Imogen's decision now had a major impact on my own future, so I knew this was necessary.

"Make a space for me." Lump walked along the hedge and began pushing his way into the gap.

"No!" I pushed back at him. "There are plenty of places here to hide. Find your own."

"The Monarch wants to remind you not to make a sound while Imogen is here, not to let her know you are listening."

"I remember. Now go away. If you squeeze in here, I'll breathe on you, and I'll tell you now, my breath is terrible."

Lump frowned, but he walked on and found another gap in the bushes nearby.

Minutes later, Imogen arrived, wearing a simple blue dress and, with her hair pulled away from her face, outshining Wilta in every possible way. Imogen gave a polite bow, and Wilta held out an arm, gesturing to a chair across from her. "Please sit."

Imogen's chair was almost facing me. I wondered if I stared hard enough at her, would she somehow sense that I was here? Maybe not, but it was worth a try.

"I am glad for this chance to speak with you," Imogen began. "There was a time when I thought we could have been friends."

"That was before you helped Jaron blow up my ships." In the same cool tone, Wilta added, "You've proven to be every bit as strong and clever as Jaron. Tell me, do you consider Castor Veldergrath to be a worthy leader for Carthya?"

Imogen lowered her eyes. "Castor would like to believe that of himself."

"Yes, but what do you think of him?"

Imogen looked up again and slowly shook her head. "He is not the leader that Carthya needs."

"Is that why you have still refused to give him an answer about marriage?"

Imogen hesitated. "It is very soon after Jaron's death, Monarch."

"Do not try that lie with me! You know very well that Jaron is alive. You have spoken with him yourself, is that true?"

Another hesitation, then Imogen slowly nodded. "Yes, I know that he is alive."

"So you will be glad to hear that tonight I am offering you a choice —"

"Before you do, I ask you to consider one other option." Imogen spoke quickly, as if she had forced the words out before she was ready.

"Oh?"

"I have recently learned that I am a daughter of royalty, through Faylinn, one of the original three rulers of Carthya. Jaron's line has held the throne since the time of the three rulers ended, but I have a royal bloodline of my own. I ask you to give *me* the throne, make me the queen of Carthya."

I hadn't expected that answer from Imogen. It was brilliant, but risky. As queen, Imogen had no need to marry Castor. But I also knew Castor would never walk away from the throne, not now when he was so close.

"Queen?" Wilta leaned back in her chair. "That's an interesting suggestion. You would agree to my terms, become subject to me?"

"I will agree to everything Castor has already agreed to."

"What will Castor do, if I remove him as steward?"

"He'll be angry, but I can deal with him and his armies."

"That isn't good enough. I cannot risk Castor's armies seeking revenge on you, or on me. He and all his armies will have to die." When Imogen failed to respond, Wilta leaned forward. "Does that bother you, to order the deaths of hundreds of soldiers?"

"Allow me to set their punishments, Monarch."

"If I did, what would you do about Jaron? He will never stop fighting against me."

Imogen opened her mouth to answer, then closed it. She didn't seem to know what to say to this.

And Wilta took advantage of that moment. "Every ruler must at times make difficult decisions. This will be your first test so that I know what kind of queen you would be. I will allow you a choice: save the lives of Castor and his Stewardmen, or save Jaron's life."

"Why must there be a choice?"

"Because Castor will not rest until you are married to him. And if you marry Castor, Jaron will never rest again."

"If I choose Jaron, what happens to Castor and his armies?"

"Mass execution, at the moment you are declared queen. I find Castor intolerable anyway."

"If I choose Castor and his armies, what will happen to Jaron?"

"I must separate him from Carthya, and from you. So Jaron's reputation with the people must be destroyed. If you choose Castor, the price is that you will speak in public for all the people to hear. You will say whatever is necessary to make the people hate Jaron, to make them glad that he is gone. Then Jaron will enter into my service, working closely with me to find the treasure."

A long silence followed. I studied Imogen's face, her eyes darting back and forth as her mind raced to get ahead of Wilta's schemes.

Finally, Wilta continued, "This seems to be a difficult choice for you. Let me make it easier. What are your feelings for Jaron?"

"I . . . care for him, of course."

"Do you love him?"

Imogen fell silent, for far too long, and asked her next question as though she already suspected the answer. "Does Jaron know about this?"

"That doesn't matter. You asked to be queen, and with that role comes the responsibility to make these types of decisions."

"I need time to consider this."

"No, Imogen, time is the one thing I will not give you. Tell me now who you choose. Choose Jaron, and tomorrow morning, Castor and the Stewardmen will face the executioner. Or choose Castor, and disconnect yourself forever from any future with Jaron."

"Monarch, this is an impossible choice."

"But the choice must be made! If you do not choose, I will decide for you. It all comes down to a simple question: What are your feelings for Jaron?"

Still more time passed, in which my heart was pounding so hard I worried I might not hear Imogen when she spoke.

Finally, Wilta said, "Very well. You force me to choose —"

"I choose Castor."

In those three words, my heart shattered. Imogen's words echoed in my ears, replaying in an endless loop that dug deeper into the remains of my heart with each round.

Wilta leaned back in her chair and laughed. "That wasn't so difficult, was it? We will delay any further talk of marriage while I consider your request to become queen."

"Thank you." Imogen was silent a moment longer before she stood, clasping her hands behind her. "I am not hungry, Monarch. You must excuse me."

Wilta merely reclined in her seat and smiled. "Thank you for coming. I have learned a great deal about you tonight."

"I understand you better as well." Imogen turned and left the gardens, passing almost beside where I hid but never realizing I was there.

Hours seemed to pass between the last footsteps I heard of

Imogen's, and Wilta's soft laughter as she sat at the table. Perhaps it was only a matter of seconds, but it was certainly enough time for the full weight of Imogen's words to sink inside me.

Without moving from her seat, Wilta said, "She did not choose you."

No, she hadn't. I stepped out from where I was hiding and crossed over to the table, slumping in the seat across from Wilta. I asked, "When will you make her queen?"

"When I have something to gain from it. But for now, I have a bigger problem." Wilta glanced up. "Why do you look so glum? Imogen still loves you; that was obvious. But she chose Castor and his Stewardmen, which means she has a plan of her own to defeat me. She will find that I am not so easily tricked." She pushed Imogen's plate of food toward me. "Eat that. I know you're hungry."

I had been, until a few minutes ago. Now I only picked at the food, barely tasting what I ate and caring nothing for any of it.

Wilta looked up at Lump, who was standing behind me now. "I will consider what to do about Tobias. In the meantime, Jaron gave me a promise. Take him to the library and give him the Devil's Scope to study. I'm going to my room to sleep, but if Jaron does not figure out where the treasure is located before dawn, I want you to kill him." She sighed. "For her own sake, Imogen should have chosen you."

· THIRTY ·

I probably fell asleep sometime after midnight, or at least, I tried. Every time I closed my eyes, Lump kicked me awake. "You're here to think!" he'd say each time.

Finally, I shouted back, "That's the problem, Lump! I need a rest from thinking!"

He left me alone, but I was fully awake by then, my head aching with too many ideas competing for my attention. Most of them had nothing to do with Wilta's treasure.

Lump settled into one of the more comfortable chairs in the room. "You know that Imogen had to choose Castor. Otherwise, all the Stewardmen would've been killed tomorrow."

"Let's only talk about the treasure." I had no wish to discuss Imogen with him, or with anyone.

"You're too young to know anything about love. You should consider the Monarch's offer to join her. I think she likes you."

"Six months ago she liked Roden." Since we were having an absurd conversation anyway, I turned to Lump. "I'm curious. What would it take for you to switch loyalties and serve me instead?"

He chuckled. "I serve the Monarch."

"Yes, you do *now*. But what would it take for you to switch loyalties? For example, as a reward for joining me, I could allow you to choose another name."

"My name is fine."

"Rosewater? No, it's not fine at all. Imagine if I were named Peach Fuzz. Do you think anyone would take me seriously if I were King Peach Fuzz?"

"I don't take you seriously as king now."

"Why not?" I crossed the room and leaned against one of the pillars near him. "Didn't I defeat the Prozarians when we were in Belland?"

"And yet here we are again."

"If I defeat you twice, will you take me seriously then?"

He grunted. "You were right before. Let's talk about the treasure."

"Agreed. Though I still believe that you'd fare better in service to me than with what Wilta can offer you."

"Why?"

"Because in the end, she won't care about your life." He smiled and began to look away, but I added, "I'm serious about that, Lump, and you know it. She has servants, but she knows nothing about friends."

He shifted his position in the chair. "You and I are not friends."

"We could be. Most of my friends began as enemies. And I've been thinking about how Lord Stench —"

"Trench."

"How he offered himself to Castor as a high chamberlain.

Eventually, I will get my throne back. Once I do, I'll need a high chamberlain too, and it won't be Stench."

Lump shrugged. "It won't be me either."

"Obviously not." I grinned over at him. "You'd be miserable in that role. Kerwyn was a genuinely good man and someone I've known and respected all my life. Mott should be my high chamberlain. Until now, he's been my companion-at-arms, and he's done a superior job. But he was injured almost a year ago and he's not as quick as he once was. You should be my new companion-at-arms."

"No." Lump gestured to the scope. "You're running out of time. Solve that."

"Where do you think the treasure is?" He hesitated, and so I picked the scope up off the table and brought it over to him. "Have you never been asked for your opinion? This is proof of how little respect the Monarch has for you."

All three lenses were already in their slots. Lump took it and began turning it over in his hands. I asked, "What do you see when you look in it?"

He shrugged. "A lot of lines and dots. Is it another language?"

"Maybe."

Lump studied the markings on the top of the scope. "What do these mean?"

I pointed to the Carthyan symbol engraved there. "This is my country. Levitimas believes the treasure is somewhere here in Carthya, and maybe that symbol is the reason why."

Lump pointed at the other two symbols. "What are these?"

"I think it's a message that the treasure isn't limited to Carthya. This one, in the center, is Mendenwal. And the one on the far end represents all known kingdoms. It is possible that all we will find here in Carthya is another riddle that will require a search elsewhere."

Lump turned the scope around. "So you think these symbols are some kind of message?"

"Yes, but you're holding it backward now." I reversed the scope. "If the symbols are read as a message, then it would say that one is greater than three. It might be an indication that all countries must unite to defeat a single common enemy."

Lump shrugged again. "Maybe you've got it backward. What would the symbols mean if reversed?"

Curious, I took the scope from him. "Whoever buried the treasure wouldn't have meant it that way. Because then it would read that Carthya is greater than all the countries around it."

"That's what it would say if a Carthyan created the scope."

"Yes, but whoever buried the treasure was not Carthyan."

"How do you know that?"

I turned the scope over and showed him the writing beneath the scope. "That is not a language I know. I'm not sure anyone knows that language."

Lump pointed to the books surrounding us. "If it exists, I bet the language is in one of these."

"I've searched these books, Lump!"

"When?"

In truth, I had asked Tobias to search them weeks ago. When I checked on him, I found him in here reading poetry to Amarinda. I'd tried to avoid the library after that.

I sighed and walked to the far corner of the library. "Then I guess I'd better get started."

I didn't have to wait long. The candles were burning low, and I made no effort to change them, nor to add any other light to the room. I made sure to be as quiet as possible, and as boring as possible, as I sat in a single spot, pretending to read a book that had nothing to do with the treasure. I did learn some interesting theories of astronomy, however.

After a while, Lump sat lower in his chair. His head gradually slumped forward. Then he fell asleep entirely.

Two minutes later, I slipped out the library door, the Devil's Scope in my pocket, wearing my servant's hat and wig once again. The castle was quiet, though vigils were posted at nearly every turn. So rather than try to figure out a way past them, I simply snuck up on one who was near the ruins of my former study, knocked him unconscious, then slid outside into the darkness. Also, I took his hat and coat.

Which made it relatively simple to move about the grounds. It was too dark for anyone to recognize me, and all I had to do as I passed by a vigil was to say, "Lord Trench asked me to check on you. See any problems out here?"

No one had. But if I had my way, their answers would change soon.

Vigils were also in the stables. I walked in, but they quickly blocked my path.

"What are you doing?" one of them asked me.

"I'm carrying with me something highly valuable to the

Monarch. It's urgent that I deliver it, so you had better help me saddle that horse."

"What are you carrying? Who are you?"

I straightened. "Who are *you*? Give me your names, and I'll ask the Monarch whether either of you is worth this delay."

They looked me over. "Let's see what you're carrying."

"Not a chance, you moonwart. Now help me saddle that horse or stand aside."

He looked at his companion; then they shrugged while one reached for the saddle and the other the bridle. I grabbed a satchel from a nail in the wall and slung it over my shoulder, quietly placing the Devil's Scope inside.

The one who had first questioned me said, "What did you say your name was?"

"Some people call me Sage. I came in with Commander Coyle days ago."

"I was in that company," the other vigil said. "I never saw you."

"Because I was in back, by Haddin. Do you know him?"

"A little." That seemed to be enough for them because they returned to their work.

As soon as the horse was saddled, I climbed onto its back. This was a horse I'd ridden before named Night Runner, a name that seemed perfectly appropriate tonight. But I'd only barely grabbed the reins when the other vigil said, "I recognize that sword; it belonged to a friend of mine. Where did you —"

I turned and kicked him in the face, knocking him backward into the second vigil, then raced out of the stables toward the gates. I had hoped to find it quiet at this time of night, but instead, the gates were lined, this time with the Stewardmen.

I didn't dare get too close, so from a distance I tried the same excuse as before. "I am on urgent business for the Monarch."

"The Steward's orders are for no one to come in or go out after dark," a man called back.

"Your steward has no authority over the Monarch's orders," I said.

"Wait here," the man said. "Lord Trench passed by a few minutes ago. I'll find him and ask his permission."

"Lord Trench would be very surprised and angry to find me still here," I said. "Neither of us wants that."

"Wait here."

Another Stewardman stepped forward, and now I smiled, recognizing Captain Reever. "I heard Lord Trench issue the order. We can let this one pass. Open the gates."

I nodded my thanks as I rode past him but picked up speed when the two Prozarian vigils came running out of the stables, screaming for the gates to close on me.

The castle gates did begin to close, but I made it free and raced down the road into Drylliad. If anyone tried to follow me, I could easily get lost in this city.

As I'd expected, the streets were quiet at this time of night, but blue ribbons hung from many of the doorways, a symbol of a great loss to Carthya, and something I had not seen since the death of my parents. Confused, I slowed my horse, until I realized the ribbons were hung for me. With few exceptions, I was still believed to be dead.

It was a chilling thought, and my discomfort pushed me onward, away from Drylliad and on to Farthenwood.

Other than meeting Imogen, I had almost no good memories of Farthenwood. Here was where I'd first been told of the deaths of my family. I'd been whipped here, subjected to every humiliation. During the war, I'd nearly been killed here, and Conner had lost his life here to save mine.

Every furlong closer to Farthenwood filled me with increased anticipation. More than anything, I hoped that Roden would already be there when I arrived, along with all my armies, and Darius and Mott. With a little extra luck, perhaps Amarinda and Harlowe would be there too. I also hoped this was where Fink would go. Lump claimed he had been released.

I imagined how my welcome might go. Surely Fink would have already told them I was alive, and they knew I was coming by tomorrow. I hoped they'd have food available for me tonight. I should have eaten more when Wilta offered it.

But every wisp of hope I'd had quickly evaporated as I approached Farthenwood. From a distance, I saw the entire estate was dark. Coming closer, I saw no horses, no vigils at watch, no candles left burning. Certainly there were no signs that anyone was here, or had been here in months. The disappointment I felt tasted like acid in my mouth and burned equally harsh in my chest.

I dismounted and left Night Runner near some grass and water, then cautiously went inside Farthenwood, armed with the sword I had taken from the vigil and the knife I had stolen from Wilta, but neither was necessary. The house was empty.

I knew where Conner had once kept a flint and steel

behind a brick in the fireplace and used that to light the remnants of a candle. I placed the fire kit in my satchel in case I found another candle. There wasn't much left of this one. It would easily burn out before dawn.

Everything of value had long been stripped away from the home. With the candlelight, I saw where robbers had come to take parts of the home itself, the moldings, carved wood mantels, nearly all the doors. The house was decaying, and no one would mourn its loss.

I wandered from room to room, though I knew by now that nobody was here. Finally, I ended up in Conner's former bedroom and was surprised to see that nearly half his books still remained.

I held up the candle and let the light brush across the spines of the titles, finally settling on one particular book. This was the book that had first suggested to me the way my parents had been killed, poisoned by oil from the dervanis plant.

I carried the book with me back downstairs and into the front entry, where the moonlight that spilled in would give me some extra light, and where dawn would arrive first. If anyone came by morning, I wanted to be here and ready.

I sat down against one wall and began to look through the book's pages until I found what I was searching for. I leaned back and closed my eyes to think more about what I'd just read, but must have fallen asleep only seconds later with a dozen new questions that seemed to have no answers.

One question lingered in my mind longer than any other. Why had Imogen chosen Castor?

· THIRTY-ONE ·

I awoke early to the cheery sounds of birds outside, including one that somehow had gotten inside and was fluttering around, trying to find an exit.

I sat up and went first to the window, hoping someone had arrived, though it was apparent that no one had.

And very likely that no one would.

After some time, it occurred to me that my hunger was becoming desperate, yet there was no point in thinking about it too much. Nothing was here.

I went outside to drink some water from the river and found a berry bush that did little to fill my empty stomach, but I felt a bit better afterward. Then I wandered to every corner of the estate, looking into the countryside beyond, hoping to see signs of anyone approaching.

When I'd freed the soldiers from the dungeon two days ago, I'd told them to find Roden and have him meet me here today. Maybe they hadn't found Roden yet, or Darius. Or Mott.

Maybe they had, but Prozarians had found them first.

Maybe no one was left to be found.

By midday, I had begun to ponder the rarity of a king ever

having the chance to be truly alone. There were vigils at every door, servants in every room, and regents and nobles waiting for any opportunity to walk at my side, offering false compliments in hopes of earning my favor. I could escape to my study and shut the door, or retreat to the King's Gardens, or even my own room, and still they could find me. How often I had complained of that, resented it, sought out places I could go to get away from everything and everyone, but it was all in vain.

Now here I was. Completely alone.

And nearly everyone I knew believed me to be dead. The last time this had happened, my father had made it clear that I was no longer a prince.

Maybe I wasn't a king any longer. Castor had my ring and my sword.

Back inside Farthenwood, I spent the afternoon studying the Devil's Scope and comparing it to every remaining book in Conner's library. When that grew dull, I created a map of my castle and its grounds in the dust, using sticks from outside to design a plan of attack. I knew that Imogen had a plan as well, and I hoped her plan was better than mine, made of something sturdier than sticks and dust.

Maybe Imogen had found a way to contact Roden or Darius. She had suggested that she knew where they were. Captain Reever was supposed to be out looking for them, but I had seen him last night at the castle gates.

And Fink had never made it here. It was possible that Lump had lied to me and Fink was still sitting in the dungeons.

By evening, my hunger and despair had finally caught up with me. I needed to get back to the castle and do what I could there. I went outside again and was nearly finished saddling Night Runner when a rider in the distance caught my attention.

Amarinda.

I waved to her, but she didn't wave back, although I was certain she saw me. So I climbed into the saddle and raced toward her. When I got closer, I realized she was not alone. Harlowe was riding behind her, though his head was slumped over and he was leaning heavily against her back. Amarinda looked exhausted and dirty and was almost emotionless when she saw me.

She merely said, "Mott told us to have hope that you were still alive. I thought that was too much to ask."

"Nobody told you to meet me here?"

"No! I just didn't know where else to go. Jaron, you've got to tell me what is happening. We've had so little news from the castle."

"I'll tell you everything. What help do you need right now?"

Her eyes drifted ahead to Farthenwood. "Are you here alone?"

"Yes."

"Tobias . . . ?"

She said nothing more, and I didn't offer any information. I didn't know where Tobias was now. I didn't know even if he was still alive. I couldn't give Amarinda hope for him when I had so little of it myself.

I leaned over and took her reins and carefully led her horse with mine back to Farthenwood. Once there, I pulled Harlowe off the horse. He was heavily bandaged and barely responsive. I heard him mumble my name, but nothing more.

"That's the most he's said in a day," she said. "Let's get him inside."

We carried Harlowe inside Farthenwood, though there was nowhere comfortable for him to properly rest. Amarinda checked over his wounds while I found a cup to fetch water from the river for Harlowe and then Amarinda.

When she was satisfied that Harlowe was resting as comfortably as possible, she finally sat back and closed her eyes. For a moment, I thought she was asleep, but she mumbled, "Are things at the castle as bad as I think they are?"

"Yes. And everything I try only seems to make things worse."

"You will solve this, Jaron. You always do."

I shook my head at her. "No, not always." Concerned, I leaned forward. "Where is Mott? Why isn't he with you?"

"He left us in a home in Drylliad that he thought would be safe. But Castor Veldergrath had supporters in the city who heard where we were and turned us in. Mott stayed back to give us time to escape. I don't know what ended up happening to him. I haven't seen anyone else." She exhaled and on her next breath asked, "Where's Tobias?"

"He's still at the castle."

"If Castor finds Tobias, he will kill him. You know that he will."

"I know that he wants to, but so far, Tobias has stayed ahead of him. As you would expect, Tobias is making smart choices to keep himself alive."

She nodded. "What about Imogen?"

"Wilta is probably going to declare her queen and remove

Castor from his role as Steward. That will create some serious problems. Imogen —" My heart pounded. "Imogen has agreed to give a speech denouncing me to the people."

"She'd never do that."

"I was there. Those were the terms for her to become queen. She could have chosen me, but instead . . ." I barely could speak the words. "She chose Castor. He'll never accept losing his title as Steward, so he'll do something to force Imogen into marriage. That will make him king." I barely looked at Amarinda now. "She is going to marry Castor."

Amarinda sniffed with irritation. "Then it's part of something she's planned, some larger plot to free Carthya. She won't go through with it, Jaron."

"Imogen believes it is her duty to Carthya, but maybe it's not only that. Maybe . . ." My voice trailed off, and I kicked at the dirt with my boot. "Maybe I've become too much for her."

"I'm sure that's not true."

"I was too much for you."

She smiled. "Perhaps."

I paused and tried to hold my voice steady. "I've lost Imogen."

A long minute passed in silence before Amarinda said, "What are you going to do now?"

"I'll return to the castle. I still have to get my kingdom back."

"How? Mott isn't here, or Roden or Darius, or any of your armies. What if it's only you?"

I stood and tried to absorb that question. "Then it's only me."

Amarinda smiled again. "You are not too much for Carthya. We need you, just as you are."

"I'd still feel better returning with an army behind me."

Amarinda sat up. "You're leaving already?"

"I've got to."

"You look as though you can barely stand on two feet. Sleep, Jaron. You'll need that for tomorrow."

I knew I needed to be at the castle, but I also knew there was almost nowhere I could go there and truly rest. I tried to lean against the wall but felt the sting in my back when I did. I drew a sharp breath and stepped forward until the worst of it passed.

When I looked at Amarinda again, she was staring sadly at me. "Does Imogen know?"

I nodded, but there was nothing more to be said about that. Imogen knew, and that same night, she had chosen the person who caused the whipping to happen.

"I can wrap your wound. I have bandages."

I shook my head. "It's beginning to heal on its own."

"Wounds will do that, if cared for properly." Amarinda offered me a gentle smile. "Imogen loves you with her whole heart. If there is a wound, it can be repaired."

"Do you really believe that?"

"Of course I do. Here, take this." Amarinda reached into her bag and pulled out some bread. "It's dry, but you look like you need it."

I stared at the bread for a moment, then shook my head. "You and Harlowe need it."

"When is the last time you ate?"

"I . . . uh . . ."

"If you can't remember, it's been too long. Take the bread, Jaron."

I took what she offered and pulled off a piece of the end, then passed it back to her. The piece I ate sat like a lump in my stomach and became a reminder of how hungry I was. But it would do for the night.

"You sleep first," Amarinda said. "I'll keep watch over Harlowe."

I wanted to argue that, but I was already finding it impossible to keep my eyes open. I lay on one side and was asleep almost instantly.

I awoke early to relieve Amarinda so that she could rest, and split my watch between Harlowe and the window to the main road. Both were far quieter than I wished they were.

Harlowe coughed, and I hurried over to offer him some water, though his lips barely parted to receive it. I brushed his hair from his face, heavy-hearted. Harlowe felt very much like a father to me, and even more so with the loss of Kerwyn. I couldn't bear to lose them both.

"He'll be all right, Jaron." Dawn had come, and Amarinda must have awoken and seen me watching him. "As long as no one finds us, Harlowe will live."

"I'll do what I can to make sure they don't find you." I looked over at her. "Thank you, for talking with me last night."

"You can fix this, Jaron. I know you can."

I grabbed my satchel and left Amarinda with the knife I had taken from Wilta in the library, then headed for the door.

I turned back long enough to say, "Take care of him. Take care of yourself. I'm going to end this."

"Do you know how?"

"For now, I only know that I will. Be safe, Amarinda. Tobias will be eager to see you again soon."

I walked out the door from Farthenwood, saddled my horse, and began riding back to my home. I had no army, no fixed plan, and no base of my own from which to launch an attack.

But none of that mattered. I was ready to end this, once and for all.

· THIRTY-TWO ·

It was midmorning when I approached the castle gates again. I could have ridden faster, but hunger was gnawing at my every thought, so I swiped a meat pie from the market, with a silent promise that I would repay the seller tenfold when this was over, and possibly offer him a position as a cook in the castle. The meat was done to perfection.

It was a simple thing to get inside, using the same method as always, coming through the gate, then up through the kitchen.

Cook was in there, as she usually was. This time she was stirring a large vat of . . . I really didn't know. But it smelled terrible.

"What is that?" I asked.

She smiled when she saw me. "Lard. We can't put it in the river or it would gum up the gates. We save it and try to keep it hot so that we can use it in our cooking. Are you hungry?"

I still was, actually, but I'd suddenly lost my appetite for anything that might come out of that vat.

"Are there any changes from the last day or two?" I asked.

"A big fight between Castor and the Monarch two nights ago, and they haven't spoken since. Apparently, Castor returned to his room to find a threatening note beneath his pillow. He demanded to see the Monarch, and when she refused him, he barged right into the small dining room where she was eating and said that if she did not share the treasure with him, he would take all of it for himself. I was there — I heard every shouted word!" Cook squinted one eye at me. "Do you know anything about a treasure?"

My only answer was to smile; then I added, "How did Wilta respond to his threat?"

"I thought I saw smoke coming from her ears, she was so angry. She ordered Castor's immediate execution, but he got to his knees and begged for his life. Finally, he agreed to new terms for Carthya. Our taxes to the Prozarians have been doubled, and we must now give up half our men to her armies. If you ask me, the Monarch was already going to change the terms; I heard her tell her mother that only minutes before Castor entered. He just gave her a good excuse."

"Has there been news from Castor and Lady Imogen?" I asked. "Any . . . announcements?"

"Not that I'm aware of, my king. But there was one other odd thing, now that I think about it. Captain Strick came in here yesterday asking for every potato bag we had. I gave her twelve and said that was all we have, even though we really have about eighty." Cook winked at me, clearly proud of herself.

"What did she want with potato bags?"

"I have a guess. Captain Strick also wanted to know where Carthya stored its gunpowder. I think the two questions are connected, but don't worry. I told her as far as I knew, we had no gunpowder."

I had every reason to worry about that. Carthya did have gunpowder, though it was stored at a good distance from the castle walls, to prevent any accidents. Mostly accidents caused by me.

I thanked Cook and gave her the satchel I'd been carrying, asking her to keep it hidden. Then I picked up a tray, exchanged my Prozarian coat for a servant's coat hanging in the kitchen, and started toward Imogen's room. The morning was busy, with more servants and soldiers working at castle repairs. Other servants roamed the halls with morning duties, and I did my best to blend in with them, holding the tray against my shoulder.

I took the servants' staircase to go upstairs and from there slipped into the maid's room. I used the connecting door to enter Imogen's room, hoping to speak with her, but the room was empty.

From the sitting room, I heard Castor yell, "Tobias is gone! Did you arrange that in your supper with Wilta?"

He was loud enough that I didn't need to lean against the wall to hear them.

"No, we never even discussed him," Imogen replied.

"What did you discuss?"

"As I told you yesterday, that is between Wilta and me. If you want details, you should ask her."

"She isn't speaking to me. And the last time she did, she refused to answer any questions, then called me her puppet!"

"Calm down, Castor," Imogen said.

"She called me her puppet! Told me I had no right to think for myself, that she would do the thinking for me, and that I should be grateful she was even allowing me to live. I've done nothing wrong!"

"You stormed into her supper and accused her of writing a note to threaten you!"

"Someone close to her must have written it. But it doesn't matter. My plan will stop her."

"If we are to rule together, I should know your plan."

"We rule together after the marriage. No more delays, Imogen. Let us go before the priest right now."

More silence followed, too much. Enough silence that I darted into the corridor and pounded on the sitting room door.

"What is it?" Castor asked.

Lowering my voice, I said, "The Monarch wishes to see you immediately, Steward Veldergrath." As an afterthought, I added, "You are to come unarmed."

I was fairly sure he must have kicked something in the room, which was confirmed when he limped out, barely looking at me, though with my dipped head, he wasn't likely to recognize me.

Once he was out of sight, I ducked into the room, only to see Imogen facing forward with her arms folded, as if she had been expecting me. I stopped where I was as my mind emptied of everything I'd intended to say to her. Maybe that was for the best. Judging by Imogen's expression, I knew we had a very different conversation ahead.

"You'd better close the door," she said. When I did, she asked, "Where were you yesterday? I didn't see you all day. Do you know how worried I've been?"

"I went to Farthenwood. I saw Harlowe and Amarinda. But I had hoped to see Roden and Darius. Have you been in contact with them?"

"No. I sent a messenger out in hopes of contacting Roden, but he hasn't returned. I don't know where to begin searching for Darius."

We stared at each other a moment longer; then Imogen said, "I spoke to Wilta the night before last —"

"I know. I was there."

Imogen looked away but said nothing. So I walked farther into the room and grabbed my sword. I wished I could have found a reason to force Castor to leave the king's ring behind as well, but getting that back would not be so simple.

Imogen said, "I had to choose Castor. It's the only way I'll ever get control of his armies."

"Do you think it will be that easy, that Castor will step back and let you take the throne without him?"

"I never thought it would be easy, but it's the best option I had."

"And when will you give your speech denouncing me?"

"Jaron, if you were there, then you heard what my choices were. What would you have done?"

I stopped. "I'd have done the very same thing. That's the hardest part about this, that I understand every decision you've made."

"None of it is what I want. Do you understand that?"

"Sometimes." I kicked my boot along the rug. This time it left a scuff mark. "But I don't know what you want anymore."

Imogen only frowned back at me. "You must know. Jaron, I want you as you truly are. Without secrets. Without anything false." Her eyes darted at a sound in the corridor. "It won't take

Castor long to figure out that Wilta never sent for him. It isn't safe for you to be here."

I nodded and began to leave, then huffed and closed the door once again. I had decided last night to give Imogen exactly what she wanted, but my stomach was churning now to carry out this decision. I stood where I was for several seconds, my hand on the door to leave, unable to turn around, because I really didn't know where to start. I only knew how awful things would be when it ended.

So with my back still to Imogen, I just . . . spoke. "One day when I was still very young, Darius and I were about to begin lessons with our tutor. Just before he came in, Darius told me he had nearly sawed in half the legs of our tutor's chair. He expected that when the chair fell, we'd all have a great laugh, but instead, the tutor fell backward, crashing against the wall and becoming seriously injured. Darius ran and hid, but I was brought to my father. He asked who had done this, and I told him the truth — the full truth. I was punished for lying and disciplined before the entire court. Even when Darius finally confessed, my father said that Darius was only protecting me and then doubled my punishment."

"That's a terrible story." Imogen crossed the room and touched my shoulder, asking me to look at her, which I did. "But I don't understand why you're telling it to me."

"There was another time, a few years later. Shortly after my father sent me from the castle, I became so hungry one night. I saw some older boys around a fire, cooking a fish they had caught. I asked to join them, and they refused me. And even though it was against my father's orders, I told them who I was. I told them the full truth. They beat me so badly for my claims, my right eye was swollen shut for almost a week."

"Jaron —"

"I was not always this way. But in my life, truth has too often been rewarded with pain and punishment. And so it will be again. I am going to tell you the full truth now."

I paused, again barely able to look at her. I could make jokes with every breath and hand out insults like candy drops. I knew how to issue orders, how to speak the language of diplomacy and of war, and I usually said far more of my thoughts than I ever should. But I had no idea how to tell Imogen this secret.

Finally, I began, "After one of the times I was kicked out of the orphanage, I wandered to an area near Tithio. I knew a regent named Bevin Conner owned a great deal of land in the area, so I figured if I stole a little food from him, he'd hardly notice. The same day I arrived, a woman passed me in a wagon, going so fast that mud splashed all over me, and nearly ran me off the road. She didn't stop or apologize, or even look back to see how I was. She should have looked back, because in her hurry, she failed to realize that her purse had tipped over and several garlins had fallen out along the roadside.

"I followed behind and picked up the coins, every one of them, and stuffed them into my pocket. After a few minutes, she returned and demanded to know what I'd done with the garlins. I should have returned them. I knew even then that I should have given her those coins, but I was angry, still dripping with mud, and I'd been barefoot for a month. I told myself that

I needed the money more than her. I lied to her, Imogen — I looked her straight in the eye and told her I had no idea what she was talking about. She knew I was lying, but I darted off the road and disappeared with her money. That is the truth."

Imogen seemed to have frozen, and now her eyes were brimming with tears, but she wasn't speaking and that made me nervous.

Finally, she said, "I remember the night my mother came home and said that she was unable to pay our rent to Conner. I hadn't worried all day, because although we had almost nothing left, we had managed to scrape together the rent. But now she was telling me she had no other choice, that to pay the rent, she had made an agreement with Conner, and I was to be sold into service at Farthenwood until I had earned back enough to pay the debt. I begged her not to send me there; then I accused her of having used the money for herself, because I knew we'd had enough when she left home. She told me the garlins were stolen by some boy at the side of a road. I accused her of lying . . . about you."

I could barely breathe. I had known how hard it would be for Imogen to hear the truth, but the expression in her eyes was worse than I could have imagined. She had suffered dearly at Farthenwood, entirely because of my pettiness at the side of a muddy road. I had never felt lower in my life, more ashamed of all I'd done wrong, or even of the very person I was.

Forcing myself to speak, I said, "You were right before. The secrets I keep are not to protect you, or anyone else. They protect me. I keep secrets. . . ." I inhaled, trying to steady myself. "I keep secrets because in my past, the truth has cost me so much. If it costs me a future with you, then I am the only one to blame. I need you to know that I was sorry then — that's when I decided I would never lie again, if possible. But to continue to be Sage, I had to find ways around the truth. Maybe that part of me is still there, but now it's to continue to be Jaron. I am sorry, Imogen."

Her eyes widened. "I've never heard you apologize before."

"Then let it matter that much more. You have every reason to walk away from me, and I have no right to ask you to stay. But if I still have any hope for you, please tell me now."

A softness warmed her smile. "Your body takes beatings and rises again and again. Your mind brushes away insults like they are harmless flies." She took my hand. "But your heart is different. It bruises deeply and is slow to heal."

"Do not stay with me out of pity, or because of any past obligation. Stay only if you can love me, even with what you now know."

"Jaron —"

"All Stewardmen to the courtyard," a voice called from out in the corridor. "Castor Veldergrath orders all to attend."

Attend what?

I started to the door, but before I reached it, Captain Reever opened it and said to Imogen, "Forgive the interruption, my lady." He noticed me. "And my king. Tobias has been found. Veldergrath isn't taking any chances of losing him again. I won't be able to stop this."

"I understand," Imogen said.

When Reever hurried on, I began exchanging my servant's

coat for Castor's Stewardman coat left on a nearby chair. Imogen touched my shoulder. "They shouldn't see you yet."

"They have Tobias!"

"This is mine to solve. Stay here."

She brushed a kiss across my cheek before hurrying out the door. Only seconds later, I followed.

· THIRTY-THREE ·

Imogen should have made it outside ahead of me, but to my surprise, she wasn't here. My concern for where she had gone turned to genuine worry when I saw a crowd of Stewardmen gathered around Castor. He stood on a wood block and must have told some kind of joke because everyone was laughing.

I remained on the castle steps, craning my head until I got my first look at Tobias, kneeling in front of Castor. He wasn't moving much, so either he was injured or he was terrified.

Castor's tone sharpened now. "Am I not the Steward, the governor of this land?"

"Hail, Steward Veldergrath!" a man in front shouted, his words echoed by most of those around him.

The words seemed to bolster Castor's confidence in what he was about to do. "This regent, and anyone else who remains loyal to Jaron, are traitors to me!"

The irony of Castor accusing anyone of treason rang in my ears. Keeping my head down, I walked toward the group. They were pressed so close together, I didn't know how I would get anywhere near Tobias without announcing who I was. And if I did, I was more likely to join him than rescue him.

Castor looked down. "Do you deny the accusations against you, Regent? Get on your feet so we can all hear you."

In the center of the group, Tobias stood tall, and the Stewardmen backed up to give Castor space to question him. I held my ground so at least now I was closer to Tobias than before.

Tobias spoke loudly, and with surprising boldness. It reminded me of when he had first escaped the inner keep and had been backed into a corner with a sword he could not wield. "Do what you want with me. I serve the true king of Carthya, no one else."

Castor placed one hand on Tobias's shoulder. "I will be the true king very soon." His voice was so calm, it sent a chill through me, and I saw Tobias shudder as well. "You and Rulon Harlowe are the only two people in my way. You should have resigned when I gave you the chance."

Tobias looked around at the group of Stewardmen. "Are you not all Carthyans, the same as me? Then why do you wear coats in any other colors? If I could wield a sword, I would protect this castle and all it stands for. If I was a fighter, I would fight for Carthya, not against its king." He turned back to Castor. "The true king. Jaron."

"Perhaps you wish to die the same way Jaron did. Where's my archer?"

I was already pushing my way toward the center of the group. But I hadn't gotten far when Imogen ran from the castle and yelled, "Castor, stop!"

He lowered his hand, signaling for his men to part for Imogen.

She marched directly toward Castor, her eyes blazing with anger. "We had an agreement!"

"An agreement based on you answering the one question I have asked of you," he countered. "If you will not answer, then you force me to act now."

"That's true." Imogen's voice softened. "I have not been fair to you. I will give you my answer."

"You are only answering now in hopes of saving Tobias."

"Yes, Castor, I am. But I do have an answer."

From where I stood, I had a good view of both Castor and Imogen. A better view than I wished, actually.

Tobias said, "Imogen, you don't need him. You know who you are."

That was true enough. Imogen could declare herself queen and order Tobias to be released, but she didn't do that.

I pushed farther forward. Imogen saw me and very subtly shook her head, warning me not to act.

Instead, she said to Castor, "I accept your offer of marriage."

Castor's smile was cautious. "Yes?"

"Yes." I thought Imogen might look my way this time, but she didn't. Instead, she was staring at Castor as if no one else existed but him, while the best I could do was remain on my feet.

Imogen was correct that my heart bruised easily, but what she did not understand was that with a bruised heart, my body and mind became equally broken. I truly did not know what I should do next.

The men around me cheered with her announcement while

Castor stepped off the crate and took her hands. "I confess that I thought all hope was lost for us." He kissed her hand, though I had to turn away, even for that. Then he said, "Cheer for me, Stewardmen. We shall be married at once!"

Another cheer rose up around me. I looked around at each man, trying to determine who seemed to be fully loyal to Castor and who was only cheering out of fear. I was so blinded now, I could not tell the difference.

"But you must release Tobias," Imogen said. "With our marriage, he is no threat to you."

And there it was, Imogen's sacrifice. She had been waiting until the marriage was necessary to save someone's life, but Carthya itself was far from being free. If the time came that she would have to bargain for her own life, she had nothing left to offer.

"Very well. Release Tobias," Castor ordered. "I care nothing for him now."

A Stewardman beside Tobias cut his binds. Imogen excused herself long enough to take his arm and walk him through the crowd.

They stopped at some distance away, standing close together in an exchange of whispers. I would have liked to know what they were saying but I had to stay near Castor, who had gathered us in once again and spoke in a lower voice than before.

He said, "Somewhere within these walls is the younger brother to Jaron, named Fink. Find him and bring him to me."

I turned back to Imogen and Tobias, wondering if they had heard that too, and it appeared that they had. Imogen whispered one thing more to Tobias, then took his hands and gave him a quick embrace. He nodded grimly and walked away, headed toward the stables.

Was Fink hiding in the stables?

Back again on his wood box perch, Castor called over to Imogen, "Send for your ladies-in-waiting, my dearest. I will have someone fetch the priest. There's no reason to delay another minute."

Imogen met my eyes again before speaking to Castor. "I don't have a proper dress. And my mother is concerned about the silver pattern for the guests."

"The wedding is all that matters. Captain Reever will escort you back to your room to prepare."

Imogen frowned at me, as if to say that she had known all along her fate would come to this. I was not so willing to give up and tried to communicate that to her with a forced smile. That was the best I could do.

She opened her mouth as if to speak but stopped at the sound of a trumpet overhead.

Like everyone else, I looked up and saw Mercy on the balcony. The burns around his eyes were still evident, but the bandages were gone, and he squinted against the bright daylight. He raised his hands for attention and said, "How convenient that all the Stewardmen are gathered here now, for this announcement is for you. Hail your Monarch!"

With little cheer or enthusiasm, Wilta walked out onto the balcony, arms raised to greet a people who loathed her almost as much as she did them. It wasn't only the Stewardmen out here. Naturally there were several watches of Prozarians and handfuls of servants going about their business for the day. Everyone stopped their work to offer the required bow.

Everyone but me. Instead, I walked alongside one of Strick's archers and quietly pulled a ball arrow from his quiver, one designed to hold fire when it was launched. I had other plans for it.

Castor pushed past me to stand beside Imogen. I saw him whisper something in her ear, but she only shrugged and looked up.

"I have an announcement that will be greeted with much happiness," Wilta began. "Lady Imogen, will you step forward?"

I froze in place, worry rising in my chest. In that instant, I knew what her announcement would be. It was no accident that Wilta had timed it for this very moment.

With only a few words, she would destroy Castor, mark Imogen as a target, and solidify her hold on Carthya once and for all.

· THIRTY-FOUR ·

Imogen had no choice but to obey the Monarch. She left Castor's side to stand directly below Wilta's balcony. She obviously knew what announcement was coming as well, but looked as if she had no idea what to do once the words had been spoken.

Castor, however, definitely knew that he wouldn't like whatever Wilta was about to say. His eyes seemed to be turning red with anger, and the rest of his face had become stone.

Meanwhile, I casually walked toward the stables. My instincts were telling me not to make my face visible right now, and besides, I needed to speak to Tobias. Also, I still had that arrow in my hand.

From the balcony, Wilta said, "The Prozarians came to Carthya offering the opportunity to become part of a larger empire. Castor Veldergrath promised to help us fulfill this dream, yet he has been a disappointment as Steward. Because of his failures, I must ask for a greater tribute, and more of your men to join our armies."

I rolled my eyes as I opened the door to the stables. I loathed

Castor, but her words were lies. She was always going to change the terms of the agreement and blame him for it.

"Monarch!" Castor called up from the courtyard. "I beg your forgiveness. I will do better."

"You had your chance, and you failed."

I ducked inside the stables. "Tobias!"

"Jaron?" He peeked out from behind a stall, pieces of hay in his hair.

Outside the stables, Castor continued to beg. Meanwhile, I stuck the end of the arrow into a pile of horse manure, spinning it to collect as much as possible.

"What are you doing?" Tobias asked.

"Collecting manure onto an arrow. What are you doing?"

He grunted. "I need to get to Farthenwood. Castor knows Amarinda and Harlowe are there. Imogen is worried that he will send someone after them."

Outside, Wilta said, "Lady Imogen, you will kneel."

Tobias said, "But I couldn't leave without speaking to you. Levitimas sent me with a message for you, from the dungeons."

I turned back to Tobias. "Can this wait?"

"No. Levitimas and I were talking more about the history of Carthya, about each of the three original rulers —"

I spotted a crossbow hanging on the far wall. A full set of weapons was always stored inside the stables for a rider's use when necessary. "Give me that."

Tobias passed me the bow. "Levitimas said that Linus, your line of kings, created the scope and lenses, as a warning to other countries about their own downfall."

I paused from my work to look at him. "And?"

"And I thought that was interesting."

"It's not. But this will be."

I walked outside, angling until I saw Imogen kneeling on the ground, directly below Wilta on the balcony.

The pit in my stomach grew heavier. Wilta had warned me that she would have to stop Imogen's plan, and she was doing it in the most devious way — by giving Imogen the very thing she had asked for.

Wilta announced, "I have recently learned that Lady Imogen has a bloodline unknown to Carthya until now. She is no commoner. Carthya was founded by three rulers, one of them a woman named Faylinn. When fighting broke out between the rulers, Faylinn was killed . . . but her family was not, including a daughter who survived. A thousand years later, this daughter of many daughters kneels before me now. I give you Queen Imogen!"

Amid the cheers of the crowd, I watched Castor. His fists were clenching and unclenching so fast, I had a good idea of the turmoil that must be happening inside him. He knew what was coming as well as any of us, and there was nothing he could do to stop it.

Wilta continued, "Therefore, we have a logical successor to the throne. Castor Veldergrath's services as Steward are no longer required. In his place, I am assigning Lady Imogen as your new Steward, with all the powers and privileges of a queen, subject to me. Imogen, do you accept this?"

Imogen blinked a few times before standing again. "I accept."

Wilta turned to Castor. "Will you place the Stewardmen under Imogen's command?"

"I will not." Castor clearly sensed his opportunity. "The Stewardmen are mine, and I alone command them." He crossed to Imogen and took her hand. "However, we are to be married within the hour, and then Imogen and I will rule together."

"Is this something you want?" Wilta asked Imogen.

"It's a promise I have given."

"I accept your removing me as Steward," Castor said. "Because very soon, I will be king."

By then, I had climbed into the lower branches of a tree, which was no small trick, given what I was carrying. I had a good angle for the balcony, but before I was ready, Wilta said to Castor, "You are not king yet, Master Veldergrath. Lord Trench, give my orders."

He bowed to her as she walked back inside the castle, then strode to the center of the balcony and raised his arms.

I lifted the bow, with the arrow notched into place. My aim wasn't the best, but I'd been practicing, and considering what was on the tip of the arrow, even if I came close, I would consider this a success.

Mercy said, "Castor Veldergrath, you will send the Stewardmen to stand at watch on the curtain wall. Our spies in the countryside report that an attack on the castle is coming soon. Your Stewardmen will be our first line of defense."

"Yes, Lord Trench."

Captain Reever used the moment to approach Imogen and whisper something in her ear. She nodded before giving him a quick reply. He stepped back in line with the Stewardmen.

Mercy wasn't finished. "Before anyone returns to their duties, Lady Imogen, your queen, wishes to speak to the people about the former king of this land, Jaron."

Imogen looked around the area, as if unsure of what she should do or say. Finally, she met Captain Reever's eyes, drew a deep breath, then stood on the same crate where Castor had just been.

"My people!" she said, loud enough for everyone in the courtyard to hear. "You know me as Lady Imogen, once betrothed to King Jaron. Indeed, we would have been married now, if things were different. I can tell you that no one knew Jaron better than I did; nobody understands how he thinks, or why he does the things he does, as I do. If at any time, he might have done something to put Carthya at risk, I would know it."

I glanced up at Mercy, who was smiling down, eagerly anticipating the worst of what Imogen might have to say about me. I felt less eager. Imogen did know me better than anyone, and there were more than enough of my failings she might share.

Imogen's voice grew louder. "So I say this to you, Carthyans everywhere. At all times, Jaron has loved you. At all times he has served you, sacrificed for you, and risked his life for the lives you have."

"That's enough!" Mercy shouted.

Imogen did not flinch. "We will *not* accept these invaders; we will not kneel to a Prozarian Monarch. We will not pay a single coin of tribute, not while I am queen. Carthyans, an army is on its way here. If you can fight, I call on you to fight!"

"Stop her!" Mercy ordered.

That's the moment I released the arrow. It flew surprisingly well, though slightly heavy in front due to the amount of manure I'd loaded onto it. I'd aimed for Mercy's face, but it hit him in the chest, which was plenty good enough. Manure splattered everywhere on him.

Mercy's screech of anger was loud enough that the Prozarians who were headed toward Imogen paused, just for a moment, but it was enough time for several of the castle servants to get between them, armed with pitchforks and shovels and anything else they could grab.

Mercy stumbled back inside the castle while fighting broke out in the courtyard, though the Prozarians easily had the advantage, in their numbers, training, and weapons. I dropped out of the tree onto one soldier and used the bow to pull another man to the ground by his neck.

Castor shouted at his Stewardmen, "All of you, get to the curtain wall and remember my orders!"

I remembered them. Castor had told the Stewardmen that they were not to fight in any battle between the Prozarians and my armies. Castor was very happy to put his men on the curtain wall, away from this battle.

While the Stewardmen raced toward the curtain wall, I reached Imogen as she was hurrying into the castle, striking at a Prozarian who tried to get between us.

She saw me, and then together we entered the castle and exited again into the King's Gardens. I rolled a rock against the main gate between the other gardens while Imogen propped the castle door closed with a nearby stick.

We found a place to hide in the far corner of the gardens and there sat, breathless and staring at each other.

"That wasn't a bad speech," I said, smiling.

"It was easier to list your few good qualities than to go on and on about your failings," she said as her mischievous smile widened. "I hope you enjoyed my time as the Steward. I'm sure that will be the shortest reign in history."

My tone became far more serious. "Wilta will not forgive you for this, nor will Castor."

"And you shot Wilta's highest counselor with manure. That is a far worse offense."

"But you have promised to marry Castor."

Imogen reached over and took my hand. "Then we must hope that our armies arrive soon enough to save us both."

· THIRTY-FIVE ·

Imogen and I began talking, comparing what each of us knew and expected to happen.

She said, "I was on my way out of the castle to save Tobias when Wilta stopped me. She said she had made her decision and would name me as queen in the next few minutes. I had to accept Castor's offer of marriage before she did. Not only to save Tobias, but to save my own life."

Much as I hated it, I understood her decision. If Imogen had not agreed to the marriage, Castor would have ordered his Stewardmen to go after her.

"You said that an army was on its way," I said. "Is that what Reever reported to you back in the courtyard?"

"Yes, his messenger finally found them. Roden is coming from the east. The curtain wall is still damaged from when the Prozarians attacked, so he'll have no trouble getting in. Darius will come through the main gates at nearly the same time. Their plan is to surround the enemy."

"Castor won't allow the Stewardmen to fight. I think he intends to let Roden and Wilta destroy each other's armies, leaving him the last one standing." I had come to think of Castor as a special breed of mudworm, but he wasn't the stupidest mudworm.

From out in the courtyard, orders were shouted: "All Prozarians to arms! The battle is coming! Everyone to the east wall!"

Imogen and I looked at each other. The Prozarians must have seen Roden approaching, but no one was speaking about defending the main gates. Darius was not there.

I gave Imogen my extra sword, then began climbing the castle wall to reach the lowest ledge, where it was wide enough to sit. I'd been in this exact place once before when Roden attacked me. Now I was sitting here in anticipation of another attack, one on the Prozarians.

In the distance, I saw what appeared to be an army of soldiers approaching from the east. It was difficult to see their colors from here, but I caught a hint of gold on a banner. It had to be Roden and our armies.

I called down to Imogen what I was seeing, but she shook her head. "Roden and Darius must arrive at the same time. Otherwise, the Prozarians will easily defeat Roden and then be ready for Darius too."

"Could Darius be coming in secret?"

"No, he was supposed to be ready outside the gates. My job was to hang blue fabric from my window as a signal that Roden had entered. We have to let Roden know he must wait." Her eyes widened. "I've got to get back to my room, and you've got to warn Roden."

I nodded. "I can light the spire. If he sees it, he'll know that something is wrong."

"You'll never get to it, Jaron. All Prozarians have been called to duty. The castle will be filled with them."

I glanced up. "There's another way to the spire."

Imogen shook her head. "You are *not* going to climb the entire castle wall!"

"Then you are *not* going to your room. You'll stay here where it's safe."

Imogen frowned. "I have to go, for Carthya." Her shoulders fell. "And so do you, I suppose. Don't you dare fall!"

"Don't you dare get caught!"

Imogen ran inside while I began climbing. I was already nearly to the top of what would be the main castle floor, but there were two more stories to climb, and time was not on my side.

I had to choose carefully which holds to trust, though the recent damage to the castle both helped me and hurt me. I did find more places for grips than usual, but many of them might not hold my weight.

Below me, several Prozarians stormed into the King's Gardens, using the hedges and trees as hiding places in preparation for Roden's attack, so I quickly moved sideways, rounding the castle's corner to be more out of sight. Before long, I was at the third-floor ledge.

I glanced around the area, but from this side of the castle, I could no longer see Roden or his armies. I couldn't see anyone, except —

"There you are!"

I glanced down and saw Lump far below, staring up at me. I waved at him, though that nearly cost me my balance, so for now, I was forced to be impolite and keep climbing, even faster than before.

Lump shook a fist at me or something equally threatening, then ran back inside. He had three flights of stairs, and I had one wall left to climb. If I hurried, I still had a chance to get there before him.

At last, I reached the roof by climbing over the parapet, with the muscles of my arms and legs shaking from exhaustion. By now, Lump would be pounding his way up the main staircase.

I sank to the floor and leaned against the parapet, then stared at the spire. It was in the center of the castle, a large dome kept ready at all times with oil and dried wood to quickly light as a warning of danger to all of Drylliad. I could only hope that Roden would see it and understand its meaning.

But first, I had to light it, and though it only required one climb up a ladder, that seemed like more than I could do. I wasn't even sure I could still walk.

Nor would it be so simple. A Prozarian came around the spire, and I realized he'd been posted here as a vigil.

"What is a Stewardman doing up here?" he asked.

I reached for my sword but remained where I was. "I'm exhausted. As a personal favor, would you climb that ladder and light the spire for me?"

"Light the spire?" His face twisted. "We were sent up here to stop anyone from lighting it."

"Yes, I'm sure you were, but if you don't light it, you and I will have to fight, and I will win."

"You said you were exhausted." He looked over the edge of the parapet. "Did you just climb the side of the castle?"

"You'd be exhausted too, but I factored that in before I challenged you. Seriously, will you go light it?"

He chuckled and started toward me. Bracing myself against the parapet, I kicked at his legs, and he stumbled backward. I was instantly on my feet and grabbed him as he went to his knees, putting my sword to his chest.

"I know who you are," he mumbled. "I saw you plenty back in Belland."

"Say my name aloud and I'll really hurt you. How many others are stationed here?"

"Two others. One is in the privy. The other ran downstairs when we saw you. He's gone for help."

"Perfect." I cursed under my breath. "Then you'd better hurry and get up there."

"The Monarch will have my head if I do."

"Think of what will happen if you don't."

He nodded, and I released him so that he could begin climbing. While he did, I locked the second vigil in the privy by rolling a loose cannonball against the door and bracing it with a rock. From there, I looked out over the eastern wall of the castle. Roden's men were getting closer. If Roden didn't stop when he saw the spire, he would enter a battleground where he had little hope of winning.

I waited until I saw the spire light up, then began running for the door to take me back down the main staircase. My timing couldn't have been worse. The instant I opened it, Lump pushed through and hit me hard enough that I fell back to the ground.

"Did you think I was stupid? That I wouldn't know where you were going?"

"I never thought you were stupid. I just thought you'd be slower on the stairs."

I shook my head, hoping to clear my vision, but the stars hadn't yet faded before he drove another fist into my gut. On instinct, and still doubled over, I rolled and must have moved just in time because this time he punched the stone stairs. I knew that hurt because of how he wailed and drew his hand against his body.

I scrambled to my feet and stumbled back up the steps, but Lump was close on my heels.

"There's no need for any demonstration of your strength," I told him. "I already believe you'd make a great companion-at-arms."

He growled and lunged at me, getting hold of one leg and flattening me to the ground. "Help me," he shouted at the soldier who had just climbed down from lighting the spire. That man picked up his sword and hurried toward me. I swung around and used my sword to swipe at his legs, but I still had Lump to contend with.

He stood and began dragging me along the rooftop by one leg. I tried kicking at him with my other leg, but that got me nowhere. Finally, near the edge, we passed a pole holding one of the flags of Carthya. I twisted around and got hold of it. Lump paused, then yanked hard in an attempt to pull me off. When it didn't work, he walked in closer to pull on my legs again, but this time, I was able to kick him, which I did with every bit of strength I had.

He released my leg and stumbled back. I stood, but there wasn't much left in me, and I knew I'd never make it anywhere fast enough to escape.

So I turned toward Lump and raised my sword, holding him back, at least for now.

"My offer still stands to officially rename you," I said. "At least you are better named than Lord Stench."

"Stop talking or I'll hurt you again," he said.

"No, you start talking," I said. "Accept my offer, or by this time tomorrow, I might not feel as generous. Answer me while you can."

"For the last time, I serve the Monarch!"

"All right, so you want to think about it a bit longer? I understand."

"You have nowhere to go up here," Lump continued. "Lower your sword. I'm bringing you to her, as she ordered."

He had been slowly backing me toward the edge. Or rather, I had been slowly backing toward the edge, and he was following me. "How will she punish you when you fail to get me?" I asked.

He chuckled. "How can I fail? The only choice you have now is to jump."

"Perhaps you're right." I replaced my sword, leapt onto the edge of the parapet, and raised my arms before I jumped over the edge of my own castle.

THIRTY-SIX

Climbing up a castle wall is difficult and risky. Jumping off one is the greatest possible act of stupidity.

But this wasn't my first jump.

The first time I ever went over the edge of the castle roof, I was nine. In my defense, at the time, I had thought there would be a balcony only one floor down. The tutor I had been running from caught me by the wrist before I was fully over the edge, which he still claimed to this day had saved my life. My father had offered to double his salary as a reward, but instead, he quit the same day and changed professions, becoming a tailor instead. It was four months before another tutor took the position.

The second time I'd gone over the edge was an accident. Yes, I had fully intended to run along the parapet, but I had never planned to lose my balance. Fortunately, my belt snagged on a flagpole posted on the side of the castle. Darius had pulled me in.

I'd learned a lot from that last experience, namely, the exact place where I should jump.

My aim this time was good, but my speed was faster than

I wanted. My fingers slipped past the flagpole directly below me, but I did catch the fabric of the flag. That stopped my fall momentarily, but with my sudden weight, the flag had torn.

The good news was that I was no longer falling. The better news was that Lump stared down at me, utterly furious that I was out of his reach. But nothing so sweet could ever be all good. The flag was still ripping.

"I've got to put out that fire up here," he called to me. "But when I get down to you, I'll finish what I started."

"Take your time," I called back up. "You'll need it to think about my offer."

He left, and I immediately began trying to work out a plan to not fall to my death. Very carefully, I climbed the flag. With each pull, the strands of the fabric separated farther. Finally, I rotated my body upward and wrapped my legs around the pole. The fabric continued to tear, but now I no longer needed it.

I curled up to hold on to the pole with my hands and scooted closer to the castle wall, but the nearest window was still closed. I didn't want to kick through it — the glass was thick, and I risked a fall by kicking too hard. For now, I needed to be patient.

How familiar this felt to my childhood when I would get myself into trouble and have to wait for someone who didn't hate me to come along and offer help. Sometimes I had to wait a very long time.

But time was not on my side now. Lump would be here soon, and he wouldn't come with offers to help.

"King Jaron?"

Cook opened another window farther down the corridor,

then closed it and immediately darted to the window beside me. She opened that too.

"How did you —"

I pressed a finger to my lips to quiet her. Something had begun happening directly below me. The balcony was filling with Prozarian archers, but they were ducking low so that no one on the ground would know they were there. They were going to pick off Roden's men one by one as they came through the broken wall.

As quietly as possible, I angled my body through the window. Cook grabbed my legs to steady me at the end. I sank to the floor, mumbling, "Thank you, Cook."

"Always at your service, my king. I was actually sent up here in hopes of finding you."

"By whom?"

"Well, that's just it. There are pirates in my kitchen, dozens of filthy pirates! They came up through the riverway below, the way you always enter."

I smiled. That must have been where Roden disappeared to after the attack. He had gone to ask the pirates for help.

"Do the Prozarians know they're here?"

"No. But they're certain to figure it out. Pirates are quite loud."

"Find a pirate down there named Teagut." I paused, still waiting to catch my breath. "Ask him to take a group to find Imogen and help her get to safety, as well as any servants who are trapped inside."

"Very well. Anything else?"

"We should start moving." I stood, and as we began walking

along the corridor, I said, "I've been thinking about that vat of lard in your kitchen."

She arched a brow. "You were thinking about that? Was that before or after you jumped off the roof of the castle?"

"Both. But mostly after. I need you to gather enough people to carry that up here. Open the window again, then dump that lard all over the archers below. You can drop the pot too, if you want. Then go and hide until the battle is over. Can you do this?"

Cook smiled. "I've been wanting to do that since the moment they stormed this castle."

"Then make it worth your trouble. Thank you, Cook."

We parted on the second floor. The area was full of Prozarians following whatever orders they had been given, but despite their hurry, I could easily be recognized now. With my head down, I crashed straight into Errol, of all people, hurrying toward one of the rooms with a long towel draped over his arm.

"Pardon me, sir," he said; then his eyes widened as he looked at me. "Jaron? You're still alive?"

In my life, I'd been asked that question a surprising number of times. But it had become far more meaningful lately.

"You knew I was alive."

A corner of his mouth turned up. "That was two days ago. A long time for you."

"Fair enough." I added, "Where are you going with the towel?"

"Lord Trench is in the bathtub cleaning off some . . . well, he smelled very bad, sir. He's been stuck in there since we had word of the attack, waiting for me to come with a towel, but as you can imagine, I've been distracted."

I grinned. "He's going to wait even longer. I need you to bring me all his clothes."

Errol's eyes widened. "His clothes? Why?"

"Go and get his clothes for me. Hurry."

"I wouldn't know how."

"Really, Errol, you've watched me steal for almost two years. Don't tell me you haven't learned anything in that time."

Now Errol smiled too. "I think I could be a very good thief, if I practiced."

"Wonderful, but don't you ever practice on me. Now go."

Errol nodded and ran into the room. I stood in the corner and kept my head down until he snuck out again, with everything in his arms, even Mercy's cane and boots.

I carried them into the neighboring room and put on Mercy's coat, and donned his hat to help shield my face. With his cane in one hand, I walked out again, finding the entire floor thick with Prozarians.

Ahead of me, I noticed Batilda hurrying down the steps. The last thing she should be doing in the minutes before an attack was going out into the courtyard. Both curious and concerned, I followed.

Any uprising by those who had heard Imogen's speech seemed to have been mostly controlled by now, but at least half the Prozarian strength had to be in the main part of this courtyard. So either Roden's approach didn't worry them, or else they were more worried about something here.

From the courtyard, Batilda crossed into the stables. In her hand, I saw the tip of a note.

I was halfway to the stables, ignoring the occasional soldier who addressed me as Lord Trench, when the stable door opened again, but this time, it wasn't Batilda or even Tobias who had been hiding here. It was Fink who walked out the doors, wearing a Prozarian coat and hat. If anyone gave him a second look, they'd see how young he was.

Sticking out of Fink's pocket was the same folded paper that had been in Batilda's hand. She followed him out of the stables, edging along the wall back toward the castle. Fink walked in the opposite direction.

"You there, get in line!" A Prozarian officer gestured at Fink, who lowered his head just as I had been doing.

He started toward the line, but I bumped against him and grabbed his arm, pulling him with me. The officer began to object, until he noticed the cane.

"Apologies, Lord Trench," he called after me. I only waved the cane without turning back.

Fink struggled against my grip until I had dragged him around the corner; then he looked up. "I knew it was you," he insisted.

"No, you didn't."

"Well, I figured it out before now. Jaron, I did my best to warn Roden, but I couldn't get out of the gates."

"I know. Don't worry about that."

"Then why do you look angry?"

I held out my hand. "Give me the note."

"How did you know —"

"The note, Fink."

He grunted and passed it over. What I read alarmed me. On the paper, Imogen had written, *Stop the explosion.*

I glanced up at him. "What does this mean?"

At that moment, I heard the shouted orders. "Carthyan armies are at the wall. Prozarians, this is your time to fight! Leave no survivors!"

I cursed and peered around the corner, watching the Prozarians march behind their line commanders, preparing to meet Roden's armies in the next few minutes.

Lighting the spire hadn't worked. And Darius was nowhere in sight.

We were going to lose this battle.

· THIRTY~SEVEN ·

I turned to Fink. "Take off that coat or you'll find yourself on the wrong side of this battle." While he did, I said, "Now go back to the stables, find a strong horse, and ride out of here."

"No, I can't do that!"

"I'll stop the explosion. Just tell me what —"

Lines of Prozarians continued running past us, headed to meet Roden. I pulled Fink out of their way and saw he had a sword of his own at his belt.

Fink noticed my eye on it and said, "I can do more than you think. I'm almost the age you were when you took the throne."

"Not by a year, and this is not the time or place to test your skills. Go back to the stables and leave. That is the order of your king."

"Maybe, but I have orders from my queen." Fink winked at me. "She's nicer than you are."

"Which is why you should obey me. Now go!"

He scowled and ran toward the stables while I stuffed Imogen's note into my pocket, then peeked around the corner again. Captain Strick was in the center of the courtyard, directing more soldiers toward Roden's armies, promising them, "If we win here, then Carthya is ours, its spoils are ours, and its treasures are ours."

My fists curled. I'd use my last breath to ensure that they wouldn't even get our garbage drippings.

The instant Strick rode away, I rounded the corner to join the fight, though someone must have recognized me. I heard my name and turned in time to see a sword coming toward me. Just before it landed, the man's head jerked forward and he fell. Behind him was one of my servants, an older man with a shovel in his hands.

"You're a gardener here," I said.

"I used to be a soldier, sire. It feels good to fight again."

I clapped him on the shoulder. "Then fight on, my friend."

However, he was one of the last servants to remain. Only minutes later, I saw him surrounded by several Prozarians who forced him to his knees, in line with other servants who had been captured. Other servants were being escorted out of the stables, where they must have been hiding. Fink was not among them.

I walked deeper into the main courtyard, trying to search for him without calling too much attention my way. The sun was low in the sky, which would better hide my face. But the diminishing light would also make finding Fink far more difficult.

Where was he?

My mind raced. The note was in Imogen's handwriting, but she hadn't said a word to me about any explosion, so she must have only discovered it after getting to her room. If that was true, then where would it come from? How could Fink stop it?

And why would Imogen want to stop it?

There could be only one reason: The explosion would harm people she cared about.

So the Prozarians were in no danger. They filled the courtyard and the castle. The Prozarians were nearly everywhere other than . . .

The curtain wall.

Except for the place where Roden had come through, the wall was intact. The Stewardmen stood at posts along the wall, spread out on all four sides of the castle. All of them were there on Wilta's orders.

If Wilta wanted to destroy the Stewardmen, she would explode the wall. Imogen had assigned Fink to stop it.

I began running along the perimeter, my eyes scanning for any sign of him.

The curtain wall could only be accessed through doors at each corner of the courtyard. A rounded staircase inside led to the wall walk, which was protected on either side by a chest-high stone battlement. Like square teeth along the battlement, brick merlons were cut with arrow holes. The gaps between them were embrasures, allowing soldiers to watch for an incoming enemy. A steep and narrow roof ran overhead to give them additional protection in case of an attack.

That was where I finally saw Fink, on that roof. I began running toward the wall to reach him before he fell. I'd learned from personal experience how easily one could lose their balance. So why was he up there?

Because that's where the explosion would be.

Then I stopped, long enough to watch him more carefully.

He was holding on to the roof with one hand and sawing at potato sacks with the other. Three sacks already hung over his shoulder, and when he finished the fourth, he added that one to his growing load.

Cook had given Captain Strick twelve sacks that she wanted to fill with gunpowder. She must have found where we stored it.

Now I understood. At some point, her archers would shoot those bags with fire-tipped arrows and explode the entire wall. Fink was already moving toward his fifth bag. Seven more remained after that.

The battle against Roden had begun to spill into this courtyard. Roden immediately spotted me . . . or who he thought I was.

"You!" Either he had developed a sudden loathing of me — always a possibility — or he believed I was Mercy.

By the time I realized his mistake, Roden was already racing toward me with his eyes ablaze and his sword out.

I could have revealed myself as easily as removing my hat, but in a courtyard of hundreds of angry Prozarians, that would hardly improve my situation. So I turned to face Roden, holding my sword flat in front of me. I hoped he would either recognize it, or me. But the closer he came, the more I realized he might run me through before getting a good look at my face. So when he was close enough to hear me, I said, "Don't you usually target my leg?"

Roden stopped, staring at me as if he doubted his own eyes.

"It can't be. We heard —" Then he grabbed me and wrapped his arms tight around my shoulders. "You're alive?"

"Why is everyone asking me that today? Roden, duck!"

He released me and crouched low while I swung at someone headed directly for him. Then he rose up to do the same favor for me.

We separated again as the fight intensified around us. I was having particular trouble with a large Prozarian who missed a stab at my chest only because I tripped him with Mercy's cane first. He regained his balance and raised his sword, but before either of us could strike, Roden got him from behind.

Roden knelt beside him. "Help me take his coat."

"His coat? Not his sword? Don't we prefer the things that stab?"

But I knelt anyway and got one arm released. As we worked, Roden said, "Somehow, Mercy got inside our gates as a sentry. I should have known. This is my fault."

"Not all of it," I said. "Do you know about the pirates in the kitchen?"

He grinned. "Watch for them, Jaron. You'll like what you see."

"I'd better. They probably ate the supper I'd hoped to get tonight."

Roden chuckled, then picked up his sword again. I did the same but heard a familiar cry coming from across the courtyard.

"Someone help me!"

That was Batilda, on a horse in the middle of the courtyard. I'd thought she had gone back into the castle!

"I heard that she hates you," Roden said.

I sighed. "You have no idea." Then I stood and raced toward the sound of Batilda's voice.

· THIRTY-EIGHT ·

Since I was dressed like them, the Prozarians left me alone as I ran toward Batilda. I used my sword to stop a few Carthyan blades headed my way; then I'd lock eyes with the soldier and give him a wink. He'd smile and turn elsewhere to fight.

"Help me!"

Finally, I was close to Batilda, who was barely keeping her balance on the horse as she kicked at the Prozarians around her. I fought my way through them, saying, "This is the mother of the queen. Harm her and Carthya will have its revenge."

"Carthya is finished, Lord Trench," a soldier said to me. "Their fool king is dead. Next will be the Steward and his queen."

"Their fool king does not appreciate the insult." I cut him, then swung my sword at the other Prozarians. "Back away. She is coming with me."

Batilda took my hand when I offered it, and I kept her close at my side, all the time using my sword to keep everyone back.

"You fools, that is not Trench!" a soldier shouted. Obviously one of the smarter Prozarians.

I struck at him with the sword in my left hand, but he got my arm too, leaving a deep slice behind. He fell, but I wasn't far from falling either. I was nearly nauseous from the pain flooding through me.

Now it was Batilda who put her arm around me to keep me balanced. "If you're not Lord Trench, then —" For the first time she truly looked at me. "You're alive?"

This time, I didn't answer. All I could think about was how much I hated pain.

Batilda led me into a feed stall near the stables and closed the doors while I fell onto the hay.

"Remove that coat and I'll tend to the wound," she said.

When I did, Batilda pulled the thin shawl from around her shoulders and tore a strip of fabric from it to wrap around my arm. It reminded me of the way that Imogen had cared for my wounds once, with tenderness and kindness.

I watched her work, then said, "Why didn't Imogen tell you I was alive?"

"She and I agreed that first night it was best if we didn't talk about you at all."

For some reason, that made me smile, though it quickly faded. "You recognized me as soon as you came to the castle."

"As a thief, not a king. Until that moment, I had no idea who you were."

"Nor did I know you were the one I . . ." My voice trailed off while she knotted the shawl. When she looked up at me again, I said, "What I did . . . that was the reason you had to sell Imogen into Conner's service." It wasn't a question.

"Without that money, I had no other choice. Imogen

believed I had lost it due to my own carelessness, and there was some truth in that. But I would have found it again —"

"If I had not stolen it. Forgive me, Batilda."

She drew in a slow breath and stared at me. "Back then, when I saw you on the road, I saw a thief who cared for no one but himself. But when you were in the dungeons of Elmhaven, I saw what they did to you there, and what has been done to you before. You're too young for this, Jaron." She paused in her work and stared at me. "You have no need to ask forgiveness of me. You have earned it with every wound you have taken for this country."

I nodded back at her, the best I could manage, then reached for the coat.

She took my hand, trying to stop me from leaving. "You cannot go back out there!"

"I did earn these scars, Batilda, every one of them. And if I stay here, then they will have been for nothing. But I am asking you to stay. I think you will be safe here until the fighting ends."

With some effort, I put on my coat and found her holding my sword, which she offered to me with a smile and a sincere bow. "Go and reclaim your country, my king, and then your bride."

I smiled back at her but was only halfway out the door before I bumped headlong into Tobias. My eyes widened. "What are you still doing here? I thought you were headed toward Farthenwood!"

"I couldn't get out. There were too many Prozarians." He hung his head. "It wouldn't have been too many for you. I must be a coward."

"You're no coward, Tobias. I doubt anyone could get through those gates in this battle."

"What if Castor already sent soldiers to Farthenwood?"

"Nothing is better for them if you get injured here."

He gestured at my arm. "It looks like you forgot that rule."

"I always get injured, remember? Besides, it could've been worse."

"Don't tempt the devils that way. Even without their help, we both know you're already going to make it worse. Such as when Mercy figures out you're the one who stole his clothes."

I couldn't help but grin. "Is he still in the bathtub?"

"No. I heard that he's inside the castle, running around in a blanket, shouting for someone to get him some new clothes."

My first thought was how funny that would have been to see.

My second thought was that under no circumstances, ever, would I want that image permanently burned into my head.

I pulled out my sword. "Wonderful. Duck!"

"There's a duck?"

I pushed him down low while I swung for a soldier who was headed straight for Tobias. Then I looked past him to see Fink in the corner near one tower, winding a single cut sack around his shoulders. I wondered what he'd done with the other sacks he'd collected, and how many he had left.

A horn blew from one of the Prozarian vigils on a watch at the top of the castle. Something was happening.

"Look at Imogen's window! A blue cloth." Tobias grabbed my uninjured arm and began pulling me forward with him. "Blue, for Carthya. I'll bet this is the signal that Darius is finally here."

"He can't be, not yet!" I said. "They're going to explode the gates."

Far above the courtyard, Fink continued to work. He began pulling another sack up toward him, but this time, lost his balance and slid down the steep roof. I gasped and began running, though there was nothing I could do for him if he fell.

Just before slipping over the edge, Fink dug his boot into some part of the roof that seemed to hold his weight. His shoulders slumped; then he rolled and began climbing again. Within seconds, he was at work again.

"He's as foolish as you are," Tobias breathed. "Well, almost."

Captain Strick rode near us on a horse, her eyes also on Fink. "Where are my archers? I want that wall to come down now! Start with that boy up there!"

Orders were shouted throughout the courtyard for the archers to gather. The first one to run toward her was the archer I had stolen the arrow from earlier. A dozen or more arrows filled his quiver now, all wrapped and dripping with liquid. On Strick's orders, the archers would light their arrows, then fire them directly at the gunpowder bags. They were still going to destroy the wall.

I got the first archer from behind with my sword, but other archers were already gathering around Strick. With my injured right arm, I had little chance of fighting all of them.

"Come with me," I said to Tobias, and began running.

"We're going *to* the gate?" he asked. "Jaron, you just saw —"

He must have given up on arguing and followed. I ran into the first tower and began shouting, "Abandon this wall at once or you will die here."

The Stewardmen didn't need to be told twice. They pushed past me on their way off the wall, calling out my order to others behind them. Tobias stuck close to me, all the time saying, "They're leaving. Why are we still climbing?"

"Fink is up there!"

"He'll hear the orders. He'll come with them. Please, Jaron. She's going to bring this wall down."

"He won't hear the order. And if you're worried, stop talking and climb faster."

"This is a terrible idea," Tobias said. "Whatever you're thinking, it's a terrible idea."

"But it's the only idea I've got. Hurry, Tobias."

THIRTY-NINE

As we neared the wall walk, I said to Tobias, "Find Fink and bring him to me, along with everything he's collected."

"Brilliant idea. So when they blow up the wall, we'll be right in the middle of it."

"I'll handle the sarcasm, Tobias. Now go!"

Then I hurried to the center of the wall, where the last bit of daylight was fading into a sunset. In that diminishing light, I stood on an embrasure, overlooking a battle between Carthyans and Prozarians, and a dozen archers waiting for the order to fire upon the wall on which I stood. I waved my arms, hoping it would be enough to get Captain Strick's attention.

It must have been, for someone below pointed at me and shouted something I couldn't quite hear.

I saw the captain stop and stare up at me. From the steep angle, I hoped I'd look taller than I actually was. I also hoped Mercy would not come running out of the castle right now, still wrapped in the blanket. Actually, for multiple reasons, I hoped he would not do that.

I continued waving my arms until I saw a signal from

Captain Strick for her archers to stand down. Then she called up to me, "Trench, get off that wall!"

I cupped a hand behind my ear, indicating that I could not hear her, then jumped back onto the wall walk. By then, Tobias and Fink were running toward me, each of them dragging sacks of gunpowder behind them.

"Are you insane, climbing on the roof to retrieve those sacks?" Never before had I spoken to Fink so sharply. "You could have been killed!"

"And for almost a full day, I thought you had been!" he shouted back.

"If you're going to be my little brother —"

"Then be a better older brother!" he finished.

That was a fair point. The argument was over.

"If you want me to do better, then it starts here." I pointed to the stairs in the corner. "Both of you get down and try to find someplace safe to hide."

"The whole courtyard is in a fight," Tobias said. "This is the safest place we could be."

"It won't be." I pointed out toward the Drylliad hillside, where at least five hundred soldiers were on the march toward these gates, only minutes away. Mott and Darius were at their head, riding side by side.

"We're staying with you," Fink said. "It's what a little brother would do."

"And a friend," Tobias said. "Even a cowardly one."

I stopped what I was doing and looked directly at Tobias. "You think you're not strong or brave or capable of a fight, but I've seen what you can do when your back is against the wall. I know the courage that's in you. You wielded a longsword after escaping the keep. You defended me when you thought you were about to be killed — that's who you really are. Just believe in yourself a little sooner so that you put *their* backs to the wall."

"I'm not you," Tobias said.

"Well, that's good. Because if my plans fail, it will take someone very different from me to end this. If you're going to stay, then we have work to do. Now go open the gates. Roden needs those soldiers."

Fink asked, "What should I do?"

"How many ropes do you have left to cut?"

"I have one wall left."

I hated to say this, but I had no other choice. "Cut the rest, and bring them back here, as fast as you can. But don't you dare fall!"

He grinned and ran back along the wall walk.

While he did, I began collecting the nine gunpowder bags that Fink had already left on the wall walk. I expected to hear orders to fire at Fink and was ready to wave Strick away again, but it seemed that her attention had shifted.

"Why are the gates opening?" she shouted. "Lord Trench, close and secure them!"

The Prozarians gathered at the gates and began trying to push them closed, but Mott was the first to come through. In his arms was a battering ram held sideways. He sped up on his horse as he approached the gates and splintered them apart.

Darius was the next to ride through. He stopped at the gates and began shouting orders to the others who had followed him. At least half of them were my soldiers, and the rest were

Carthyan farmers and miners and merchants, each carrying whatever they could fashion into a weapon, and all were risking their lives. I owed them their best possible chance to succeed.

"Stop them, you fools!" Strick shouted, and a wave of Prozarians rushed to meet the new arrivals. Although we were still heavily outnumbered, the new arrivals gave Roden a chance to regroup with his soldiers.

Meanwhile, Captain Strick rode closer to the wall, even as I looked down, and her eyes narrowed. I didn't hear her orders to the soldiers around her, but I saw them nod and begin heading toward the nearest tower. They were coming up here.

I pointed to a sword one of the Stewardmen must have dropped in his escape. "Tobias, grab that!"

"Why? You know I can't use it," he said, though he picked it up anyway.

"Give it to me." I held out my hand but grimaced at him. "When this is over, sword training will be the only thing you do. I'm serious about that."

He passed it to me, then asked, "What can I do?"

"Find a way off this wall. Take Fink with you."

"And leave you here alone?"

I glanced back at him. "I won't be alone. Captain Strick sent me some company."

Then I ran down the steps to greet what appeared to be twenty Prozarians coming up the rounded staircase. At least in this limited space, I didn't have to face them all at once.

The first man up the steps narrowed his eyes. "Jaron?" He raised his sword. "I'm going to cut you good."

I lifted my injured right arm. "You're too late." He swiped

at me anyway, but I dodged it and kicked him down the stairs, then stabbed the next man to come at me. Others followed, but I managed them each in their turn, until someone below finally called a retreat. They ran out from the gate, and I heard one of them say to Captain Strick, "Whoever that is, it's not Lord Trench."

I hurried back upstairs to find Tobias and Fink still on the walking wall. "What are you doing here?" I scowled. "Didn't I order you to leave — twice?"

"We stayed," Fink said.

"You know what an order is, don't you?"

"We wouldn't be safer out there," Tobias said. "The battle isn't going well."

Mott was fighting in the center of a crowd, but Captain Strick pointed to him and shouted out some orders I couldn't hear from where I was. The soldiers grabbed him and pulled him off his horse, then began dragging him toward the castle. They placed him on his knees in the center of the courtyard.

I cursed and began lowering the extra gunpowder bags to the ground. I only needed five up here. I'd save the rest for later.

While I worked, Tobias said, "Jaron, when I was in the dungeons, there was something else Levitimas wanted me to ask you."

"Can this wait? I've got a lot on my mind right now."

"I might not get another chance."

"Can you speak and work?"

"Yes."

"Then push that cannon toward me."

He grunted, but as he worked, he said, "Levitimas wants you to go and see him."

I sighed and pushed the hair away from my face. "He wants me to visit him in the dungeons, now? Shall I bring tea?"

"No, but he said it was urgent."

"I'm in the middle of something. If you think it's important, you find a way there."

"He wanted to see you!"

"Work this out on your own, Tobias. Until then, aim the cannon straighter. Fink, help me move these sacks. Hurry!"

Tobias turned to me as I continued working. "Jaron, look around you. We are losing this battle."

That was true enough. My people were fighting as well as anyone could, but they still didn't have the numbers, and no matter how many Prozarians fell, they were quickly replaced by even more Prozarians. How was that possible?

That wasn't the worst of it. With another sounding of the Prozarian trumpet, the main castle doors opened and at least two dozen Prozarians soldiers entered the courtyard, with Mercy at their center. He was fully dressed, thankfully. Other than his cane and hat, he looked as he usually would, though far more angry. I ditched his hat and coat in the same moment that I saw him, leaving me only in a shirt and trousers. There was no point in wearing any sort of disguise now, and I hated his smell anywhere near me.

"Carthyans, on behalf of the Prozarian Monarch, the time has come for your surrender!" Mercy shouted.

The fighting seemed to pause as each side looked to their

leaders for instructions. Darius waved his hand for calm, then wheeled around on his horse to face Mercy. When it was clear the fighting had stopped, Darius shouted, "We meet again, Lord Trench. I am the eldest son of King Eckbert. I am Darius, the crown prince of Carthya. With the loss of my brother, I have come home. I am here to claim the throne."

Mercy only laughed. "You were a fool to come here, Darius. With your death, the house of Eckbert will be finished forever."

"Where is your monarch?" Darius shouted. "Does she cower behind the castle walls, hiding in fear?"

In that moment, the upper-floor balcony doors opened. The doors themselves had been replaced from the original attack on the castle, though no glass was in them yet. Wilta walked out with Castor at her side, though there clearly was no friendship between them. They stood as far apart as possible on the balcony.

"Why would I ever listen to you?" Wilta called down to Darius. "This is my castle now, my kingdom. These are my people. *You* are the foreign invader, not me. You may be the king of Belland, but you are nothing here in Carthya."

"And I am the Steward of Carthya —" Castor began.

"Ex-Steward," I muttered to myself.

"You are a traitor and a coward!" Darius shouted. "I know you, Castor Veldergrath. I've known you since we were boys. You cheated your way through every game of Queen's Cross we ever played, and you are a cheater now, in hopes of gaining the throne. *My* throne!"

"You speak boldly for someone who has just lost the battle," Mercy replied. "Your armies are surrounded, the castle has fallen, no one is left to fight with you." He raised his voice now. "Bring him before the Monarch!"

A swarm of Prozarians surrounded Darius, pulling him from his horse. He fought them at first; then someone got hold of his sword, and almost instantly, he ceased fighting.

"Why did he stop?" Tobias asked. "He knows what they'll do to him."

"He knows what he's doing," I mumbled. I understood the plan now.

Darius was dragged to the center of the courtyard beside Mott, with a dozen Prozarians around him. He stared up at Wilta, and though I couldn't see his face, I saw defiance in his posture. He wasn't finished yet.

Nor was Mercy. He yelled, "Captain Roden, are you certain that you want to continue fighting?"

Roden struck down the first Prozarians to reach him, but three others had already surrounded him. One grabbed his sword and the other two forced him to the center of the courtyard to stand directly beside Darius.

"What are you going to do?" Tobias asked me.

"Nothing." I returned to my work. "They can handle this."

"Look at them!"

I did, in time to see Darius shout up to Castor, "You are a traitor and a pretender to the throne. I invite all Carthyans to join me in the fight against these invaders."

"What invaders?" Castor Veldergrath raised his arms. "My people, I am no invader, nor is my soon-to-be wife, Lady Imogen, a descendant of the original queen of Carthya. Lower your weapons and kneel to me, as I kneel to her."

Castor waited for his orders to be obeyed, and I wondered for a moment if I actually saw smoke come from his ears as his temper began to burn.

Because not a single member of my army, or any of those who had come with Darius, went to their knees. Instead, they stood tall, raising their swords straight in front of them, their eyes on Darius and Roden.

Castor screamed, "You fools, you leave me no choice! Jaron is dead; I gave the order myself. And I will do the same to Darius if you will not kneel!"

Tobias turned to me. "Jaron, you've got to do something!"

"I suppose I do. Are you ready, Fink?"

He smiled. "Ready!"

"Ready for what?" Tobias paled, worse than usual. "Jaron, ready for *what*?"

"What do you think we've been doing up here, Tobias? Fink, help him load his cannon."

Tobias shook his head. "Jaron, you can't put a cannonball in there now. You know what will happen if you light it, and there's no time left to do it properly."

I clicked my tongue. "Very true. Now load the cannonball."

Below us, Captain Strick threatened, "If all Carthyans are not on their knees in the next ten seconds, the Prozarians will show you no further mercy."

Tobias craned his head toward the window outside Imogen's room. "She just changed the flag hanging there. It's black. Do you know what that means?"

"I hope so."

By then, I was finishing the knot on one of the ropes that

Fink had cut from the roof, tying it around a nearby embrasure. Two cannons were behind me, both of which directly faced the castle. Each was loaded with gunpowder and had a cannonball ready to fire.

"Jaron, don't do this," Tobias warned. "All they have to do is fire a single arrow."

"If they do, then it's your responsibility to finish this."

"Jaron, no —"

"Are you both ready? Light your torches. Make sure everyone can see them."

"The battle ends now." Captain Strick raised her hand, ready to signal the Prozarians to fight.

Then I climbed onto the embrasure and called out, "No, Captain Strick, our battle has just begun."

FORTY

Strick nearly fell off her horse when she saw me. "Jaron?" She screeched my name with a peculiar combination of disbelief and rage.

I saluted her, then shouted, "Carthya, I am Jaron, the Ascendant King. Together, we will rise up and finish this battle, end this war, and rid ourselves of the Prozarian infestation."

From below, I heard Carthyan soldiers cheer and call out my name. Darius, Roden, and Mott had all turned to me, with equal expressions of disbelief.

I continued to speak, as loudly as my voice could carry. "My people, the crown has not fallen, the throne is not abandoned, and for the record, Lord Stench's clothes now match his miserable name!"

Mercy darted to the castle steps, shouting loud enough that I could hear him. "Where are our archers?"

"I wouldn't recommend that," I said, lifting my torch again. "There are two cannons behind me, both of them ready to fire. If a single arrow comes at me, both of the cannons will be lit. One of them is aimed at you, Lord Stench. The other at the ruler you serve."

Mercy looked up that way, then quieted down. Meanwhile, Castor stepped forward. He had actually reeled backward against the castle wall when he first saw me and was only beginning to recover now from the shock. He screamed, "I saw you get hit by that arrow, Jaron. I saw you fall into the river!"

"If you thought that was exciting, you should have seen me climb out of the river. Because I always will climb out, or climb up, or ascend again. Now, shall we discuss your surrender, or will you try to survive the cannonball aimed at your chest?"

"We will not surrender," Wilta said.

"The last time you said those words, I blew up your ships. In one minute, I will fire one of these cannons behind me. Will it be the cannon aimed at you, or at Lord Stench?"

"That isn't his name. And we both know you'd never fire on your own castle."

"I would. I'm actually looking forward to it, though I'd prefer to use the cannon aimed at Stench. Getting rid of him would do us both a favor."

"Stand down, and we will let you leave Carthya alive," Castor said. "I will give you the exile that I promised before."

"That is literally the worst thing you could say — I remember your ideas about exile." I began to step down from the embrasure. "The minute is done. I'll just fire both cannons."

"Wait!" Wilta said. "I'll release one of these prisoners, any that you choose. Who will it be? Your brother, your captain, or your companion-at-arms?"

I looked them over, then pointed down to an older man kneeling in the far corner. He had not been taken in with the other servants, which probably meant he had not agreed to end his fight. "I'll choose him. My gardener."

Wilta tilted her head. "Your gardener?"

"A good gardener is impossible to replace."

"Very well." She pointed to him. "You may leave."

The gardener stood and looked up at me, then gave a deep bow before hurrying out of the courtyard gates.

I turned back to her. "I should have mentioned that I'm still going to fire one of these cannons. Choose. Will I aim at you or at Stench?"

Her response came quickly. "Lord Trench, then, or anywhere in the courtyard."

I paused for some time, genuinely confused. "You'd choose those who've pledged service to you?"

"It is their duty to die for me. If I lose a hundred here, I'll get a hundred more next week."

A few of the soldiers began to back away, but Captain Strick yelled, "You will all stand your ground. Let your fate be what it is."

"I'm sorry you both feel that way." I turned to Tobias. "You and Fink get off this wall and find a safe place to hide, outside the castle gates if you can. Fink, light your cannon!"

Fink did; then he and Tobias began running. When it fired, it hit its target, the parapet of the castle roof. Stone tumbled down the front of the castle, directly over the balcony where Wilta and Castor had stood. I heard Wilta scream but had no time to see what had happened to any of them.

From below, Roden called out, "Pirates, now!"

At his command, the Prozarians watching over Darius, Mott, and Roden removed their coats and hats, revealing themselves. The pirates tossed weapons back to their former prisoners, and the Carthyans who had fought rushed forward to gather their weapons again. In that moment, our numbers felt almost equal.

I dove from the embrasure to the rope with the intention of sliding to the ground, though with an injured arm, it was more of a controlled fall. Or, more accurately, it was a fall.

From the ground, I stared up at the balcony. Thanks to the cannon fire, it was almost entirely gone, but there was no sign of Castor or Wilta. They must have gotten inside.

Mott found me first and pulled me to my feet. He gave me a brief embrace, then said, "That must be the biggest fool thing you've done in a long time."

I shook my head. "You should've seen me earlier today." I pointed to the bags of gunpowder I'd dropped from the wall walk. "We need to get these in our possession."

Mott reached for one; then I saw a deep cut in his side. I grabbed his arm. "Someone else can get these. You need to get that wrapped!"

"I can move them," he insisted, picking up two bags and piling them on his shoulder.

"Jaron!"

Darius rode up to me, leaning low to offer me a hand. I took it, and he pulled me into the saddle behind him. As he continued riding, I stretched out a sword on either side of the horse, striking at every Prozarian we passed.

Gradually we left the battle behind, finding quiet at the far side of the castle. Darius slid out of the saddle and so did I; then he gave me a warm embrace. When he stood back, tears filled his eyes. "You're alive? Imogen sent us messages. She should have told us —"

"We couldn't risk anyone finding out if the note was intercepted."

He smiled through the tears. "This is a great relief, you know. I didn't want to be king of any castle that looks like this one. If only Father could see this."

"He'd be angrier than usual with me." I sniffed and glanced back to where the sounds of fighting were continuing.

Darius pressed his brows together. "Are you all right?"

I shook my head. "I've felt their absence lately, Mother and Father's. A week ago, I realized that I'd have no parents to stand with me at my wedding. Now their paintings have been removed from the gallery, Castor is using Father's room as his own, and I just fired off a cannon at our own castle. I think if Father could see me now, he wouldn't have stood with me at the wedding anyway."

Darius put a hand on my shoulder. "Father might not approve of how you've fought the Prozarians, but I know he would approve of you. And I know you're going to fix this."

I made myself smile and gave a half shrug. "Not if I stay here when all the fighting is on the other side of the castle. We need to go back."

Darius climbed into the saddle, and I followed behind him. We rode toward the main courtyard, which took us almost directly beneath Imogen's window. I looked up and saw that she had once again changed the cloth hanging from it. I said to Darius, "What does a yellow flag mean?"

He glanced back at me. "Yellow? Are you sure?"

"What does it mean, Darius?"

"She's in danger!"

· FORTY-ONE ·

Darius rode us faster toward the castle entrance. When we were closer, I slid off the back of the horse and dove into the crowd of vigils there. As they surrounded me, someone shouted, "You fool, do you want to be actually killed?"

I looked and saw Roden had somehow appeared, as if he'd cleared a path from the courtyard directly to me.

"Need help?" he asked.

"Absolutely. I need to get to Imogen." In my condition, I was slowing down, and at the worst possible time. I swung hard and fierce, but Roden still fought off twice the Prozarians as I did as we tried to get into the castle.

"You're fighting like an old man!" he said, grinning over at me.

"You have two good arms. I don't."

"You have two swords."

I hated it when he was right. We were about to enter the castle itself, but the doors opened and Teagut stumbled out, nursing a wound on his right side,

Roden caught him as he fell to his knees, and I crouched

beside him. "Eight of us were protecting her," he said. "I'm the only one left."

"Where is Imogen?" I asked.

"Forgive me, Jaron. I don't . . ." Teagut drew in a sharp breath. "I don't know."

Mott crouched beside us, pressing a hand to the wound.

I looked up at Roden. "I've got to find her."

"Don't." Teagut grabbed my arm. "I only made it this far because they allowed it. They wanted me to find you. Jaron . . . it's a trap."

"I know." I turned to Roden again. "Call a retreat of our soldiers. All of them."

Roden turned to me. "What? No, we can still win this!"

"They have Imogen, and if our soldiers are here, they'll use her to force our surrender! Now go call a retreat. Get everyone out of the courtyard while you can!" He continued to object, but I said, "Those are my orders."

"Yes, Jaron." Furious, Roden bit into his words, but he put an arm around Teagut to help him onto the nearest horse, climbed on behind him, and signaled for a retreat.

Once they were riding, I ran behind a pile of rocks near the front steps, formed by the fallen balcony. I'd seen Tobias and Fink dart behind here to hide.

Startled to see me, Tobias raised a sword in his hand, facing the proper direction. That was progress. "I just called a retreat," I said. "You both need to leave immediately."

"I have a different plan." Tobias straightened. "You told me to trust myself and defend Carthya. That's what I'm going to do."

"At any other time, I'd admire your ambition. But for now, you need to leave."

Fink had been peering out from the side of the rock pile. He turned and looked back at me. "Jaron, we have a problem!"

I scrambled up to the top of the barricade and saw a handful of Prozarians pushing both Mott and Darius up the steps into the castle. Roden was riding out through the gates. So many of our people were leaving, I wondered if he knew that not everyone had made it out.

My attention returned to Tobias. "Tell me your plan."

He frowned. "You're not going to like it, but —"

"Your armies have abandoned you, Jaron!" Captain Strick rode toward me, stopping almost directly in front of where I stood on the barricade.

Mercy had found his own horse and joined her. "You have lost," he said. "It's over."

At least a hundred Prozarians still remained on the ground, standing in silence, watching. But even more were on the curtain wall, so thick they were nearly shoulder to shoulder. Only a single gap remained, to allow for the second cannon, now aimed directly at me.

Mercy saw where my attention had gone and began laughing. "You left us a loaded cannon, already aimed perfectly for where you now sit. I wonder how it must feel to realize that what is about to happen is your own fault."

I stared straight back at him. "It feels fine, thanks for asking."

"This is our final revenge for what you did to the Monarch and our Steward."

"Ex-Steward," I muttered.

"Except you will not survive this," Mercy added.

"Your men on that curtain wall will not survive this," I said. "Don't let them fire that cannon."

From behind the barricade, Tobias hissed, "Jaron, that cannon is aimed straight at you, at all of us!"

I ignored him and kept my eyes on the captain. "I suggest a compromise. Aim the cannon at Stench and we'll both be rid of that thorn."

"Give the order, Captain," Mercy said. "Finish him!"

I leaned forward. "Captain, you do not want to do this."

She only laughed and raised her hand. "Oh yes, we do. Goodbye, Jaron." Then she closed her fist, giving the order to fire.

Mercy and Strick quickly rode away, trying to get as far from me as possible. I saw them light the cannon, but I remained exactly where I was.

I had no intention of dying today.

· FORTY-TWO ·

Fink had cut down a dozen sacks of gunpowder from the roof over the curtain wall. The contents of one sack had gone into the cannon that fired on Wilta. The contents of four more were in the second cannon, far more gunpowder than a cannon of that size could handle. It wouldn't launch the cannonball inside. The cannon itself would explode first.

And so it did.

The explosion completely destroyed the main curtain wall and took down two towers and parts of the adjacent walls. It shook the ground beneath me and sent rocks tumbling throughout the courtyard. One landed closer to me than I would have liked, but I remained in my place. I suspected nearly half the Prozarian soldiers still here in the courtyard were now injured, or worse.

I leapt off the barricade and said to Fink and Tobias, "Follow me!"

Amid the chaos, we ran inside the castle, pushing against Prozarian soldiers who failed to notice us in their rush to see what that explosion had been. They followed me down the main steps into the cellar.

I said to Tobias, "Go into the kitchen and ask Cook for the satchel I left with her."

"Aren't we looking for Imogen?"

"I need something to bargain with. Meet us at the crypt. Now go!"

As Tobias ran in one direction, a line of five Prozarians started toward us from the other, one of them shouting, "That's Jaron!"

I turned to Fink. "You said you wanted to fight."

He grinned. "I'm ready."

Fink and I ran toward the Prozarians with swords drawn. I kept one eye on him, but he was fighting as well as any of the soldiers here. I knew he'd spent a great amount of time practicing, but until now, I hadn't realized how talented he was. We finished off the last man together just as Tobias ran up behind them with the satchel in his hand.

I slid it over one shoulder as we continued running, rounding the corner where the dungeon entrance was, and there we stopped. The doors to the crypt should have been here. Instead, so much rock had collapsed, it had buried the entrance and blocked us from going any farther. We were trapped.

Heavy footsteps had been following us, but no one came around the corner. I simply heard Captain Strick say, "It's time to end this, Jaron."

"I agree. Enough of your people have died fighting me. I accept your surrender."

"You will surrender. We have Darius, and Mott, and Imogen."

I closed my eyes and tried to think through what options I had. Nothing was good.

Strick continued, "I'll give Tobias one minute to talk some sense into you. After that, our prisoners will begin to pay for your stubbornness."

Even as I continued to think, Tobias frowned at me. "Jaron, you have to surrender."

My brows furrowed. "Why?"

"We're trapped. In less than a minute, she will kill Mott and Darius, and maybe even Imogen. Then she'll come for us."

"I'm sure she will."

"And we have no army."

"I understand that. But what's your point?"

"My point is that you've got to surrender."

I turned and stared at Tobias. "Do you think it will be any better if I give up now?"

"At least we'll be alive. Three people you love will stay alive."

"When have you *ever* known me to kneel in surrender?"

"You don't. You won't. But it's different this time."

"No, Tobias, it is never different. If I kneel once, my legs will learn to bend. I have lost many battles, but this is the war, and I will not give in. Hear me now because I will never repeat this again. I will *not* surrender!"

Tobias's eyes filled with tears. "Then you have doomed us all."

"Oh, no. We are not dying here. Let me think."

"Your minute is over," Strick called. "Jaron, what is your answer?"

"You want me to show courage before I am backed into a corner. That's exactly what I'll do." Tobias looked at me. "I know you cannot surrender, Jaron, so I hope you will forgive me for this one day." He walked past me with his arms held high. "Captain Strick, I surrender! And if you agree to keep us all alive, I will turn over something of value to you." He reached into a pocket and pulled out a leaf. "Keep us alive, and I'll remain silent about this leaf."

I was so angry, I could barely speak, so I merely stood there, watching Tobias give away our last chance for victory.

"Very well." Captain Strick must have spoken to other soldiers. "Put Mott and Darius in the dungeon. Fink too; I know he's back there. Tobias will walk with me. The Monarch wishes to see both him and Jaron."

Soldiers rounded the corner. Fink passed me his sword, swallowed hard, then walked forward to meet them. The soldiers who took him knocked on the dungeon door, which was opened by Haddin.

The other soldiers who had come took either me or Tobias. I sheathed my own sword but offered them the other two I now held, as a sign that I would not fight.

Both Lump and Mercy came around the corner. The smirk on Mercy's face struck me like a slap in the face.

A slap that had come from Tobias. I hadn't surrendered, but thanks to him, I felt just as awful as if I had.

· FORTY-THREE ·

Mercy and Lump walked on either side of me toward the main staircase. I clicked my tongue. "So the Monarch is still alive?"

"She is alive. And very angry."

"Ah, her usual mood, then."

"Ow."

I had been slowly drifting closer to Mercy as we walked, forcing him to scoot closer and closer to the rough walk wall. Finally, his leg hit an outcrop of a rock near his shin.

Lump pulled me back to the center of the hall, and he was hardly gentle about it. "This is a terrible way to treat your king," I said.

"Just wait to see what the Monarch has planned for you," he replied. "And you are not my king."

"Jaron isn't thinking about the Monarch," Mercy said. "He is more worried about what Castor has planned."

"Castor is still alive too?" I had never intended that cannon to kill either Wilta or Castor. Any aim directly at them also risked Imogen's safety, since her room was near the balcony. But

I wouldn't have minded hearing that Castor had at least broken a fingernail or something.

Mercy grinned at me. "In fact, I have another duty to tend to once we're upstairs. I have a message to pass on . . . to the priest."

"So Castor is ready to beg forgiveness of the saints? I wish him luck."

Mercy laughed. "No, Jaron, the message came from Imogen. She requested the priest, as a final preparation for the wedding."

It turned out that I wasn't particularly good at hiding my feelings. I stopped at the base of the stairs. "*Imogen* asked for the priest?"

Mercy smiled again. "Why should it matter to you? Your captain abandoned this castle, leaving you with an army consisting of a single regent who just betrayed you for his own survival. Your castle has fallen, or it soon will, literally. And once you've found the treasure, the Monarch will be finished with you. The rest of your life can be measured in hours."

"That's a relief." I steadied myself and began walking upstairs. "I'm measuring yours in minutes. I wonder if you'll even live long enough to see the treasure."

"Ow!" Mercy must have realized only then that once again I had been forcing him nearer to the wall. He shoved me to the center, then scoffed, "You have no more idea of where the treasure is than any of us."

I glanced over at him. "You still haven't solved it?" I let out a low whistle. "Even Lump knows. How embarrassing for you."

"Lump knows nothing."

I shrugged that away. "It must be torture to think that Lump is smarter than you. He was the one who started me in the right direction."

Lump grinned back at Mercy as we walked up the stairs. It was true that he had helped me. I had believed the symbols on top of the scope read that one was greater than three, but Lump had suggested I was reading the symbols backward. If he was correct, the message would have been that Carthya was greater than all other countries. I doubted that was the exact message, but Lump did get me thinking in a different way. The symbols on top of the scope weren't a message; they were a tribute to the three original rulers of Carthya.

Strick brought us into the throne room with Tobias still at her side. Castor and Wilta each sat on their respective stolen thrones. Both wore bandages and had small cuts, but neither appeared to be seriously injured. That was a disappointment.

One of the soldiers who had been in the cellar with us went onto the dais and whispered into Wilta's ear. I used the time to glare at Tobias, who was making every effort not to look back at me.

Within seconds, I'd had enough of the whispering. I broke free of Lump's grip and said to Wilta, "Where is Imogen?"

She frowned and with a wave of her hand dismissed the man who had been whispering to her. As he rejoined the group, she said, "I summoned *you* here. I captured *you*. I will ask the questions and *you* will answer."

"Fine." My tone sharpened. "Where is Imogen?"

Castor stuck out a bandaged arm. "Why are you tolerating this, Monarch? After the last conversation you had, he shot a cannonball at you."

"Actually, you were my target," I said. "Wilta just happened to be standing too close."

Wilta shook her head. "That went too far!" she shouted. "I am finished with your tricks, your games." She gestured to Lump. "Kill him."

I stepped back, holding up a hand to keep Lump at a distance. "I am here to keep my promise to you, Wilta. I will take you to the treasure."

Her brows lifted. "You know where it is?"

My eyes shifted to Castor. "Why is he still here? He's not your steward anymore."

"I am soon to be king," he said. "I have every right to be here."

I ignored that and continued to address Wilta. "We both know you hate him, and he's hardly on my favorites list. You and I must talk alone."

"Alone?" Wilta didn't flinch. "You can't be serious."

"Not entirely alone. I want Tobias to stay." Even if I was angry with him, I had to keep Tobias here; otherwise, Captain Strick would take him for questioning. "Lump can stay too, if he steps back to where he was. He's almost as loyal to you as he is to me, so he'll be fair."

"I am only loyal to the Monarch," Lump said, to which I shrugged and added, "We'll call it even."

Wilta hesitated, and I said, "While anyone else is here, I will not say another word about the treasure."

Wilta frowned but did not take her eyes off me as she said, "Castor, you will leave us."

"That's not good enough. I want Castor locked in his room,

just as he did to Imogen." A corner of my mouth turned up. "Admit it. You want him locked in there too."

"What?" Castor nearly exploded. "Imogen has sent for the priest! I'm to be married as soon as we're finished here."

"The wedding must wait until *I* am finished here." Wilta gestured to her mother. "You will take Castor Veldergrath to his room. Stay there until I summon you back."

"You will not send me away," Strick said to Wilta. "I am here for your protection!"

"Leave," Wilta said. "Everyone, leave!"

Strick protested almost as loudly as Castor, but she did escort him out, followed by the entire crowd of Prozarians who had been in the room. It left me standing directly in front of Wilta as she sat on my throne. Lump stood in front of the dais and off to one side. Tobias was somewhere behind me.

I began by nodding at the door as the last Prozarian closed it, then asked Wilta, "How did you do that?"

"Do what?"

"Get them to obey so easily? Every order I've made lately seems to require an argument."

"I kill people who don't obey me."

"Ah," I said. "I sometimes deny them dessert."

Wilta's smile soon faded, and she turned to Tobias. "You were the one who surrendered to my mother. I understand that you showed her a leaf, and that caused her to back down."

Tobias widened his stance but said nothing.

"Tell her," I said.

"Jaron, she's the enemy."

I threw out my hands in frustration. "This is what I mean, no obedience to my orders. No dessert for you, Tobias."

He said, "I cannot tell her, Jaron. I swore to Captain Strick that if she kept us alive I would never discuss that leaf."

I snorted. "*Now* you show honor?" I turned back to Wilta. "I made no such promise to your mother. I'll tell you all about that leaf *after* you release one of the prisoners."

"Choose one, then."

"Set Mott free." He was injured, probably worse than he had let on, and I was worried for him.

Wilta gave a slight nod to Lump, who walked to the doors of the throne room and spoke to someone outside. When he closed the doors again, he reported, "It is done. Mott will be escorted safely beyond the castle walls."

Ready to keep my agreement, I reached into my satchel and pulled out the book that I had brought from Farthenwood. Only two pages after the one that had solved the mystery of my parents' deaths was a drawing of the same leaf Tobias had shown to Captain Strick. I showed Wilta the picture. "Ever seen something like that before?"

Wilta shrugged. "It looks like any other leaf."

"Not at all." I pointed to spots on the back of the leaf and then to a drawing of the tree itself. "This is from the gilbrush tree, not the most common tree in the land but hardly rare. Touching the leaves is harmless. Eating one or two might be equally harmless, but over time, it builds up in the body, creating rashes and sores on the flesh that leave terrible scars behind. With enough time, the leaves will cause death."

Wilta's eyes had widened as I spoke. "You're suggesting that someone has been feeding them to me?"

"Ask yourself why your mother became so nervous when she saw Tobias with that leaf."

"These are lies! My mother would never —"

"My lady?" Lump looked as if he was having trouble swallowing. "After Lord Trench was sent here, I began delivering your tea, prepared, as always, by your mother. One morning, I arrived earlier than usual and saw your mother pull that same leaf from the teapot."

"Didn't you say that you trusted no one other than your mother and Lord Trench to prepare and deliver your food?" I asked.

Wilta nodded and lowered her head. After a moment, she straightened and took in a deep breath. "Say nothing to my mother. This is my problem, and my problem alone."

"But it is not your only problem. Stench is in league with Castor."

"Stop calling him that. And I already told you, I sent him to that meeting as a spy."

"You did, but his request to serve Castor was sincere."

"Can you prove it?"

"When I had the cannon aimed at him, I told him that the second cannon was aimed at the leader he serves. He looked up at Castor, not at you."

Wilta's face hardened. "That's hardly proof. My mother, however . . ." After a brief dab at each eye, she looked at me. "I assume you also have the Devil's Scope in that satchel? I know you stole it the night you escaped from the library."

"I can't steal what is already mine," I said. "But yes, it is here."

"Give it to me."

"I need it to gain access to the treasure."

"Then let's go get it, right now."

"First, I want you to release Imogen."

Wilta laughed. "Prove that you know where the treasure is."

"It's accessed from the cellar. Release Imogen, and I'll tell you the rest."

Tobias stepped forward. "Monarch, I cannot stand here another minute and listen to Jaron lie to you."

I turned, certain I had not heard him correctly, but before I could say a word, Wilta said, "You told me that Jaron never lies."

"He has no idea where the treasure is. The cellar is a trap."

"What sort of a trap?"

I folded my arms. "Yes, Tobias, I'd like to hear this too."

"He's going to tell you the treasure is inside the crypt. But the entrance is completely blocked by fallen rock. You'll never get inside. Jaron was just down there. He knows this."

Wilta looked at me. "Is that true?"

I sighed. "Which part?"

"Is it possible to enter the crypt?"

"It would be far too dangerous to try."

"But is the treasure there?"

"Yes, I think so."

"That's why I had to say something." Tobias's voice grew more desperate. "When you see how dangerous the entrance is, you'll send Jaron, or Fink, or me instead. The first rock that rolls beneath our feet will create an avalanche of rocks that will crush us."

I glared over at Tobias. "Wonderful suggestion, Tobias.

Maybe you can see if she wants to lay hot coals beneath our feet at the same time."

Wilta rubbed her hands together. "That's exactly what I'll do. We'll go down to the cellar, and you three will be the first to test for an entrance."

I snorted. "No, we won't."

"Then you must know another way in!" she said. "Let's bargain, Jaron. I'll give you what you want if you tell me how to get inside."

I was still busy glaring at Tobias, but I said, "For this betrayal, I want Tobias placed in the dungeons."

She laughed, delighted to see our quarrel unfold. "That's it? Of course he should go to the dungeons, but before he does, I have one question for him." She turned his way. "Only two days ago, you told me that Jaron was both your king and your friend. But now you disobeyed his orders as king, and have betrayed his friendship. Tell me why."

Tobias eyed me but quickly looked away. He merely shrugged and said, "Sometimes, Jaron must be saved from himself."

Wilta waved at Lump. "Take him."

Lump grabbed Tobias, but before they were out of the room, Tobias said, "He won't give you the information you want, Wilta. He is deceiving you!"

Wilta turned to me. "Tell me how to get inside."

"No, I won't." I shrugged. "Tobias is right. I was deceiving you."

"Then you will go to the dungeons too!" she screeched. "I'll give you one hour to tell me how to get inside the crypt, or Tobias will suffer for your stubbornness."

"I'll tell you right now how to enter. You've got months of repairs ahead before it will be safe."

The problem wasn't merely that a lot of rock had fallen; it was the way it had fallen. The wreckage was stacked unevenly, heavy stones balanced on thin edges, creating pressure on weaker stones that might collapse at any minute. Dust and debris lodged in between could give way with every stone moved from above, filling in gaps of air.

Wilta turned to Lump. "Commander Coyle, gather all our available soldiers at the entrance to the crypt. I want them to find a way inside."

I stepped forward, urgency rising in my voice. "Listen to me, Wilta. It really is too dangerous there. The treasure is not worth anyone's life."

"It is worth all their lives! We will not give up now." Her eyes were fiery when she looked back at me. "But if you care so much about them, tell me how to get in."

"Tell her, Jaron," Tobias said. "Don't let her send us to the dungeons again!"

I merely set my jaw forward and stared back at her.

"One hour." She looked over at Lump. "Take them."

Lump began to lead us out of the throne room, but Wilta added, "This had better not be a trick."

"Oh, it absolutely is," I called back to her. "Trust me on that."

"I will do whatever it takes to get inside. And if you ever want to see Imogen again, it is you who must trust me."

I frowned at her as Lump led us away. I absolutely did not trust Wilta.

· FORTY-FOUR ·

I had nothing to say to Tobias as we walked toward the dungeons. The corridors were nearly empty now, with a much smaller Prozarian army at watch. I didn't know where Castor had sent his Stewardmen, but they had been entirely absent from the recent battle, so he had them in reserve for some later purpose. If any servants still remained in the castle, they were likely in hiding.

Beside me, Lump asked, "Is the treasure really inside the crypt?" I didn't answer, and he said, "Because if this is a trap, you will be the first to pay for it."

I shook my head. "Any punishment would be a clear violation of your future vow to protect me."

Lump was silent for a minute, before he leaned in and lowered his voice. "It would take a long time for you to trust me in your service."

"Then you had better start earning that trust now. Listen to me. Captain Strick is not the only threat to your monarch. Mercy is just as dangerous, maybe worse."

"How do you know that?"

Tobias caught up to us. "Don't bother asking. Jaron rarely explains himself."

"Why should I, when I know you'll do the explaining for me?" I shot back.

Lump pushed between us, still confused. "Why would you want to help the Monarch?"

"I don't. But I know you do. I won't let you switch loyalties to me with the guilt of failure on your shoulders."

I didn't say another word until we reached the dungeon entrance, and as we looked farther ahead to the crypt entrance, Lump said, "If you know another way into that crypt, tell me now. Otherwise, she'll sacrifice as many of us as it takes to get in."

"You've got to stop her from doing that," I said. "Lump, do not be part of Wilta's plan!"

"Then tell her what she wants to know!" His face tightened. "You don't care about us any more than the Monarch does."

From there, we were led down into the dungeons themselves, a place I was far too familiar with by now. Haddin opened the door for us and grabbed the keys to open our cell doors.

One other vigil was already down there when we arrived. Tobias was placed in the first cell, rather unkindly, by Lump, who said, "There's no honor in what you just did to the person you call your king."

"What did he do?" Fink was in the next cell.

Darius was in the cell closest to Levitimas and glared at Tobias, though it didn't mean much tonight. A glare was his usual expression for Tobias.

"When other Carthyans find out, Tobias won't be safe out there," Lump answered.

"So true," Levitimas said. "Nowhere is safer than a good dungeon!"

I pointed to the cell with Levitimas. "Put me in there."

But he put me directly across from Levitimas, then said to Haddin and the other soldier, "You both stay down here and watch them all, especially Jaron."

Lump started to leave, then stopped long enough to say to Tobias, "If Jaron doesn't talk within the hour, I'm coming for you first."

I grabbed the bars of my cell, trying one last time to get his attention. "I'm serious, Lump. Do not carry out Wilta's orders."

But it seemed we were already too late. Lump had not even reached the top of the steps before we heard the rolling sound of a rock and the cries of a man for help. The crypt entrance had claimed its first victim. Lump's footsteps paused, then continued on.

My attention shifted to Haddin and the second vigil. "Eventually they'll come for you two. You're lower-end soldiers. They'll waste your lives before they risk their senior officers."

Levitimas sighed. "How many will die trying to access that treasure?"

"One is too many," I said. "None of this would be happening if you had told me where the treasure is."

"They would have only died sooner."

There was another cry from up in the corridor. Seconds later, the dungeon door opened and someone called down, "You there, vigils! Captain Strick wants whichever of you is the smallest to come upstairs."

Haddin was slightly larger than the other vigil, who gulped with fear, then began walking upstairs, visibly trembling.

I turned to Haddin. "You'll be next. If you're smart, you will give me the keys to this cell, then sneak upstairs and run as far from here as you can." He hesitated, and I added, "Among my enemies, you're the closest friend I've got. I'm trying to help you live."

Haddin thought about that for only a few seconds before he tossed the keys into my cell and hurried up the steps.

I immediately unlocked my cell door and went next to the cell Tobias was in, flashing him another glare. "Did you think that was brave, that accusing me of lying in my own throne room was some great act of courage?"

Tobias tilted his head. "Yes, Jaron, I do think that."

My face melted into a wide grin. "I think so too." I finished unlocking his door, then offered him a hand to get back to his feet. "I admit that at first I was genuinely furious with you for surrendering. I was equally angry when you showed Captain Strick the leaf. I'm still angry about that, in fact. But I remembered our conversation on the wall. You said that Levitimas wanted to see me, and I told you to solve this yourself. Well, you did."

Tobias heaved a sigh of relief. "I'm glad you figured this out. I was nervous."

"You should have been. I don't appreciate being called a liar in my own throne room."

Next I unlocked Fink's door. He said, "As long as you're not angry, I helped with the idea."

"I am angry," I said. "You should have given me a hint."

Fink sighed while I unlocked Darius's door. He said, "Mott told me where he hid all the remaining bags of gunpowder. I can use them to threaten the rest of the Prozarian armies. We can cut their numbers almost to nothing."

I nodded. "The only terms we accept are that they leave Carthya, forever."

"What about you?" he asked. When I only shrugged, he put one hand around the back of my neck. "Be safer than usual, all right?"

That was the most he could ask, and I nodded a quick promise to him before turning to Levitimas. "You wanted to see me?"

Levitimas sighed. "If I tell you how to get the treasure, will you keep your promise to get the book for me?"

"This is my castle, Levitimas. If there were another way into the crypt, I would know it."

He chuckled to himself, though it ended in a dry cough. "Arrogant boy. There is so much you do not know. Do you want to see the treasure or not?"

I took a deep breath. "Yes, I will get the book for you."

"Then this is your way into the crypt." Levitimas scooted aside to reveal a hole in the wall behind him. My mind flew back to the first time I had seen Levitimas in this cell. I had offered to help him escape. Now I understood why he had refused that offer.

Levitimas shrugged again. "It wasn't all my work. I simply finished what other prisoners began, probably years ago." The half of his face that smiled began to beam. "They would have escaped the cell where they were meant to die, only to find themselves in a room for the dead."

I looked past him through the hole into a tunnel so narrow that a person would have to crawl on their belly to get through it. It appeared to be longer than I was tall, though I couldn't be sure because it was completely dark on the other end. I had no idea what to expect.

"Get a torch ready," I told Fink.

"You can't be serious about going in there," Tobias said.

"We're all going in there." I took a deep breath, ducked my head into the tunnel, and began to crawl.

Behind me, I heard Levitimas say, "After so many years, victory is nearly ours!"

Hardly.

Far from believing I was on the verge of victory, I was more certain now than ever that I had lost everything but my life, and even that could not be far off.

· FORTY-FIVE ·

The crawl through the tunnel only took a few seconds, but I was fairly sure at one point I wriggled over some bones, belonging to my ancestors, obviously. I hoped it was someone we hadn't liked much in the past. I also figured it was better not to tell Tobias and Fink about them until after they had come through. Fink shoved two unlit torches ahead of him, then said, "It's my turn now."

While he did, I pulled out the fire kit that I had taken from Farthenwood. After a few tries, the torch lit, and I used it to scan the crypt room. The usual entrance to the crypt was far to my right, at the top of a narrow set of stairs that led to this wide underground cavern. I had been here several times in my youth, usually as part of a tutor's history lesson on what some great king or queen had done. I never understood why it was important to stare at the gray stone boxes where they were buried to learn about their lives.

My feelings had changed after my parents were buried here. Everyone here had been loved, and lost, and deserved to be remembered.

Most of the royals from Carthya's thousand-year history

were entombed here as well. One day I would join them, though I hoped that was still a long time away.

My parents' tombs were close to the entrance. I saw damage to the corner of my father's tomb where a stone had broken loose from overhead and knocked off the corner. That bothered me. This was one of the few places left where I could come to feel nearer to my parents.

Wilta would eventually get inside, which would destroy the sacredness of this place. The fact that I couldn't stop it felt like a betrayal, disrespectful to all those who were buried here.

Fink popped out through the tunnel, and I helped him get his balance on the ground.

"Did I just crawl over —"

"Don't ask, and yes."

"Disgusting."

Tobias came through with a slightly different reaction. "What a fascinating thing the human body is," he said. "I wonder how old those bones were."

"Don't ever wonder that around me," I said. "I don't want the answer to that question." I lit the second torch for Tobias and passed it over to him. "Let's go."

"What about me?" Levitimas asked, poking his head through.

I turned and sighed. "It's not safe here."

"I've waited my whole life to get this far. You won't leave me behind now!"

Tobias turned back toward the tunnel. "We need to hide the entrance."

"No, we don't."

"Jaron, in one hour, the Prozarians will come for you. When they see that tunnel, they'll follow us."

"I'm sure you're right. We'd better hurry." I glanced back at Levitimas, who was struggling to get down the slope where we stood. "Take his arm, Fink."

"He hasn't bathed —"

"Neither have you. Do it."

I led the way through the maze of tombs, rows and rows of them, toward the back of the crypt. There, at the farthest end of the cavern, were three raised granite blocks for the original rulers of Carthya: Ingor, Faylinn, and Linus. Long before my time, a gate had been installed to keep anyone from coming too close to their tombs. It was said that the floor beneath their tombs was not safe, that the floor moved.

I wondered about that now.

My tutors had always explained that because the three rulers had died in violence and jealousy, the moving ground was a curse that had fallen over their tombs.

I had never believed in the curse, but I figured now that if there was a curse, the devils would somehow excuse me for testing it.

Maybe they already had. When I was seven, I went past the gate, and even jumped on the ground to see what would happen. Nothing did . . . until my tutor saw me there and fainted to the ground. Darius had run from the crypt, yelling that my tutor had died as a result of my crossing behind the gate. His cries brought a dozen servants and soldiers into the room, but by the time they arrived, my tutor was sitting up and perfectly well. However, the rumors persisted for years that tutoring me could cause death.

When I crossed around the gate this time, I looked back to see if anyone with me had fainted. So far, everyone was on their feet, but Tobias looked particularly nervous.

"I heard the ground is cursed," he whispered.

"Come over here and find out for yourself," I replied, which he did, testing every step one foot at a time.

I held my torch closer to each tomb as I walked around it, but it was Tobias who made the first discovery. "Look at this, Jaron! The symbols!"

Ingor's tomb bore the traditional mark of Carthya, the circle divided into equal thirds. Ingor had wanted Carthya to pursue trade and become wealthy, and indeed, he had gained great wealth for a time, though all of it disappeared with his death.

"That is a powerful symbol," Levitimas said as he crossed past the gate. "It suggests that all people are equal. The king is no better than those he serves. If he understands that, his country will prosper."

Fink pointed to the symbol on Faylinn's tomb. It was engraved with the second symbol on the scope, a circular arrow with a beginning but no end. "Do you know this one, Levitimas?"

He smiled. "Ah, that is my favorite. That is a symbol of knowledge itself, which must begin somewhere, but which will never end."

The third tomb belonged to my ancestor Linus, with the triangle symbol of strength, representing his belief in weapons and war.

Levitimas looked over at me. "Ask your third question, Jaron."

I had been staring at the symbol and only shook my head. "I'm not sure that I want to."

"I have no ability to see the future. I only know the past and I carefully observe everything around me. But to answer the question you will not ask, I do not believe your future will always be one of war and battle. Peace is coming to this land, and it will last for a long time. There are many ways of being strong. Fighting is the lowest form of strength."

I thought about that while Tobias and Fink continued to explore the area. Levitimas, however, simply held out his hand.

"Let me see the scope. I assume you have it in that satchel."

I withdrew the scope from its satin pouch. All three lenses were still in their slots.

I held the torch close to the scope while Levitimas compared the writing from the scope with marks on Linus's tomb. They had the same lines and half circles as the third lens, but the symbols were different.

"It's the same unknown language," Tobias said.

Levitimas arched a brow. "Is it? Hold the torch near the tomb." Fink did, and Levitimas lifted the scope to his eye, aimed directly at the writing on Linus's tomb, and his smile widened. "Half of a language is on the tomb. Half is on this lens. Viewed together, this is a complete language."

"May I?" Tobias took the lens and aimed it toward the tomb as well, then soon lowered it. "I still can't read it."

"It's the original language, as the founders of Carthya would have spoken it," Levitimas said. "But some of the letters are too small for my eyes. If someone tells me what they are, I'll translate them."

Tobias began, while Levitimas closed his eyes and listened, then said, "Turn the tomb."

I squinted back at him. "Huh?"

"There are no details. Just the instruction. So turn this tomb."

Tobias and Fink took one end of Linus's tomb and Levitimas and I took the opposite end, and together, we began to push. My injured arm throbbed, but slowly the ground beneath us shifted. I realized the tomb was on a circular floor that slowly opened to a narrow hole.

"So the floor does move," Tobias mused. "Does that mean we have now opened up a curse?"

"Probably." I lay on my belly and lowered the torch through the hole. The fire flickered but showed me what appeared to be a steep and narrow staircase made of rough-hewn stone. I couldn't see the end of it, nor anything beyond.

We did hear running water below, which amazed me. The Roving River ran beneath the castle at the cellar level, but this had to be a second, lower river, one I'd never known existed.

I looked over at Levitimas. "How deep underground does this go?"

He shrugged. "A thousand years ago, this might not have been so deep. The land was mounded up higher over Drylliad when the castle was built. During the time of the three rulers, that crypt might have been the highest structure in all the land."

"I admit, Levitimas, you were right." I grinned over at him and shifted around to put my feet through the hole. "I don't know everything . . . yet."

I lowered my body to the top step, a landing wide enough for two people, if they stood close together.

"This is a terrible idea," Tobias said.

"I'm just glad he's going down and not us," Fink said.

"Both of you need to stop talking," I snapped. Then, with a deep breath, I started down the steps but had only gotten to the third when my torch went out. I reached for the fire starter again, but Levitimas shook his head. "It won't work. Do you feel the cold breeze coming up at us? It will put out every fire we try to light."

"I'm not going down there without a torch," I said.

Tobias peered behind him. "It won't take the Prozarians long to figure out where we are."

"I'll come help you." Fink began to lower himself down, but a sharp glare from me ended that conversation.

"We still have a chance," Levitimas said. "I saw instructions for how to enter the chamber on Ingor's tomb. If Tobias continues to give me the letters, I will translate them."

"And I will pass them on to you, where you can hear me," Fink said.

My stomach began churning with nerves, partially because I was headed into a pitch-dark cavern, possibly for the first time in a thousand years. But also because my instructions for how to do it safely would come through Fink.

I looked back as Levitimas pointed to the scope in his hands. "Jaron, the other symbols engraved here are warnings that you must remember."

"Is there any warning about walking into an underground cavern without a speck of light?"

"Yes, in a way." Levitimas turned to the underneath side of the lens. "This asks you to remember what matters most, or you will lose your way, and be lost forever."

"That's comforting. Thanks for that, Levitimas."

He only offered a crooked smile back while I turned toward the staircase once again. "Let's begin. How do I get down there?"

· FORTY-SIX ·

The instructions were very specific, I soon learned.

I knew from feeling my way forward that I was on some carved stone steps, with a rock wall on one side of me and absolutely nothing on the other side.

The torchlight from the crypt had been helpful for the first few steps, but it was useless to me now. I raised my hand in front of my face and saw nothing.

"Levitimas says everything here is made of layers of symbols." Fink's voice echoed, which told me something about the size of this cavern. "It took strength to move Linus's tomb. Maybe that explains his symbol."

"I really don't care about that right now," I called back to him. "What am I supposed to do here?"

"The second symbol is for knowledge. Levitimas says that the tomb reads, 'Walk in darkness to find the light.' I guess you need to walk."

"That's what I'm doing."

I took the next step, thinking that if everything here was a symbol, then walking into this cavern certainly felt familiar to me as far as my own life. Nearly everything I ever did was taking a step forward in the dark without any idea of where it would lead. Levitimas had said that I needed to remember what mattered most, or I would lose my way.

"Jaron, stop," Fink said. "We have a problem."

I turned back to see his face poke down from the hole through which I'd entered the cavern. In what little light he held, I saw how grim his expression was.

"What's wrong?" I asked.

"How many steps have you taken?"

"I don't know. You never said to count them!"

"Sorry. I was supposed to tell you that."

"I don't know how many steps, Fink. Does it matter?"

"I'll ask." He disappeared for a moment; then I saw his face again. "Yes, it matters a lot. Could you have gone twelve steps?"

"Yes. Or maybe thirteen."

"No, at thirteen steps, you'd be dead already. Is it twelve steps?"

I closed my eyes and tried to estimate the count. "Yes, maybe. Are these real instructions?"

"I'm telling you what Levitimas said to me. But he mumbles."

"*I'm* not mumbling, Fink. Tell me what to do!"

"You won't like it."

"I don't like any of this. What am I supposed to do?"

"Jump."

"Jump where? To what?"

"I don't know."

"Fink, do I jump straight ahead or turn and jump? Do I jump up or down?"

"Yes, try that."

I cursed and didn't care if he heard me. "Nothing is ahead of me, Fink."

"You don't know that. Jump!"

"If you're wrong about this, I'll kill you."

"If I'm wrong, the jump will kill you first."

I whispered a request to the devils to ignore me for once, then crouched low and jumped into open air, clutching for an edge of rock, or a rope, or anything to keep me from falling. I found nothing, and for a brief moment, I was certain that I had failed. Then I landed on something solid. I crumpled to my hands and knees, and all was silent.

"Fink!" I called. "Fink, answer me!"

"Did that actually work?"

"Maybe. What happens now?"

Silence. Then, "Eight more stairs to the bottom." While I walked them, Fink added, "When you get there, you should find something nearby like a stone basin."

Eight steps later, I touched what felt like solid ground. In the darkness, I felt around until my hands touched what seemed to be a stone pillar. I followed its curve upward until it was about waist high. Inside was an oily liquid. "What now?" I called back, but after a long silence, I decided to solve this one on my own. I pulled the fire kit from the satchel, lit Imogen's note that I had stored in my boot, and let it land on the oil.

Instantly, the flame lit, traveling faster than I could watch it move, along an oil-filled gutter from one basin to another until light filled the entire underground room. And just as quickly, what I saw took my breath away.

I was standing in a room about the size of my library but much taller, and other rooms appeared to branch out from there, divided by carved stone walls. I didn't know what was around every corner, but what I did see left me utterly speechless. Before me was more gold than I had ever seen in my life, in all its forms: gold bars and coins, finely crafted bracelets, and three crowns on three pillars, one, I assumed, for each of the three rulers.

Littered among the gold pieces were silver trays and dishes, precious gems — wealth beyond anything I had ever imagined.

"Jaron?"

I didn't answer, not yet. But I did turn back to look at the stairs I had come down. Indeed, in the very middle was a gap that would have created a hard fall to the bottom if I had taken another step. Dividing the staircase in a pitch-dark room must have been one way of preventing someone from accidentally discovering the treasure. They would have had to learn to read the writing on Linus's tomb.

Near me was another set of stairs, on wheels, designed to fill the gap. I pushed it into place, creating a complete staircase, then stood back to get a better understanding of this room.

The river we had heard earlier flowed against the far wall. It was narrow here, but the current appeared strong, so it must run deep.

"Jaron?"

I heard Fink's call, but I was far too consumed with everything around me to answer back. How could I possibly describe all this?

Levitimas had said there would be a book down here that

he wanted, and I had promised to deliver it to him. But for all the wealth I saw, there was no book.

Near the back of the cavern, I found something different: weapons with designs I had never seen before, never even imagined before. Some were models for catapults and cannons that, if built to full scale, might be capable of collapsing entire castles. There were bags of powder that I suspected had an explosive power far beyond anything I had seen until now. The destructive capabilities of these weapons were beyond my comprehension.

Yet there was still no book.

Levitimas had told me once that the treasure would offer what I thought I most wanted, but in the end, it would take what I most valued. Now he had added an extra piece to the riddle. If I forgot what I truly wanted, I would be lost down here forever.

Levitimas wasn't the cheeriest sort of person to have around.

"This cannot be."

I turned and groaned as Wilta lowered herself through the same hole beneath the tombs and began walking down the stairs, her eyes wild with greed and anticipation. "Nothing I imagined compares to this," she said.

"Has it already been an hour?" I called up to her. "Because I meant to tell you that I found another way in."

Wilta smiled. "We figured that out."

"Be careful, Monarch," Lump said as he lowered himself in behind her.

But Wilta didn't listen. She was already hurrying down the steps, so focused on the gold around her that she nearly tripped and fell more than once.

Behind Lump came Mercy, whose glare at me dissolved only when his greed demanded his attention. Levitimas followed with Fink and Tobias, and Captain Strick behind them. When they were at the bottom, Strick called up, "All of you may come down. We'll need help to carry out this treasure!"

At least sixty Prozarian soldiers entered the room, trying to keep their expressions even, despite what they were seeing. Most of them failed.

I looked over at Wilta. "Honestly, is there anyone you did *not* invite down here?"

"Imogen," she said flatly. "I turned her over to Castor so they could plan the final details of their wedding."

I began to argue that with her, but there was no point. Wilta was so consumed by what she was seeing, she had almost forgotten I was here.

I stood back to stare at the scene around me. Tobias and Fink were assisting Levitimas in searching for the book he wanted. Prozarians soldiers were sliding gold coins into their pockets when they thought no one was looking.

Wilta was off to my right, brushing her hand over a stack of gold bars as if they were delicate rose petals. "This . . . must be more wealth than exists in all the lands combined. We are not wealthier than any other country. We are wealthier than all other countries together."

"The gold is the least of it." Strick had just discovered the same weapons I had seen before. "There is power down here, true power."

"Levitimas said there would be a book." Mercy turned to him now. "A book of all knowledge. Where is it?"

Levitimas offered his usual half smile. "Perhaps the book of all knowledge could tell us where it is."

Levitimas's idea of a joke, and one Mercy didn't appreciate.

He raised a hand at Levitimas, but I darted between them and grabbed his arm to stop him. "You are a devil's coward," I said. "How could he possibly know where the book is?"

"We've found the treasure," Mercy said to Lump. "Let us finally be rid of Jaron!"

Lump widened his stance, then folded his arms. "I will not take his life, nor allow you to take it."

"We'll see." Mercy eyed me, then continued deeper into the room to explore.

If Wilta and Strick were aware of Mercy's threat, they showed no sign of it. Instead, Wilta was still staring at the room, trying to take in everything she was seeing. Strick began studying the weapons more closely, no doubt planning her next conquest with them.

"You there," she said, pointing at a group of Prozarians clustered together. "We need to start moving this back into the crypt."

"You must take only what matters most," Levitimas said. "The rest will destroy you."

He was right. I was surrounded by everything I would have thought I'd want in life: wealth and power, and victory in battle. But the items down here had destroyed the original three rulers. I would not follow in their paths.

"Everything in here matters!" Captain Strick shouted. "Your silly warnings mean nothing to us."

"Then take what you must, but leave me the book."

Levitimas's tone turned to begging as he stepped my way. "You swore to get it for me, Jaron."

"He should not have promised what he cannot provide. The book is ours," Mercy said. "With it, we can obtain knowledge long lost to all other civilizations."

"They must be conquered first," Strick said. "The weapons will give us control, and then we can take their wealth, their knowledge. Everything will be ours."

"There is no need for all that trouble," Wilta said. "We have more wealth here than we might need in a lifetime. Nothing else matters."

"The Prozarians are conquerors," Strick said. "That is what we do; that is who we are!"

"I am the Monarch," Wilta said. "The Prozarians are whoever and whatever I decide they are."

"Jaron has softened your will to make war." Strick pointed a knobby finger at me. "You have developed a fondness for each other. You wish to remain here in Carthya with him."

"To be clear, I have no fondness for Wilta," I said. "I only despise her less than some of you." I began counting on my fingers, keeping my eye on Strick. "Mercy is the worst; you're a close second, obviously. And then Wilta." I held up the three fingers. "It's my personal rule to have no fondness for anyone until at least fourth place. That's Lump."

"Enough of this!" Strick approached Wilta, her hand gripping her sword. "Give the order to kill him now, or I'll do it anyway."

Wilta frowned. "You will do nothing without my permission."

"I was right; you do like him. You are a spoiled, selfish child! If not for me, you would have destroyed our people already!"

"You are a jealous mother who would rather see me dead." Wilta raised the sleeve of her dress. "Leaves from the gilbrush tree, correct?"

Strick's eyes widened, and all color drained from her face. "I have never . . . would never . . ." When it was clear that her protests weren't working, her features instantly sharpened, and she withdrew her sword. "It pains me to say this about my own daughter, but you are a failure as a Monarch. You want to be a conqueror, but you lack the courage to achieve it. You want respect but achieve fear. You think having a pretty face and a sharp tongue is enough to return the Prozarians to the empire we once had. No, Wilta, for the sake of the Prozarians, your rule ends here. Only two votes are required to remove you as Monarch: mine and that of your chief counselor. Lord Trench, do you agree with my decision?"

His smile over at Wilta was cold. "I agree." He raised his voice. "Prozarian soldiers, you will no longer recognize Wilta Strick as your Monarch. You owe her no allegiance, no respect, no obedience."

Lump crossed between them, raising his sword. "Wilta is the Monarch, and I will fight for her until the end."

"Your loyalty is admirable," Strick said. "But before you speak so boldly, you should consider which soldiers I brought in here. They will fight for me, not her."

Wilta tossed her hair behind her defiantly. "I will not be

removed from power. Those who are loyal to me, raise your swords now and fight!"

She looked around, obviously expecting the soldiers to cross to her defense, but only one man stepped forward. He offered her no bow. "We were there in the courtyard when you told Jaron to fire the cannon at us. You said if you lost a hundred here, you'd just get a hundred more. Wilta Strick, you had better hope that next hundred comes to your aid soon. We will not."

Wilta seemed to have crumpled further with each word he spoke. She backed against the wall, angry but also defeated and utterly helpless. She looked to me for help, but I only stared back at her. I had warned her of this, that her defeat would come at the hands of those she trusted most.

Strick raised her sword. "I am your monarch now. Serve me, and you will share in the spoils of this treasure!"

The same soldier who had spoken before said, "Are you any better than your daughter? Did you not say that we were to remain in the path of the cannon fire, that our fate was set?"

Strick's eyes darted. "I was only following Wilta's orders. I would have saved you!"

Lump turned to Wilta. "Monarch, run!"

She began running deeper into the cavern while Lump withdrew his sword. "All those loyal to the true Monarch, follow me."

Ten soldiers stepped to his side of the cavern, but the last man had not fully crossed over before a fight broke out.

Immediately, I grabbed Tobias and Fink, gesturing for

them to follow me into a quiet recess of the cavern, away from the fighting. From there, I peered around the corner, keeping my sword in my hand and hoping I wouldn't have to use it.

Wilta didn't have numbers on her side, but she definitely had the greater talent. As the battle heated, Lump put his eye on Captain Strick.

"Captain, by order of the Monarch, your fate is sealed!" Lump shouted to her.

Strick retreated toward the weapons. She bent over to pick up something I had not yet seen: a weapon the length of a sword, but it turned out to be a hollow tube instead. She should have kept running.

Before the weapon was in her hands, Lump caught her with his sword, and she fell dead, on top of the very devices she had thought would make her unconquerable.

With the fall of Captain Strick, those who had fought for her looked at one another, confused. I was equally confused. Did this mean that Wilta was their monarch again? Or did Mercy now assume that title?

Whatever they decided, the fighting began again, and I realized it was no longer for or against any preferred monarch. Everyone down here knew the winners would walk out with the treasure.

Levitimas had been right. Their greed was destroying them. I had to make sure it would not destroy us as well.

FORTY-SEVEN

From behind me, Tobias peered out at the fighting. "You wanted this to happen," he mused. "This is why you left the tunnel open, to defeat them here."

"I knew they would defeat themselves. That's why I left it open."

"What is he doing?" Fink pointed to Levitimas, who was dodging the fighting soldiers and continuing to search behind stacks of gold bars and dig through piles of coins.

"He lectures us on the treasure, then risks his life for a book?" I scowled. "Nothing in here is worth any of our lives. I only want —"

I stopped there and drew in a breath. I only wanted Imogen to love me again, if she could. I'd seen for myself how quickly wealth could come and go, that war brought nothing but misery. And I was an utter fool who knew only a single thing: I loved Imogen.

"Victory is ours!" one man shouted. Only fourteen Prozarians remained, half who had sided with Lump, and the rest who had simply put down their weapons. More than two-thirds of their fellow soldiers had fallen here, making this chamber its own crypt now.

The soldiers who remained began to openly stuff coins into their pockets or satchels, whatever they could carry. They emptied out one pile so fast that Levitimas suddenly brightened and knelt on the ground. He dug farther into the coins, then reached down and pulled up what appeared to be an ancient book. It wasn't nearly as large as I'd imagined, considering that it was supposed to contain all knowledge. But he still drew it to himself, and tears began streaming down his face.

Mercy had seen it too. He hurried across the room, raising his sword to Levitimas as he stood with the book clutched to his chest. By then, I had my sword out and aimed toward Mercy.

I said, "If you give him a single scratch, I will kill you."

"Tell him to give me the book, or I will order our soldiers to kill you."

"Don't be rude, Lord Stench. Levitimas asked for the book first."

A knife crossed between us. Wilta stepped forward with it and said, "Did you think I'd given up so easily? This treasure will be mine. All of it, including that book."

Lump was with her and began removing both my swords. I continued staring at Mercy, whose eyes were darting about as he tried to figure out if Wilta was angry with him or not. Lump answered that question by raising my swords at him, and Mercy immediately fell to his knees before Wilta.

"Why do you kneel to me?" she asked. "Didn't you vote to remove me as monarch?"

He outstretched his clasped hands. "I only wished to

expose those who were disloyal. As always, my lady, I serve as your loyal counselor."

She arched a brow. "Then advise me. Of all this treasure, what do you think is the most valuable?"

He paused, obviously confused. "I believe it is the book, Monarch."

Wilta walked over to Levitimas and pulled the book from his hands, then dropped it in front of Mercy. "I will give you a choice. Take the book and leave here on your own, my payment for your years of loyal service, or you may stay here and continue to serve me."

Mercy looked from the book up to her. Finally, he picked up the book and stuffed it into a leather bag at his side, saying, "Obviously this is difficult, but I must choose this treasure and leave."

"Then you choose death." Wilta looked up at Lump. "Kill this traitor, then give me that book. If it is that valuable, then it is mine."

Mercy's head shot up, and this time a knife was in his hands. He swiped at Wilta, and when she jumped back, he began racing toward the steps. I followed and even wrenched the leather bag from his grip, but he turned and with a hard kick sent me to the ground.

"This is not finished!" he yelled, then ran the rest of the way up the stairs, hoisted himself through the open hole back into the crypt, and disappeared.

"Shall I go after him?" Lump asked.

Wilta shook her head. "No. The treasure is all that matters."

"He'll come back," I said to Wilta. "And he won't be alone."

"Then we must hurry. I am about to become the greatest monarch the Prozarians have ever known!"

Tobias cleared his throat. "I don't wish to cause offense, but I don't think you are the monarch anymore."

She only laughed. "Once I leave this room with piles of gold, my people will gladly restore my title."

I wasn't sure about that. One look around the room at the surviving Prozarians suggested they had other ideas. Other than Lump, none of them had stepped forward to defend her from Mercy, nor had they pursued him. And no doubt, every soldier here was already planning what they would do if even a portion of this treasure was theirs.

Wilta turned to me. "You kept your promise to me, Jaron. You brought me here. And so I will keep my promise to you. If you leave now, you might have a chance to stop Imogen's wedding. I will even allow you a satchel of coins in my gratitude."

I crouched down to begin filling my satchel to the top but added, "Allow Tobias, Fink, and Levitimas to come with me, and the rest of the treasure is yours."

She considered that for a moment, then said, "Agreed. But leave Lord Trench's bag here. I still want that book."

I placed his bag on a nearby pillar and said to my friends, "Let's go. Our battle is over."

Levitimas shook his head. "There is nothing left for me. I will stay here."

"Levitimas —"

He merely sat on a stack of gold bars and lowered his head, no longer listening to me.

With no other choice, I climbed the stairs with Tobias and

Fink behind me. When I was at the top, I looked back one last time, hoping Levitimas had changed his mind, but the delay turned out to be a mistake. A foot shot through the hole and kicked me down a few steps, sending Fink and Tobias even farther down.

Tobias stood first. "Jaron, are you all right?"

"Get Fink and run as far away from me as you can," I hissed. "Now!"

Tobias nodded. He and Fink began running just in time for Mercy to descend through the hole in the floor again, but this time, Castor was with him. He held a sword in one hand and a torch in the other. That worried me.

Castor's glare burned hotter than the torch ever could. "Did you think you were clever for firing a cannonball at me?"

I was still a few steps below him, and I slowly rose to my feet. "Very clever, yes."

"This will be your last chance to survive, Jaron. Kneel before me now, acknowledge me as the king of Carthya, and beg for my mercy."

"No, Steward Veldergrath," Mercy said. "Don't give him the chance to trick you. Let me kill him now."

"Wait!" I held up my satchel. "This is filled with gold. If you don't kill me, this is yours. Consider it a wedding gift."

Mercy reached out his hand for it, but Castor slapped it away and said, "Bring it to me."

Cautiously, I walked up the stairs and put my satchel directly in Castor's hand, but I kept hold of his hand, yanking hard enough that it should have pulled him down with me. Instead, he kicked me away and said, "Didn't I tell you that I would have the ultimate revenge on you? I have your crown, your castle, your wealth, and, very soon, the girl you love. Kneel to me and acknowledge my victory."

From the room below, Wilta said to Castor, "No, you will kneel to *me*! I am your monarch!"

"You all have a lot of details to work out. I'll just wait at the bottom." I began backing down the stairs, with Mercy following me down each step.

"You are no one anymore," he said to Wilta. "As soon as he leaves this room, Castor Veldergrath will be married and crowned as king. I will be his high chamberlain."

"And all this will be mine," Castor said, looking over the treasure in the room. Still at the top of the stairs, he glanced down at Wilta. "Didn't I warn you that if you would not share the treasure with me, I would take all of it myself?"

Wilta's attention was on Mercy as he reached the bottom step. "Why would you betray me, Lord Trench? After all I've done for you?"

"I only had to tolerate you long enough to reach this treasure. The book is mine again!" He picked up the bag that I had grabbed from him before and looked inside. "Where is it? Where is the book?" His eyes went straight to Levitimas. "You stole it!"

"A lost book is hardly your biggest problem, Lord Trench." Castor glanced down at him, smiling in a way that shot terror through me. "You swore loyalty to me, but I care nothing for you. You carried out the orders to plant gunpowder on the curtain wall. Now you will die in the way you planned to kill my Stewardmen!"

He looked up through the hole into the crypt, and someone I couldn't see passed down to him one of the bags of gunpowder. Somehow, he had found the extra bags from the curtain wall.

Forgetting his bag and the missing book, Mercy fell to his knees, directly on the steps, far below where Castor stood. "That was never my plan, my king. Those were the Monarch's orders, I swear it."

"Then you should give this to her." Castor lit the fuse on the bag of gunpowder and tossed it down the stairs, where it landed just in front of Mercy. "Farewell to you all. Especially you, Jaron."

Castor immediately lifted himself back into the crypt and dropped a second bag of gunpowder onto the steps, its fuse already lit. The only sound that remained was the hissing of the fuses, followed by the heavy creaks of Linus's tomb being pushed back into place, closing the hole and removing our only chance to escape.

Every person in the room knew what was coming, but we had nowhere to run.

The explosion was worse than I'd expected. It destroyed the steps and the ramp, and several large rocks fell to the ground. One of them landed on my foot, trapping me. The bigger sounds turned to smaller cracks and thumps, followed by a rain of pebbles and dust filling the room, choking all of us. The oil-filled basin that I had first lit upon coming down here was cracked, and oil from all the channels began pouring out of it, bringing fire into the room.

Everywhere we heard moaning and cries, and then a horrible sound of silence as everything settled.

From my right, a soldier lunged toward me. "This is your fault!"

Fink darted between us, raising his fists. "You will not touch my brother!" he shouted.

The soldier began to swing at him, but Lump grabbed the soldier from behind and yanked him off his feet, dropping him on the ground beside us.

"There will be no more fighting among us!" Lump said. "We need to work together if we are going to survive."

The survivors in the room quieted down, allowing Lump and Fink to move the rock that had fallen on my leg. "How bad is it?" Fink asked.

I sat up and gingerly tested my foot on the ground. It hurt, but I could use it, a little. However, I had a much bigger worry.

"Where is Tobias?" I asked.

"Maybe it doesn't matter," Fink said. "I don't think this can get any worse."

I wished he hadn't said that. Words like that only begged the devils to answer, and they did.

With Fink's words still lingering in the air, the fire consumed the last of the oil from the basins. The room went completely dark.

· FORTY-EIGHT ·

I don't suppose this was part of your clever plan," Fink whispered.

"Does this feel like a clever plan?" It had felt rather clever, until Mercy fled. I knew it would only be a matter of time before he returned with Castor. I also knew that Castor would find a way to finally make his move against Wilta. But he had destroyed our escape, which I had not anticipated. That was definitely a problem.

And everyone around us knew it. Although no doubt several Prozarians had been killed in the explosion, those who remained were calling out names, asking who still remained alive, and crying out with their injuries, or their fears.

"Silence!" I commanded in the darkness.

Almost immediately, they obeyed, and I said, "As carefully as you can, check the area around you. Where is Wilta?"

There were shuffling sounds, the frequent bump of someone's leg or head against rock, and then, "I found her!" far to my right.

That was Tobias's voice. I began to breathe easier.

"Is she alive?" Lump asked.

A beat passed. Then, "Yes, but she is not moving."

"Levitimas?" I asked.

He answered, "I've already said that I will stay here."

"No, you won't. If necessary, I'll have Lump carry you out of here. Lord Trench?"

There was no answer, but in the silence that followed, someone shouted, "What about the rest of us? Can you help us?"

"I can get myself out of here," I replied. "And I can do it without any of you realizing I've left, or where I've gone. Let me demonstrate."

Then I went silent. And not just for a few seconds, or even a minute, but until the survivors around me began murmuring, then calling my name. Until even Tobias was calling for me. But not Fink. He knew this game.

Then the same person who had spoken before said, "He left us! We're doomed."

"You are doomed," I said, letting the gasps of surprise follow. "Unless you pledge complete and immediate loyalty to me, in which case, you will survive. But I will not take one step in the right direction until I hear your pledge."

"Hail King Jaron," someone said, quickly echoed by a dozen others.

People started making their way toward my voice. I felt their hands on my back or shoulder, or even my leg. With each touch came the words, "All loyalty to the king."

"Lump?" I called.

"I serve the Monarch," he answered.

And a very weak voice said, "If he will save her life, the Monarch kneels to Jaron, the king of Carthya."

That was followed by several more voices, repeating, "Hail to Jaron, the king of Carthya."

I smiled. "Everyone join hands and follow my voice. Lump, I want my swords back, both of them."

They were passed to me in the darkness. I called for Fink and Tobias to walk beside me, and gave the second sword to Tobias, then whispered to them both, "With my foot, I won't be able to defend myself."

"Then I should have that sword, not Tobias," Fink said.

Tobias quickly agreed, but I ignored them and walked on. I led us in the direction that the river flowed, carrying the survivors deeper into the cavern, far past the treasure. The cave walls began to narrow here and ran lower to the ground, forcing us to stoop to avoid hitting our heads.

"Are you sure this is an exit?" someone behind me asked.

"I'm sure that it was at one time." That was the best I could offer.

The three rulers had created this room a thousand years ago, long before the castle existed. Back then, this cave could have functioned as an early place to live. As Levitimas had suggested, over time, the land would have been built up, and a castle had risen directly over the tombs. Eventually, this cave would have been forgotten.

Except by Linus, who must have preserved this place along with all the wealth and knowledge and weaponry that the three rulers had managed to gather during their time. But he could not have been proud of this treasure. Instead, he had hidden all of it away, ashamed of what it had led to: murder and jealousy and greed.

But he had created the scope so that a person could find their way back to it. For all the trouble it would have taken to decipher the scope, Linus must have hoped the effort would have given the person respect for what they would find in the end.

Tobias was at my side, helping me walk with the injured foot. He asked, "Do you know where you're going?"

"No. Do *you* know where I'm going?"

"This river must go somewhere."

"Could it go farther underground?"

"Yes. Which you would know if you had paid attention in the regents' meeting about a month ago. I told you all about it."

"You didn't."

"I did."

"If you had, I would remember because I would have found a reason to avoid it. Now let me focus."

"Jaron, the water is rising," Fink said.

Technically, the ground was sloping downward and the walls of the cave were narrowing, forcing the river to deepen.

"He's going to drown us," someone called from behind me. "He doesn't care about our lives."

"Stay on your feet!" I called back. "You'll need to be alive to apologize to me later."

Our path had been slowly bending. Finally, I saw a hint of

light ahead, and the sound of falling water. Now I knew where we were, though it wasn't great news.

I stopped and turned around. "You know that the castle sits on a hill overlooking Drylliad. We have reached the end of that hill. In another hundred steps is a waterfall. From the sound of it, I believe it will require a long jump. Is everyone comfortable with that?"

"No," someone behind me said, echoed by a chorus of similar responses, including at least three distinct insults to my intelligence for even suggesting this idea.

"Well, we're still jumping," I said. "I will go first, so if it's too shallow, I'll be the one to find out. The rest of you will follow."

One hundred steps later, I stood alone at the edge of the cliff, wondering how I had lived in Carthya for my entire life and failed to know this was here. I took a deep breath to jump, then felt a blade at my back.

"Thought you'd leave me behind?" Mercy asked.

"I'd hoped so." When we had walked through the darkness, I'd known he might be in our group. I had a solid grip on my own sword, but the foot I would need to pivot toward him was injured. I wouldn't be fast enough to stop him from acting.

"I will do what Castor Veldergrath could not," he said. "You will not survive *this* fall into the river below."

He pulled the blade away to strike; then I heard a sharp gasp and Mercy fell to the ground. Behind him stood Tobias with the sword I had given him outstretched. He was pulling in great gulps of air, and his eyes were wide and full of fear.

I put a hand on his shoulder to help steady him and smiled in gratitude. "You saved my life."

He managed a faint smile. "Just in time for you to risk it yet again."

"Then this is in your honor." I dipped my head at him, leaned forward, and jumped.

· FORTY-NINE ·

A one-second jump is simple, and the landing is easy. A three-second jump brings a guaranteed sting from the water upon entry. I counted to six before I hit the cold lake water, and it felt a little like splashing onto stone.

My lungs were ready to burst before I reached air again, and I immediately began shivering from the icy water. I waved up to the next in line and shouted, "That was easier than I had expected." Which was true only in the sense that I had expected to also hit rocks down here. I gestured for the next person to come.

Fink jumped in after me, rising to the surface spitting out both water and a few choice curses. I had reached the edge of the water by then and said, "You better look up and wave or no one else will come down."

He frowned, then looked up and excitedly waved his arms, still muttering at me, "One day, I'll take my revenge for that."

"No, you won't. Keep waving."

A pair of soldiers jumped next, coming to the surface as furious as Fink had been, though he quickly pointed at me for an excuse. I threatened them the same as I'd threatened Fink, and once again, they encouraged others to follow.

The next pair held hands to jump but separated somewhere underwater, and when one man rose to the surface and the other did not, Fink and I dove back in to find the one who was lost. As we pulled him back to the water's edge, the man said to me, "Why are you helping us?"

"The fight is over," I said. "Let us have peace now."

One or two at a time, those who had survived the cave got out, until at last there were Tobias and Levitimas, who had stayed behind with Lump to help Wilta. Levitimas had somehow found a long rope that he tossed over a protruding tree limb, and he and Tobias began lowering Lump, who carried Wilta in his arms. After they were down, Lump set Wilta on the ground, propped against a large rock, then untied himself while soldiers gathered in a tight circle around them.

"Jaron says the fight is over," one of the men said. "What does the Monarch say?"

Wilta closed her eyes and turned her face away, but Lump said, "You all know what happened up in the cavern. The Prozarians no longer have a monarch. You will listen to Carthya's king now."

All heads turned to me. I said, "You will leave Carthya at once. Do not return to Drylliad; do not stop anywhere to rest. If I hear that you have made trouble for a single Carthyan on the way, I will send an army after all of you. Now get out of my country."

Bows were offered to me, and they seemed respectful enough, but I felt better when the soldiers turned and began walking eastward, the fastest way out of Carthya, and out of my life.

However, Lump still remained, ever protective of Wilta, who lay limply against the rock. He watched his fellow soldiers leave, then said to me, "With no one left to lead us, I don't know what will happen to my people."

I looked over at Wilta. "Your people have abandoned their loyalties to you. Give the crown to someone who can help the Prozarians rebuild."

She turned to Lump. "It must be you. But do not be a monarch; do not rule as I did."

Lump's eyes widened in disbelief, then he slowly nodded. "I accept."

I placed a hand on his shoulder. "If you're going to be the ruler of another country, I'm afraid I will have to release you from my service."

"I never—"

"It's all right." I smiled at him. "I never thought we'd have to say goodbye either."

Lump rolled his eyes at me, then turned back to Wilta, offering her a low bow. "I will do what I can for them. I promise to rebuild our people to be something other than conquerors." Lump smiled. "With your permission, Jaron, I had better follow the people I am going to lead."

"If we are at peace, then go," I said.

By then, Tobias and Levitimas were nearly to the bottom of the rope. I was waiting there when they landed, still dripping wet.

"You might've told me you had rope!" I said to Tobias.

"I did tell you. Maybe you didn't hear me."

"Don't start this again. I hear everything, Tobias. You wanted to see if I would actually jump."

A grin tugged at the edge of his mouth. "I already knew you would jump. But watching you was all the thanks I needed for saving your life. I should go check on Wilta."

While Tobias tended to her, Levitimas glanced back up at the top of the waterfall. The sadness on his face was evident. "The book is gone."

"You never stole it from Lord Trench?" Fink asked, and he shook his head.

I said, "You told us to take nothing from the cave but that which was most important. You have your freedom now, and your life back. Isn't that more important?"

He only sighed. "Why else have I remained in captivity for all these years but to have the chance to add to that book, and then to pass it on? No, I would have chosen the book, if only for a few minutes to read it before I died."

Tobias turned to me. "Wilta's leg is injured, but I've bound it enough that she can walk. I'm not far from Farthenwood if I leave from here. May I go?"

"You must, and may you find that Harlowe and Amarinda are perfectly well."

Tobias turned the sword I had given him over in his hand. "When this is over, I should study sword fighting. Really study it."

"Agreed. Now you'd better hurry."

He nodded, then pointed to my foot. "I'll fix that when I get back. And whatever else you did to yourself."

He ran off, leaving me beside a lake beneath a steep waterfall somewhere far below the castle hill, exhausted and injured. And with Wilta, Fink, and Levitimas for company.

She tried smiling at me. "At least you only despise me third most."

Fink said, "Except your mother and Mercy never made it out of that cavern. That makes you the one he despises most."

Wilta turned to me, clearly worried. "So will you leave me here to die? I won't make it back on my own."

I sighed. "Fink, I need your help."

"Anything, Jaron."

"Run on ahead to the castle. Delay the wedding, if you can."

"What are you going to do?"

I looked over at Wilta. "Levitimas and I will help her."

FIFTY

N ow that I was walking on land, I realized that my foot was more injured than I had thought. Every step shot pain up through my leg.

Wilta was in even worse shape. I had one arm wrapped around her middle, and her arm was slung over my shoulders. She was walking but crying out with nearly every step. I couldn't see any obvious injuries, which worried me. If they were internal, then we had little hope of saving her.

Levitimas walked beside us, offering encouragement and occasionally clearing something from our path, but he seemed lost in his thoughts, discouraged at having lost the book.

"I'm not sure what I will do now." Wilta tried smiling at me. "Any chance you'd appoint me as your high chamberlain?"

"None."

She was silent for several minutes more, then said, "After my people leave Carthya, how long will you wait to go after the treasure?"

"Probably another thousand years." I looked at Levitimas. "You were right. I was so focused on the scope, I lost sight of Imogen. I won't make that mistake with the treasure."

Levitimas lifted his head. "Perhaps *you* have a lesson to teach me as well. Maybe I will never read that book of knowledge, but I can at least begin a second book of knowledge for future generations."

My smile fell when I stepped wrong and my foot twisted. I fell to one knee and tried to steady my breathing. The sun was rising higher in the sky. At least three hours had passed since Castor collapsed the entrance to the cavern. The wedding would have been finished even before we reached the waterfall.

"You're thinking about Imogen," Wilta said. "I can tell by the look in your eyes."

"Yes."

"At supper that evening, she chose Castor. He was the one she wanted."

"I remember."

We returned to walking and became silent again until Wilta added, "You argue everything, Jaron. Why won't you argue back when I tell you something we both know is a lie?"

"Was it?"

"If you don't see how much that girl loves you, then you do not deserve her. Oh!"

Wilta grabbed her side and clutched my arm for support. "This isn't working; I can't keep going."

"Let's rest a minute."

Yet within that minute, I heard the sound of marching coming toward us. More Prozarians. I was exhausted, hungry, brokenhearted, but most of all in that moment, I was nauseous at the thought of having to see any more Prozarians.

I stood up straight, trying to take pressure off my injured

foot. I reached for my sword, though I was so tired, it felt heavier than I'd be capable of wielding.

"There he is!" one of them shouted. "He's captured the Monarch!"

Dozens of soldiers abandoned their lines and ran toward us, swords out. I backed away as best I could, trying to find stable footing, but it wouldn't be enough. I had no fight left in me.

"You fools, step back. Jaron saved my life!" Wilta grimaced as she made herself stand and balanced herself by holding the trunk of the tree she had been resting against. "Go to your knees and bow at once!"

Without hesitation, each soldier fell to his knees, and shouts of "Hail the Monarch" echoed throughout the group.

Wilta frowned. "I am no longer your monarch. I am no longer anyone. You kneel before the king of this land."

The soldiers looked at one another, obviously confused. Then one man turned toward me, still on his knees. "Hail King Jaron." Others echoed his words, though few of them seemed to understand how everything had changed so completely.

I lowered my sword, then used it to point at Wilta. "She needs help."

"We'll care for her now." The soldier who had first hailed me stood. "But what about you?"

"Someone needs to help him get back to his castle," Wilta said.

"I volunteer." Haddin stepped forward from the back of the group. "I owe him a favor anyway."

Wilta took my hands and kissed my cheek. "It's not too late for you to accept my offer. We could rule together."

"It is far too late," I reminded her. "Goodbye, Wilta. I hope you find peace in your future."

"I'm not sure I have much of a future," she said. "I know how serious my injuries are."

If she was as injured as I suspected, then that explained why she had so willingly turned over her power to me. I told her soldiers to care for her the best they could; then Haddin braced me with one arm around my middle, and I slung my uninjured arm over his shoulders. Levitimas followed along behind us.

"I've lost a lot of good people over these last few days," I said as we walked. "What would it take for you to join me?"

"You must ask," Haddin replied. "Nothing more."

"Then I'm asking. I need a companion-at-arms. Would you consider it?"

His smile widened. "Well, you did say I'd owe you a favor."

"Jaron!"

I looked up and saw Mott hurrying toward me, the bulge of a wrapped bandage beneath his shirt. Darius was close behind, and with them, at least a hundred men and women of Carthya, all of them looking as battle ready as any soldiers I'd ever seen.

"How did you know I'd be here?" I asked.

"Fink passed us some time ago," Mott said.

"Besides, when we saw the collapsed entrance to the crypt, I knew you'd have to get out another way." Darius shrugged. "Your only choice would have been the waterfall."

"You know about the waterfall?" I was still confused.

He stared back at me. "Our lessons on the geography of the castle. Didn't you — No, I remember, you skipped lessons that day. You're soaked through."

"Waterfall."

"You're shivering. Wait here." Darius hurried back to his saddlebag and pulled out some clothes, which he offered to me.

I shook my head. "These are too nice. I still have to deal with the Stewardmen. I'll ruin these."

"You'll ruin whatever I give you. Now put on something dry, or I'll dress you myself."

"You won't," I said, but as I started forward, I collapsed on my injured foot. Mott braced me before I fell, but I winced when he grabbed my right arm. "You're injured there too?"

"Yes, but that happened earlier. I don't think it counts." With some effort, I ducked behind a bush and pulled off my wet clothes. My body was stiff and sore, but I had to admit that with a dry shirt and trousers, I did feel better.

When I came out again, Darius was staring at Haddin. "What should we do with him?"

"Give him a Carthyan uniform. He is my new companion-at-arms."

Mott turned to me. "He's what?"

"Well, it can't be you anymore, not if you're my high chamberlain." Mott began to object, but I said, "It must be someone willing to tell me the truth at all times, even when I hate it. It must be someone I trust as much as I trust myself, because now I will have to listen to you. The high chamberlain must be you, Mott. Please say you will do it."

Mott smiled and bowed to me. "As you wish, my king."

I turned to Haddin. "Wilta and a lot of Prozarians are behind me. I want to be sure they leave Carthya."

Haddin said, "I'll see to that."

"Our soldiers will go with you," Darius said, then turned to me. "Mott and I will see you and Levitimas safely back to the castle."

Darius gave me a hand up to ride behind him, and Mott helped Levitimas onto his horse. We rode away, not much faster than I had been walking.

"How fast can you go?" I asked Darius.

"In your condition, this is it," he said.

"Please, Darius," I said. "Go faster."

But he only shook his head. "You're barely bandaged together as it is. I don't dare go any faster."

I sighed, then said, "At least tell me you have some food here."

FIFTY-ONE

Beside me, I heard Levitimas talking to Mott about the treasure we had discovered, which in his mind consisted entirely of a single item, the book. I wondered if he'd ever get over losing it.

"I think it's too late for the wedding," I said to Darius.

He looked up at the sky. "You might be right." He half glanced back at me. "Maybe this is our fate as royals. Because of who I am, I lost Amarinda."

"It's not the same. Tobias is a good person, and he loves Amarinda. They chose each other for love. Imogen only agreed to marry Castor because she felt it was her duty."

"When Father sent you into the streets to live as an orphan, why did you do it? When I stayed in Belland to help them recover from the Prozarian attack there, why did I do that?"

I knew what he was saying. We did what was required to preserve the kingdom, no matter the sacrifices to ourselves. Imogen had proved herself to be a true royal.

But this time, that nobility had gone too far.

"Darius, if you don't ride faster, I'll get off this horse and walk there myself," I threatened.

"On that foot? I doubt it." He sped up a little but not nearly as much as I needed him to.

Finally, we entered the gates of Drylliad, but I was surprised to see the streets were empty. The last time I had come through here, Prozarian soldiers nearly lined the roads. The frightened people of Drylliad had peered out from their windows. But now I didn't see a single soldier, and even the houses appeared to be empty.

"Where is everyone?" I asked.

"Strange," Darius agreed, though he didn't seem nearly as alarmed as I was.

My question was answered when I turned onto the next road, and my eyes suddenly filled with tears. A blue ribbon was tied every single place where it could fit, around every tree and fence post, in the hair of the women and around the hats of the men. The streets were filled with people, all who bowed or curtsied low as I passed. Most of the children held some kind of flower and ran to me when we rode by, offering their stems as a gift.

"Your people are trying to greet a king, but you look like a wild boy," Darius said. "At least try to straighten your hair or something."

I finger-combed it out of my face, though it almost immediately fell back where it was. I gave up.

Mott and Levitimas had fallen behind us now, but when Darius turned onto the next road, I saw a lot of Prozarian hats and coats. My first instinct was one of alarm. I reached for my sword, but Darius said, "Jaron, look again."

Now I did, and I laughed aloud. These were the pirates,

doing a miserable job of lining the road at attention. Rather, they were leaning against buildings or wagons, and I was fairly sure that a couple were actively plotting to steal the horse from one wagon. But when I passed, they stood and faced me. Teagut, wrapped in bandages around his side, shouted out, "Pirates, this is your king!"

The pirates raised whatever weapon they had with them, or in the case of several, a mug of whatever they had been drinking while they waited. "To Jaron, king of the pirates!"

Darius shook his head. "Someday you'll have to tell me why having pirates in Carthya is a good thing."

I doubted that I could explain that, so I quickly changed the subject. "Are the Stewardmen still at the castle? Darius, this isn't over."

"No, indeed, it is not," he said. "Be ready."

And with that we rounded the final bend and onto the main road that led out of the town and made a straight upward path to the castle.

I'd been watching for the familiar walls and turrets, wondering if by now any part of my home was still standing. Obviously the main curtain wall was completely gone, but from a distance, the castle itself didn't look nearly as bad as I remembered. Yes, significant repairs were needed. Maybe after I got some sleep, perhaps for the next month or two, I would be ready to start making those repairs.

But within only a few seconds, my eyes fell to the road ahead of us, and my breath caught in my throat. "Stop, Darius," I whispered.

He did, and I slid off the horse. My foot protested every step I took, but I was determined not to let it show.

There, in the center of the road, my soldiers stood in two straight columns, facing me. We had lost many good men to the Prozarian attack, but there were more here than I'd expected, and I welcomed the sight of each one.

"Soldiers, raise your arms!" Roden ordered from the back of the column.

With perfect precision, each soldier turned inward to face the soldier across from him and raised his sword high, creating an archway.

I began to walk through the group, making sure my sword crossed with every soldier's sword here.

As I passed by, each soldier shouted, "Hail Jaron, my king!" then fell to one knee.

And at the end was Roden, who gave me a low bow and echoed the others. "Hail Jaron, my king. And my friend." He quickly added, "You look worse than usual."

"It's good to look at you at all," I replied. "I had to call the retreat, Roden —"

"You had to call the retreat to win, I know."

"We still have to defeat the Stewardmen. But I must be honest with you, I'm in no condition to fight."

"You're barely in any condition to walk. If there's a fight ahead, your army will handle it." Roden whistled for one of his men to bring me a horse, and it was as beautiful as any I'd ever seen, tall and deep brown with a single white stripe across its back.

"This is a horse fit for a king," I said.

"Then go and reclaim your throne," Roden said.

I climbed onto my horse, and while Roden climbed on his, I said, "Has the wedding happened yet?"

Roden shrugged. "Your orders were for us to leave the castle grounds, and we did. We'll find out the worst of what has happened there together. Nice flowers, by the way."

"They were a . . . never mind. Maybe I'll give them to Castor and hope some bees are hiding in them."

"There's a rumor that Castor blew up something beneath the castle and trapped their monarch inside." Roden glanced over at me. "You were there, I assume. I think part of your hair is singed."

"Don't tell Castor I ever said this, but it was a good explosion."

Roden smiled again as we approached what little remained of the castle gates. "Are you ready for this?"

I pulled out my sword and stuffed the flowers into the sheath.

"Do you think there will be much trouble ahead?"

"With you, isn't there always trouble ahead?"

A line of Carthyan soldiers stood where the gates had once been. They parted for our entry, and then we were in the courtyard.

The worst of the battle scars had been cleared away, but I feared another battle yet waited. There, in my war-torn courtyard, stood several dozen Stewardmen, all facing me in a straight row, and all of them with their swords held out flat in their hands. I lifted my sword for the fight. Then I spotted

Captain Reever at the center of the group. He shouted, "Hail King Jaron!"

With that, every Stewardman went to their knees, leaving only one person still standing.

Castor Veldergrath.

His hands were bound in front of him, his mouth was gagged, and his eyes were full of terror for what he must have thought was coming.

But I was confused. Again, I slid from the saddle and limped toward Reever, then together we looked at Castor. With wild eyes, he began shaking his head and trying to say something through the gag in his mouth.

I still didn't understand this. "Who captured him?"

Reever simply said, "We had orders."

My heart sank. Imogen would have had to marry Castor to be able to give orders to the Stewardmen.

I looked up at Reever. "Where is Imogen now?"

"I could not say, my king."

I pulled the gag from Castor's mouth. He immediately bowed, just as he had when I first saw him in the castle, only with far more sincerity now. "Show mercy, my king." He rose up again. "You are a merciful king, everyone says so."

"Nobody says that. I am the Ascendant King, not the Merciful King."

"A great king should have more than one title."

"Then shall I be the dead king? The king who was shot by an arrow on your orders? Or the king who ruins the life of everyone with the Veldergrath name? I think any of those titles are good."

"Show mercy and I will return the king's —" Castor lifted his bound hands. "Oh no." He looked up at me, his eyes wide with horror.

The fact that he hadn't noticed until now that the king's ring was missing was a reminder of how little he respected it. I held up my hand, with the ring in its place. I had pulled it off his finger when I had grabbed his hand down in the treasure room.

"I deserve some mercy," he said. "The same as you would offer to any of your regents."

I snorted. "I have only two regents, Tobias and Rulon Harlowe."

"No, Your Majesty, don't you remember? You made me a regent, in my own house."

"I said you would fit in well with the regents. I never made you one." I turned to Captain Reever. "Have the Stewardmen escort him to the dungeons. Preferably not the cell with a hole in it."

Reever bowed and grabbed for Castor's arm, but he jerked it away and said, "Here at my side is the satchel you gave me. It's full of gold, remember? Take that as my gift to you, and as a testament to my begging your forgiveness."

I lifted the satchel from his shoulder. It didn't look like a single gold coin was missing. Reever passed Castor to the rest of the Stewardmen while I turned my attention to Levitimas, who was standing behind me.

I walked back to him and said, "If I take this treasure for myself, will it destroy me?"

"Is this your third question?"

"Yes."

"The treasure is no threat to you, as long as it never becomes your priority in life."

"But you wanted the book. Wouldn't it destroy you?"

"I studied for a lifetime to prepare myself for that book and would have dedicated the rest of my life to understanding its contents. We cannot keep what we do not earn. What we have earned we cannot lose."

I dug through the coins in my satchel to pull out the book. It had been a bit of a trick to secretly transfer the book from Mercy's bag to my satchel, but hiding it in gold coins afterward assured that Castor would smuggle it out of the cavern for me.

Levitimas gasped loudly, and tears began streaming down his face.

I said, "I give this to you, as promised, and I invite you to remain in Carthya while you write the next book. In exchange, I ask you to teach me. I've realized over the past several days how much I do not know, and that is intolerable."

Levitimas accepted the book, then hugged it to his chest. He bowed to me and said, "May you earn every treasure that will come into your life so that you will never lose it."

I smiled. "That's my plan."

He nodded at the satchel. "With the gold in there, you can do better than simply repairing this castle. Build a new one as only you can."

I watched him walk away, then turned and gave the satchel to Reever. "On the outskirts of Drylliad, there is a small farm run by a man named Emmett. These coins are for him. Tell him that with these coins, he must also take on a family name and give his children a future."

Reever dipped his head at me, then said, "My king, I should have been more clear earlier. We obeyed Lady Imogen's orders because we respect her and honor her as a queen. Castor was arrested before any marriage took place." He nodded at me again, then turned toward the stables while I began limping toward the castle.

My foot ached, but my thoughts were far more focused on Imogen. There had been no marriage to Castor, but that didn't mean anything was repaired between us. I wondered if I still had a chance with her.

Errol was on the main steps of the castle, as if waiting to greet me. "My king, you look . . . as bad as I've ever seen you. Maybe worse." He sighed, pulled out a handkerchief, and said, "You could at least wipe the dirt from your face."

The handkerchief was damp, but it was filthy after I wiped off my face. I entered, and inside I found Fink. I braced myself for a greeting from him, but he only said, "Really, Jaron? Flowers where your sword belongs? You're embarrassing me."

I'd forgotten my sword was still in my hand. I exchanged it with the flowers. They'd be a good start for the apologies I still had to make.

I hoped.

"Do you know where Imogen is?" I asked.

"In the great hall. Come with me."

Fink helped to brace me as we walked. I looked around at the repairs made thus far. The castle entrance was beginning to feel almost as it once was.

The doors to the great hall were closed, but to my surprise, Harlowe was standing at the threshold.

"Harlowe?" I squinted at him. "How did you? I thought you were —"

Darius had come up behind me by then. "There's a reason I had to ride so slow. Tobias needed to get Amarinda and Harlowe from Farthenwood."

"You're like a son to me," Harlowe said. "I would have liked to walk in there with you, but Tobias has given me strict orders to go sit down as soon as you arrived."

"Yes, of course." I didn't fully understand why he would have said that, but it made more sense when Mott came up behind me, carrying a very fine coat that matched perfectly with the shirt and trousers Darius had given me earlier. That was no coincidence, I realized.

Mott helped me put it on, and said, "I have never been more proud of you than at this moment."

I looked down at the coat, then back up at him. "What moment is this, Mott?"

He smiled. "I believe you already know."

I did, and I smiled back at him. "Will you enter with me? You are a servant no more. You are the high chamberlain of Carthya."

"Actually, I was hoping to stand with you, Jaron." Darius stepped forward. "Our parents would have wanted to be here today, but if it's all right with you, I will stand in their place."

We exchanged a quick embrace, then turned forward, side by side, as Mott opened the doors for us.

· FIFTY-TWO ·

The great hall was filled with guests, both seated and standing, but a wide pathway between them was marked by a long blue carpet. I saw several officers from my armies, former regents and nobles, the castle servants dressed in their finest, and citizens of Carthya. They bowed when they saw me, but by then, my eyes were fixed on Imogen, at the other end of the carpet.

She stood on a set of wide steps leading to the dais, facing me and smiling. To look at her, I almost could not breathe.

Imogen wore my mother's wedding gown, white with sleeves that flowed long from the elbow, and with blue lace trim. Her hair was swept back and curled, with a wreath of miniature roses in her hair.

"We should walk forward, or do something," Darius whispered. "Everyone's staring."

"Oh, yes."

I caught a few familiar faces as I walked up the blue carpet. I saw Cook, and Errol, and that servant who always opened doors for me a second too late. This time, he bowed exactly as I passed.

But then I was at the base of the steps, staring up at Imogen. I opened my mouth, but no words came out.

"What happened to you?" she asked.

I smiled. "I was nearly blown up, jumped through a waterfall, and Darius rides his horse like an old man, but I'm better now and you look beautiful. Will you marry me, Imogen?"

Her laugh was soft and brought warmth to my heart. "What do you think this is?"

Now all the words that had been clogged up in my mind came loose. "I have to ask, because I need to be sure that you understand what a life with me will be like. I will be imperfect, always. I can be selfish and arrogant. I am impetuous and demanding, and the greatest of fools. The devils are far too entertained by me, and I still don't know why."

"And you have too many secrets," she added with a smile.

"But not from you, not any longer." I limped forward and gave her the flowers. "And I will never make it a secret how much you are needed here in Carthya. It will never be a secret that you are the reason for any successes I have. And it will never be a secret that you are the most important part of my world."

Imogen reached for my hand. "You should say these things to me more often."

"I say all of this, Imogen, every time I speak your name."

"Then you should join me here on these steps."

This day would long be spoken of by those in attendance. Roden sat in the front row beside his father, and by Tobias and Amarinda, sitting together hand in hand. Batilda was beside them, and her smile at me seemed sincere and warm. Mott stood behind me. I had no doubt he was already making plans to send for Trea, who was back in Belland. I hoped theirs would be the next wedding at this castle.

The priest stood between us, speaking of the saints who had come before us, of former kings and queens who had ruled well, and probably giving some advice I ought to have been listening to.

But I spent the time staring at Imogen. Levitimas was right. I gave her the truth, I gave away my secrets, and she had turned to me.

Darius stood off to one side, his eyes darting between me and Amarinda. I knew he still loved her, but I had no doubt he would find love again.

"Jaron Artolius Eckbert the Third," the priest said, getting my attention again. "Do you give yourself fully to Imogen? Your feet, to always walk beside her as your equal? Your hands, to work with her in all labors? Your shoulders, to carry any load she cannot bear on her own? Do you give her your mind, that you will think of her first in any decision that comes before you, and that you will think of her always as your companion? And do you give her your heart, to love her, to care for her, and to choose her every day for the rest of your life, and beyond, should you one day join the saints?"

"Yes."

"Lady Imogen, do you give yourself fully to Jaron?" The priest smiled. "Your mouth, to speak the truths I guarantee that he needs to hear? Your ears, to listen when he has yet again gotten himself into trouble? Your eyes, to see him every day and to love him every day, even beyond this life, when you one day join the saints?"

She smiled over at me. "Yes."

Fink walked up behind me and whispered, "I was supposed to give you the ring, but I don't have it. I'm sorry, Jaron."

I grinned. "No, I have it." I reached down and pulled off my boot, and water dumped out with it, along with the ring for Imogen. I picked it up and took her hand in mine. "It's cleaner than if there had been no water in my boot."

"This is not the way I imagined getting the ring," she said, then smiled. "But with you, I wouldn't have expected it any other way."

After we were pronounced married, I turned to our guests and said, "Hail your queen. Imogen, the Peacebringer!"

Imogen was given the warmest welcome I had ever seen in this hall, which continued after we then went outside for a larger celebration that lasted throughout the day.

For generations to come, the wedding of Jaron Artolius Eckbert III and Lady Imogen would be discussed as legend. With the passage of time, fewer people would believe we had ever been real, or that this was how it had all happened.

But when the wedding day was over and we were finally alone, I held Imogen close in my arms, with no thought of ever releasing her. Better still was that Imogen held me too. She was my family, my life, and the center of my world.

All that I knew was at peace.

THE
SHATTERED
CASTLE

· ACKNOWLEDGMENTS ·

This series has taken me on an amazing ride, but none of it would ever have been possible without the support of my family. My love to you all. Special gratitude is reserved for Jeff, my husband and the finest man I know. I appreciate him more and more each day.

Many thanks as well to my editor, Lisa Sandell, who is herself made of gold, and to the entire Scholastic family for their hard work and intelligence in helping to bring this series into the world. I am also deeply appreciative of my agent, Ammi-Joan Paquette, who continues to support and advise me as no one else ever could.

Finally, I wish to acknowledge other superfans of this series, those who proved their enthusiasm in any way that suited their talents. Many more names deserve to be here, but these few must be mentioned: Ameerah,

Bonnie, Wesley, Gideon, Solomon and Ivy, Elise and Sophie, Jenna, Jocelyn, Joshua and Sarah, Katie, Kara, Kayleigh, Mayhlee K., Minea, Olivia, and Valerie.

Thank you all for continuing to follow this series. Jaron would be amazed. I am deeply honored.

· ABOUT THE AUTHOR ·

JENNIFER A. NIELSEN is the critically acclaimed author of the *New York Times* and *USA Today* bestselling Ascendance series: *The False Prince*, *The Runaway King*, *The Shadow Throne*, *The Captive Kingdom*, and *The Shattered Castle*. She also wrote the *New York Times* bestseller *The Traitor's Game* and its sequels, *The Deceiver's Heart* and *The Warrior's Curse*; the *New York Times* bestselling Mark of the Thief trilogy: *Mark of the Thief*, *Rise of the Wolf*, and *Wrath of the Storm*; the stand-alone fantasy *The Scourge*; and the critically acclaimed historical novels *Rescue*, *Resistance*, *Words on Fire*, and *A Night Divided*.

Jennifer collects old books, loves good theater, and thinks that a quiet afternoon in the mountains makes for a nearly perfect moment. She lives in Northern Utah with her family and is probably sneaking in a bite of dark chocolate right now. You can visit her online at jennielsen.com or follow her on Twitter and Instagram at @nielsenwriter.